The Matchup

PRAISE FOR

THE *Matchup*

"Laura Walker's *The Matchup* takes the dysfunction in all of us and hits it against the proverbial fan. Pride, faith, and perseverance determine whether two wounded hearts can ever love again."

— JAN M. MARTIN, author of *Heir of Deceit*
and *Impressions of Innocence*

"A hero who has lost his way and a heroine who is struggling to stay on the right path are thrown together by an unexpected twist. Laura Walker delivers a heartfelt LDS romance, while introducing the reader to the challenges and blessings of raising an autistic child. *The Matchup* will open both the eyes and hearts of its readers."

— JOYCE DIPASTENA, author of *The Lady and the Minstrel*

"*The Matchup* is an intense story of overcoming personal demons and finding not only personal peace, but also love and happiness with the right person. I fell in love with the main characters from the beginning, and it tore my heart up as their pasts were spelled out for me. I laughed and cried right along with them as their hearts and souls were healed. A fantastic read for anyone struggling to find or hold on to their testimony."

— SARAH DALEY, author of *Drowning Sandy*

The Matchup

Laura L. Walker

BONNEVILLE
BOOKS

An Imprint of Cedar Fort, Inc.
Springville, Utah

ISBN 13: 978-1-4621-1752-9

Published by Bonneville Books, an imprint of Cedar Fort, Inc.
2373 W. 700 S., Springville, UT 84663
Distributed by Cedar Fort, Inc. www.cedarfort.com

LIBRARY OF CONGRESS CATALOGING-IN-PUBLICATION DATA

Walker, Laura L., 1975-
The matchup / Laura L. Walker.
pages ; cm
ISBN 978-1-4621-1752-9 (softcover : acid-free paper)
1. Single parents--Fiction. 2. Man-woman relationships--Fiction. I. Title.
PS3623.A4375M38 2016
813'.6--dc23
2015033112

Cover design by Michelle May
Cover design © 2016 Cedar Fort, Inc.
Edited and typeset by Melissa J. Caldwell

Printed in the United States of America

10 9 8 7 6 5 4 3 2 1

Printed on acid-free paper

To my sisters, Alana and Vonda,
whose courage in the face of adversity
has been a source of inspiration to me.
I miss you every day, Vonda!

Also to my beautiful Kayla,
whose light and wonder have helped me to see
beyond the rain.

And to the real Chad and Joy
who made a child's first time at the ballpark
a very special memory.
If I never have the opportunity to thank you in person,
know that in the next life, I will.

ALSO BY LAURA L. WALKER

Pierced by Love

This was the third time she'd called today. Gage Logan avoided verbal communication with his ex-wife whenever possible, but he knew he couldn't dodge her any longer. Impatiently, he answered his phone and barked, "Yeah, April?"

"Gage." April's voice came through sounding thin and reedy. "I need you to take Zachary this weekend."

Gage closed his eyes and cursed under his breath. He had to work this weekend. She knew that. "Why?"

The question hung in the air for a charged moment. Gage tugged at his tie and kept typing on his laptop while he waited for April's response. Her first two calls had come when he was meeting with potential clients. He really wasn't in the mood for this.

When would April get it through her head that he was no longer the naïve kid she'd married? For the thousandth time, Gage regretted ever having met April Westbrook. But then he wouldn't have his son, Zach. Still, even though he loved the little guy, Gage hated having to deal with his ex-wife. Gage had been mesmerized by her porcelain-like face and smooth-as-honey voice. Only now, it was cold and shrill.

"My friend and I are going to Las Vegas."

Vegas. After everything that had happened between them, she

was throwing *that* in his face? It stood to reason they'd be gambling on more than just the machines. At the very least, they were planning on getting smashed. She probably wasn't sober even now. His voice turned to ice. "This 'friend' doesn't happen to be your latest fling, does it? Ryker Payne, I believe?"

"Zachary told you about him?"

"Yeah," he said, scorn lacing his voice. "Hmm. April Payne. The name fits you."

"Don't be ridiculous!" April sniffed. "We're not going there to elope. I never want to try that again."

"No kidding."

"I didn't call you to rehash everything, Gage." *Everything*, meaning their brief and painful marriage. "I need a babysitter for Zachary. I know last weekend was your turn with him, but could you take him again this weekend, *pleeeze*?"

Gage sighed, recalling with a pang the trip he'd made last weekend from Mesa, Arizona, to Tucson to visit Zach. The little guy hadn't been his normally exuberant self. The sadness in Zach's eyes prompted Gage to ask him what was wrong. Zach had cried, "Mommy's boyfriend doesn't like me."

Perplexed at how a kid who'd just turned four could sense something like that, Gage had asked, "Ian doesn't like you?"

But Zach had shaken his head. "Ian doesn't come anymore. Ryker does." Further inquiry on Gage's part had revealed that the slimeball was calling Zach a brat and telling April that she would need to choose between him and Zach soon. A feeling of unease had been gnawing at him ever since.

Gage groaned. As much as he worried over Zach, he really didn't need any more complications in his life at this point. "Have your parents watch him," he said shortly.

"They won't!" she yelled back. "They gave me an ultimatum. Either I clean up my life or they'll file for grandparents' custody of Zachary." Her voice broke on the last syllable.

Gage hardened his heart against the onslaught. April's emotional breakdown seemed convincing, but he knew it was only a dramatic act. "They should. We both know that neither of us are in a position to take care of him."

Gage worked for the Arizona Diamondbacks organization as an account executive for premium sales, which meant that he was in charge of suite rentals, including the organization's swimming pool, the first of its kind at a professional ballpark. Gage loved working with a great team and meeting so many interesting clients on a daily basis. But his job, while lucrative, didn't leave much room for a personal life.

In truth, though, Gage knew that was only part of the problem. The thought of becoming a full-time father made him break out in a cold sweat.

"Please, Gage. I don't want my parents to take him. I'm tired of dealing with them. All they do is lecture me. I'm a complete failure to them."

Did April realize how pathetic she sounded? She'd never learned to take responsibility for herself. How had his life become such a mess?

His mind went back to that day three and a half years earlier when April had told Gage about their six-month-old son. Zach had been a honeymoon baby. Gage and April had divorced six months before he was born. Gage had been shocked, of course. He'd even taken a paternity test since April couldn't seem to stay with one guy for very long. The test had confirmed that Zach was indeed his child. Gage had felt completely out of his element, so when April declared that all she wanted was Gage's money, he'd gladly settled out of court, making arrangements for child support payments and monthly visitations. Then, three months ago, his guilty conscience—and a fair amount of manipulation on April's part—had finally convinced Gage to visit Zach every other week.

He hadn't been able to bring himself to involve his parents in his predicament, however. While they'd worried over his marriage to April and the fact that he continued to shun the Church, Gage had never told them about his son, partly because he couldn't handle his mother's censure and partly because everyone else's lives were neatly falling into place while his was falling apart. Shame became the driving force behind his withdrawal from his family members.

Gage softened his voice. "Your parents will come around. They always do."

It was true. April's parents always gave in to her, either by paying her bills or being Zach's surrogate parents, all in the name of love. They had doted on April throughout her entire life, aiding her in the divorce that had saved Gage's sanity but cost him his self-respect.

Or what little he'd had left of it.

"This time they're threatening to take everything away. My car, my rent money. I'll be forced to live with them again and look for a new job. Or worse. Go back to school."

Gage couldn't stifle a sardonic laugh at that. As far as he was concerned, April was a brat. Maybe April needed some time away— not just a weekend—from Zach to figure out what she wanted to do with her life.

Could I do it? Gage wondered, not liking the direction his thoughts were taking. Could he really become more than a week-end parent? When Gage had looked in the mirror this morning, he'd noticed that he was starting to look more like his own father now. Though he had Jared Logan's nose, he'd always favored his mother. But his face had filled out and his jawline and cheekbones were less prominent. When once he'd had long black hair, now the shorter strands made these changes stand out even more.

Looking like his dad wasn't something to be proud of. Jared Logan had been a successful businessman almost from the time Gage had been born. But he'd neglected his family and created emotional wounds that were still hard for Gage to talk about to this day.

Knowing that he was not only starting to look more like his father but he had, quite literally, *become* his father left a sour taste in Gage's mouth. It was hard to break the cycle.

But his little boy needed a more stable life than what his ex-wife was giving him.

"I'll take him," Gage found himself saying, surprised by the feeling of rightness that settled over him. "And, April, just so you know, I agree with your parents. You need to get your life together. I'm going to file for custody of Zach. I think I stand a good chance at winning."

Her quick intake of breath followed by an expletive let him know he'd infuriated her. "You wouldn't!" she hissed.

"Watch me!"

"Fine!" she snapped. "You know what? Never mind about this weekend! I'll grovel back to my parents before I hand my son over to you."

Something in his gut told Gage not to back down. But he needed to calm her down so she would be reasonable. Working to keep his voice even, he said, "Look, April. Go to Vegas with Ryker. Zach can hang out here. He'll be fine."

Funny how her voice became sweet as honey in the blink of an eye. "Are you sure?"

"I'll meet you at noon tomorrow. Have him ready to go. We can talk about the other stuff later."

"I will. Thanks, Gage. See you then."

"Yeah. See you."

He brought up his brother's number on his phone. It was time. Time to end this charade and face whatever consequences his stupid choices had landed him in. He needed to tell his family the truth.

Pierce's deep voice came through the connection sounding cool and confident. Gage envied that. "Hey, bro. What's up?"

"Pierce, I need to ask you a favor . . ."

Valerie Levington Hall kicked the door of the dryer closed in frustration. When would she learn to check pockets for crayons before starting a load of laundry? Now Whitney's shorts and shirts and even a dress that she liked to wear to church had purple and green streaks all over them.

Yanking the door open once again, she pulled out the marked clothing to assess the damage. Some of the articles were turned inside out, affording Valerie the first glimmer of hope since realizing her mistake. Yes, they were salvageable. Others would need to be thrown away. Hot tears formed on her eyelids. This was just a minor setback. *Keep telling yourself that.*

"Whitney!" she called. "Come here, please."

Rapid footsteps sounded in the distance before her six-year-old daughter appeared. "Yes, Mom?"

Valerie held the evidence up. "How many times have I told you not to leave crayons in your pockets?"

"I didn't!" A look of panic came over Whitney's features. "Justin did."

Cocking her brow, Valerie eyed her daughter skeptically. The evidence clearly pointed to Whitney, considering that all of the clothing in this load of laundry belonged to her. However,

Valerie couldn't discount her daughter's claim on the active five-year-old.

"Are you telling the truth?" She didn't mean to sound so harsh, but Whitney had been telling white lies lately. And since it was easy to blame Justin for everything because most of the time he really was the one responsible for the mess, Valerie was doing her best to teach her daughter accountability. Throwing ruined clothing away really hurt Valerie's budget when she could barely afford to feed and clothe her two children as it was.

Whitney's face scrunched up before her gaze turned downward. "Well . . . I think that maybe I forgot to take them out of my pocket. I'm sorry, Mommy." Whitney looked like she was about to cry. "I'll remember next time."

Valerie hugged her daughter, knowing that it hadn't been easy for her to come clean. "Did you find the invitation to Abrielle's party?"

"No, not yet." Whitney had been invited to a friend's birthday party, which was a big deal because Whitney was rarely invited to spend time with her friends outside of school and church. Valerie always appreciated others' consideration for her children, especially since she was so used to being misunderstood with Justin's learning disorder. He'd been diagnosed with a mild form of autism. High-functioning, but autism nonetheless.

"Go look in your room." Whitney scampered off at Valerie's request.

It had been a trying day. She'd arrived late to work this morning due to the tantrum that Justin had thrown when she dropped him off at school. Yesterday's tantrum had been over the milk spilling from his bowl of cereal onto his shoes. Today's had been about not finding his favorite toy car to put into his backpack. Trying to adhere to the school's policy that no toys be brought from home, Valerie had hidden it. Thankfully, his classroom aide, Miss Jamie, had stood at the doorstep to greet him and take him for a short walk to help him calm down.

Of course, Justin had a difficult time following rules and

helping others. He didn't understand the need to clean messes after he'd made them, although Valerie was working with him on that. He didn't understand about not having his favorite shirt available to wear when it was in the laundry hamper. Justin was smart—he knew his alphabet and numbers and could spell his own name—but he couldn't write it. His motor skills, both gross and fine, were something he and his occupational therapist worked on extensively at school.

With a pang, Valerie recalled sitting numbly in the developmental pediatrician's office after receiving the news of his diagnosis. While it explained why he'd been a colicky baby and such a handful as a toddler—he had not spoken a word until three and a half years of age and was potty-trained just six months ago—it explained nothing at all.

What was autism? Valerie had known nothing about it. She didn't know anyone personally with this diagnosis.

She sure knew enough about it now. More than she wanted to.

Autistic behaviors ranged on a broad spectrum from children who didn't speak at all to children who were developmentally delayed, socially challenged, or required special devices to help them cope with their environment. Earphones for the loud noises they heard, weighted jackets to help calm their nerves when they became too agitated, and music or other soothing noises to help them block outside interferences were just a few of the methods of calming these children. Valerie had learned about them as a classroom observer at the preschool Justin attended, which was designed specifically for children with special needs.

Because Justin rated in the high-functioning range, Valerie was leaning toward the idea of placing him into a regular kindergarten classroom in the next school year where he would benefit from interacting with all kinds of children. Another advantage of this choice would be that Justin would attend the same school as Whitney, who was going into second grade, therefore eliminating the need to drive from one end of Mesa to the other each morning.

However, Justin's preschool teacher, along with the school

psychologist, were advising Valerie that a better option might be to wait and give Justin the extra time he needed to mature.

Valerie was brought out of her reverie as Whitney's voice carried down the hall. "Mom, I looked everywhere for the invitation. It's not in my room."

"Go look in Justin's room. He may have gotten a hold of it." Come to think of it, Justin had been quiet for a long time. That was never a good thing.

At times like these, she lamented the fact that her marriage had come to an unhappy end, that it had never been what she'd envisioned it would be. She'd married Nick Hall in the temple, naively believing in happily-ever-afters. Since that day, however, Valerie had experienced more heartache and discord than she cared to remember. So often, she'd read about God's justice and mercy in the scriptures. But she had yet to figure out why her reward for doing the right things—getting married in the temple, honoring the priesthood holder in her home, and bearing his children—included divorce and subsequent single parenthood. Where was God's mercy in that?

Turning away from the laundry room, she walked down the hall toward Justin's room. She hated the fact that she'd become so jaded.

As an idealistic freshman in college, how was she supposed to know that Nick Hall wasn't the well-brought-up man he seemed to be? It wasn't until after they were married that his dictatorial side came to light. "Honey, that dress is too old-fashioned. Why don't you buy yourself something new?" The first time Nick had thrown her that line, along with his credit card, Valerie could hardly believe her good fortune. As a middle child growing up in a large family, she was used to wearing hand-me-downs. But Nick provided well for her as a manager at his father's golf resort. She'd felt beautiful and special in the new dress Nick had helped her pick out.

But when Valerie came home with a pair of jeans from her favorite department store, Nick insisted she take them back. "What's wrong with them?" Valerie had asked in confusion.

He snorted. "Come on, Val. As my wife, you'll go with me to work-related functions and will need to dress appropriately. Even while you're out running errands, you'll need to represent our family well."

Swallowing back a rejoinder, Valerie did as he asked, cringing at the price tag on the pair of designer jeans she purchased from the mall instead. They wouldn't be able to keep spending like this if they wanted to eat. She was careful to wash her clothing very gently to make it last as long as possible.

She soon found out that she couldn't avoid Nick's outbursts completely, however. Valerie recalled another occasion when she'd been fixing dinner and realized that Nick had used all of the cheese she needed. Turning the burner off, she quickly drove to the corner grocery store, hoping she'd make it back home before Nick arrived from work.

No such luck. His Mercedes Benz—the one they were paying a second mortgage for—was already parked in the driveway when she pulled in. Valerie hopped out and greeted him with a smile and a kiss in an effort to squelch the sense of foreboding that Nick's puckered brow had created. "Where were you?"

She held up the package of cheese. "I needed to make a quick run to the grocery store."

His eyes narrowed. "And you went without wearing any makeup? I thought we talked about this."

They had. That is, Valerie amended silently, Nick had talked and Valerie had listened. Nick had made his feelings quite clear on the subject. "As my wife, you need to—"

"Look the part," Valerie finished automatically. She knew that Nick was hoping for a promotion soon and Valerie couldn't risk it from being seen out in public with a hair or eyelash out of place.

His face softened as he pulled her into his arms. Stroking her hair, he crooned, "You're beautiful, Valerie. I want everyone else to see it too." Meaning she wasn't beautiful the way she was? She kept quiet, but underneath, conflicting feelings warred with each other, resurrecting old insecurities that Valerie had thought she'd buried.

Which were compounded when Nick suggested she highlight her hair like other women were doing. And when he gave her a mani-pedi gift package at a fancy salon for her birthday, she'd delighted in it—until she realized that he expected her to keep up with the routine. Valerie sighed. Really, she was a dirt-under-her-fingernails-kind-of-gal who had learned from her grandmother about edible flowers and the best potting soil. After they were married, though, Nick put a stop to her gardening fetish. "There's no reason to mar that beautiful face by exposing it to harsh sunlight, honey. We can afford to buy vegetables. And if you want flowers on our table, put an order in for them. Who in their right mind wants to slave away in the hot sun and dirt, anyway?"

All of this should have warned Valerie that Nick's values differed from hers. Why hadn't she paid closer attention? Valerie berated herself as she picked up a few stray school papers and toys from the floor. Because she was living her dream of being married to a handsome returned missionary. Then, when Whitney came along, Valerie dropped out of school at Nick's urging. What he was saying was true, she acknowledged. "Our daughter needs you more than you need your education. I earn enough money for my family. You don't need the stress of trying to keep up with assignments while changing diapers and waking up for 2:00 a.m. feedings."

But if she thought life with a new baby was hard, Valerie was completely unprepared for the onslaught she faced with the birth of Justin a short year later. Their feelings of joy at having a son were soon replaced with worry over his inconsolable bouts of colic. "What are you doing to him?" Nick grumbled late one night after he'd gone to bed, yanking his T-shirt down and running a hand through his disheveled hair. Justin's howling hadn't stopped since Valerie's dinner had grown cold on the table.

"Nothing!" Valerie growled, hunger and a mounting lack of sleep compounding her frustration level.

"Well, you must be doing something wrong. Otherwise, he wouldn't cry like this. Did you eat something that didn't agree with him?"

With utmost effort, Valerie held her tongue. Whitney had taken to nursing from her easily, but even two months after birth, Justin still hadn't adjusted. His little body must be hurting for all his crying. But what to do about it?

"I'm doing the best I can." Valerie hated raising her voice to be heard over the baby's wails, but it couldn't be helped. She was beyond all coherence with stress and fatigue.

"Well, make him stop! I have an early meeting tomorrow morning. I need to get some sleep." Not knowing what else to try, she strapped Justin in the car seat and took him for a long drive.

The next three months were much the same. Valerie struggled to put one foot in front of the other as she rocked Justin, fed him, and burped him. She walked up and down the hallway with him. She rocked and fed and burped him some more. She walked up and down the hallway with him again. All day. Every day. Nothing soothed him. Nap times were a blessed reprieve. However, they didn't last very long.

Through it all, Nick seemed oblivious to her plight. Valerie remembered trying to hand the baby to him when he first walked in the door from work. "Not right now," he said on more than one occasion. "I've had a long day."

And she hadn't? "Please, Nick. I just need five minutes to myself." That included three for using the bathroom. With a drawn-out sigh, Nick grudgingly took the baby.

When Nick glanced down at her, his eyes widened in incredulity. "You haven't even showered or changed your clothes." With a lethal sweep of his eyes, he took in the dining table with the breakfast dishes still sitting on it along with the sticky floor where the lid from Whitney's sippy cup had come loose. "*What* have you been doing all day?"

"Taking care of our babies," she snapped, not bothering to tell him that Justin had just spit up on him. He'd find out soon enough.

Pulling Justin's little body away from himself, Nick stared down at his son as if he was a foreign object. "Surely you could find five minutes to grab a paper towel and wipe up this mess." Shoving the baby back at her, he did just that, his jerky movements punctuating his anger.

"I-I guess I could. But then Justin would cry."

"He cries anyway, so what's the difference? That's no excuse to leave the house looking like a huge garbage can."

Valerie strove harder to keep the balance between a semi-clean home, happy kids, and a happy husband. More often than not, the scales were tipped in Justin's favor.

"You're always coddling that kid and ignoring our daughter," Nick said just after Justin's second birthday. "You shouldn't give in to his tantrums. And you need to quit allowing him to make so many messes."

"I'm trying, Nick. It's not like I want Justin to be this way. Something must be wrong, but I don't know what."

"Take him to the doctor."

"I just took him in for his checkup. Aside from a speech delay, the doctor said everything looked fine."

"Well, he obviously isn't fine. He doesn't talk, doesn't respond to me, and is totally focused on getting into stuff, even when we put it away."

"He does seem to have a one-track mind at times."

"No kidding. I'm sick of him disrupting our lives. We can't even have a peaceful dinner anymore. And we never get to spend time together." He pulled her into his arms and kissed her with a fervor that she knew meant one thing. Nick wanted her undivided attention.

As much as it hurt to hear Nick disparage their own offspring, she had to admit that what he was saying was true. But it wouldn't always be this way, would it? A frisson of fear crept in. What if Justin didn't get better?

Nick's voice softened as he caressed her cheek. "Let's get away, Val. Your passport is still current, right? My parents could watch the kids while we take a trip."

Mmm. Valerie closed her eyes and rested her head against

Nick's chest, hearing the sound of gentle ocean waves lapping in the distance. "Sounds good."

Their plane to Tahiti took off a week later. Valerie and Nick enjoyed a much-needed break away from their kids. By day, they waded in the ocean and watched surfers battling waves in the distance. By night, they walked along Teavora Beach, holding hands and stealing kisses in the moonlight. There, away from the day-to-day stresses and worries of their lives, Valerie believed she and Nick were still in love.

But reality came crashing in on them much the way the waves had in Tahiti when they landed back on American soil. Back at her in-laws' home, Valerie had almost left the guest bedroom after gathering her children's bags when she heard Nick's voice coming from the monitor. "He'll be fine, Mom. You did the right thing."

"I did exactly what you asked me to. I'm not sure it worked, though. Nick, there's got to be something we can do to straighten him out. He can't continue to climb on everything and break stuff. Nor can he be allowed to throw his tantrums."

Nick sighed. "I know. I've tried talking to Valerie but it's no use. She won't listen to reason."

"She's teaching Justin bad behavior. We didn't let him get away with it here. He spent a good deal of time in time-out with your father. At times, he had to physically hold Justin down because the boy was so distraught."

Valerie bit her lip. Talk about being distraught! A feeling of disgust and ire built in the pit of her stomach as she learned that Nick's parents had pitted their will against Justin's and undermined Valerie's parenting methods, all under Nick's sneaky direction. Spanking him for pulling down their curtains and keeping him in his bedroom until he stopped crying. Practically forcing him to potty-train when he clearly wasn't ready—and punishing him when he had accidents. What good did these methods do when the child couldn't respond in an appropriate way? How did they know that Justin understood the reason behind what they were doing?

Was it any wonder that Justin would hardly let Valerie out of his sight for the next two weeks? "That's it, Nick Hall!" Valerie shouted with Justin still clinging to her every time she tried to walk out the door just to go to the post office or grocery store, all while crying at the top of his lungs. "I will never go anywhere with you again."

Nick stalked up to her, his jaw clenched. He looked so angry that for a split second, Valerie wondered if he was going to strike her. "Oh, don't you worry your pretty little head about that, Valerie, because we're through. I've had enough of this brat. My mom tried to shape him up in the short time she had him, but you're too much of a pushover to let any real progress be made."

Shaking, Valerie asked, "What do you mean, 'we're through'?"

"Just what I said. I'll be in contact through my attorney." With that, he packed a bag and left, slamming the door behind him. Numb, all Valerie could do was stare in shock even with Whitney and Justin wailing—albeit for different reasons.

Valerie and Nick divorced soon afterward and she moved in with her parents. She worried about the possibility of a custody battle, but Nick had wanted nothing to do with "that kid," instead only opting for visitation rights for Whitney. Valerie had sought help through Arizona's Early Intervention Program to get Justin the assistance he needed, which included American Sign Language or ASL, followed by speech therapy using picture cards or PECS, occupational therapy, and even potty training in a non-threatening manner when they all agreed that he was ready. A heady sense of relief enveloped her as the tremendous burden for Justin's day-to-day care was shared with others who actually cared for his well-being.

Living with her parents wasn't an ideal situation, however. Justin repeatedly ransacked her mom's pantry and her dad's tools, scattering them every which way. They'd had to put everything under lock and key just to keep him safe. Finally, in a state of exhaustion, Valerie's mom told her, "Honey, I love my grandson, but I can't take this constant chaos any longer. Your dad and I have a solution for you. When Grandma and Grandpa Skylar leave on their mission in two months, we would like for you to move into their house. You can take care of their lawn and garden while they're gone."

The arrangement had worked out terrifically for the past sixteen months. They would need to repaint the walls to cover Justin's scribbles before Valerie's grandparents returned from Des Moines, Iowa, but Valerie was feeling pretty good about the fact that she had kept her grandparents' place in northeast Mesa in one piece. Of course, they would need to find another place to live soon, but she again pushed that to the back of her mind.

"Mommy! Mommy! Hurry!" Whitney's panicked voice carried from the hallway. "Justin got into your makeup!"

When she sprinted into the room, she came face to face with a happy little boy proudly wearing lipstick. Mascara streaked his face. Valerie almost laughed until she saw her liquid makeup smeared into the bed and carpet.

G age entered Eric and Sarah Nielsen's home in Tempe, Arizona, later that evening with trepidation. Despite the enticing aromas that were wafting from his mom's kitchen, Gage's stomach clenched. He doubted he'd be able to eat a single bite. By asking Pierce to set up this dinner so that he could explain his dilemma, Gage knew he was taking the coward's way out. But if he'd called his mom, she would have ferreted out the details right then. This was one story that needed to be told face-to-face.

"Hi, Gage." His stepdad, Eric, slapped him on the back. "We haven't seen you in a while. How's everything going?"

Gage shrugged, feeling slightly ill. He was still trying to figure out how to tell his family. Could his family members eventually come to love his little boy like one of their own?

He strode through the living room and rounded the corner where he found his mom, Sarah, setting dishes of steaming food on the table. His sister-in-law, Noelle, who was approaching her seventh month of pregnancy, was setting the table.

Remembering his manners in the company of these women, he offered, "Hey, Noelle. Why don't you have a seat and I'll take care of that?"

Both women looked up and smiled at him. "Hi, Gage." His mom gave him a hug.

"Hi, Gage. That's okay," Noelle said. "I'm finishing up now."

"Where are Pierce and Caleb?"

"They're outside, kicking the soccer ball around. The temperatures are climbing, so they're trying to get all of the outdoor time they can before summer hits."

"Yeah, I hear you. This is my favorite time of the year—and busiest."

Noelle gave him a knowing look. "The thick of baseball season. We've hardly seen you lately."

Gage had spent the better part of the spring drumming up business for the Diamondbacks, schmoozing with various CEOs of companies who wanted to offer their employees incentives for their hard work with the usage of premium seating. The suites at Chase Field usually filled up in spite of their exorbitant prices. Although some families reserved the same one year after year as a place to hold reunions, the pool remained the most popular spot for such events.

"Dinner is ready," Sarah announced.

Noelle called her husband and son inside. Pierce greeted Gage and kissed his wife before whispering something in her ear. Pierce had the look of a truly content man. And why wouldn't he with an adorable family and a career in biomedical engineering that was taking off? A lump formed in Gage's throat. He'd wanted that same ideal with April, but things had turned out much differently.

After the group sat down at the table and folded their arms, Eric offered a simple yet sincere blessing on the food, causing Gage to squirm in discomfort. When he finished, everyone passed the dishes around and started to eat. Gage filled his plate with his mom's delicious chicken Alfredo with homemade sauce and scooped a small portion of vegetables onto his plate. He took a few bites, but the queasiness in his stomach made it impossible to eat.

"Are you all right, Gage?" Sarah asked. Her food sat untouched.

He stared at her for a solemn moment. While he'd always

known that he would have this conversation with his family sooner or later, he'd do anything to avoid it right now. "I have something to tell all of you."

Sarah waited. When Gage hesitated, Eric placed his arm around her shoulders, lifting his brow at him. "Well?"

"April has been calling me a lot lately."

Sarah eyed him worriedly. "What for? She couldn't possibly be trying to get back together with you, could she?"

"No." He shook his head. "It isn't that." Clearing his throat, he tried again. "We, uh, have a four-year-old son. She wants me to take him off her hands this weekend."

Eyes bulging, Noelle turned to her husband in shock.

"Gage!" His mom gasped indelicately, prompting Gage to plunge into his explanation. He told them of April's deception after their divorce, the paternity test, and even the way he'd blown off any serious commitments toward his child.

"So that's why you were making all those trips to Tucson," Pierce said in derision. "I thought you had another girlfriend down there."

"No. Just a son named Zach."

"Just a 'son'?" Noelle echoed in disbelief. "How can you say that as calmly as if you'd bought a pet hamster?" Her voice rose a little at the end.

Pierce's brows slashed downward. "Let me get this straight. You had this kid a full year before our son was born and yet didn't bother to tell us about him?"

Gage flinched. He'd been on the receiving end of that glare more times than he could count through the years. Still, he'd hoped that Pierce, the brother he was closest to, would understand. "I'm not trying to dismiss it as if it's no big deal. I didn't tell you all before because, well, I was embarrassed about what happened, okay? I know I screwed up. But by the time I received the results from the paternity test, Zach was almost a year old. He'd been with April the whole time and I decided not to fight for him. I didn't want to get involved with her again."

"Well, you'd better rethink your plan," Eric said, neither applauding Gage nor condemning him. Considering that Eric had never been on Gage's list of favorite people, he had provided a calming influence for the Logan family. And he obviously loved Gage's mother deeply. For that, at least, Gage was grateful.

"I am. I'm going to file for full custody. Noelle, I wanted to ask you for the number at your dad's law office."

Noelle's father, Samuel Jensen, was an attorney specializing in family law. "My job is very demanding, and if I'm granted custody, I'll need to procure a reputable babysitter or a part-time opening at a day care center, at the very least."

"Be careful with day care centers," Noelle cautioned him. "The best ones will have long waiting lists."

Gage thanked his sister-in-law for her advice and added reluctantly, "Zach has already been going to day care part-time in Tucson. And speaking of childcare, I'll need to find a babysitter for Saturday and Sunday. I was able to take tomorrow off, but one day is all I get for now."

"We can watch Zach for you on those days, Gage," Noelle said. "As long as you don't mind us taking him to church."

"We're going to a different ward on Sunday, Noelle," Pierce reminded her.

"I'm sure it'll be fine." Turning to Gage, she explained, "We've been invited to a baby blessing in Queen Creek on Sunday, but we can still watch Zach."

"I'll just need to find him a suit," Gage said.

"I'll call my brother and ask if he might have an outfit that his son has outgrown. And Caleb will be thrilled to have a new cousin to play with, won't you, Caleb?" she added, turning to her son, who was staring at the adults in wide-eyed wonder.

"Uncle Gage, I didn't know that you're a dad."

Pierce looked at his son and then back at his brother before mocking, "Yeah, I wonder what else *Uncle Gage* has been hiding from us. Maybe he'll tell us next that he owns a kangaroo Down Under."

"Huh?" Caleb asked.

"Daddy's just trying to be funny," Noelle said quickly. "You know how he and his brothers are always joking around with each other."

This time, though, Gage knew this was no joke. He sighed, deciding to let the criticism go. Because even though he would like to retaliate, Gage was more concerned about his mother's reaction at the moment. Or lack of one, rather. Other than her initial outburst, she hadn't said anything else throughout the entire discussion. Gage hoped he hadn't put her into cardiac arrest with his announcement.

Looking over at her, he saws tears in her eyes. "Sorry, Mom. I don't know what to say." Which, for him, was a first. "I guess I'm just not the kind of guy you've wanted me to become."

"That's a cop-out and you know it!" Pierce yelled. "You've had the chance to turn your life around. And yet you've walked away from everything Mom and Dad taught us!"

"Oh, yeah? And what did Dad teach us?" In the heat of the moment, Gage stood and stared Pierce down. His voice held an icy edge. "That work was more important than everything else, including his own family? Seems to me I learned his lessons really well."

"Pierce," Noelle said when Pierce looked like he wanted to say something more. She gently shook her head at him, inclining it toward Sarah, whose tears were falling in earnest now. "This isn't the right time for that."

Pierce took one look at their mother and snorted before fixing his glare on Gage once again.

Gage's chest tightened. He'd been a wilder teenager than Pierce and their older brother, Craig, but had straightened his life out and had been looking forward to serving a mission. The call had come just before his parents' marriage had finally collapsed, bringing all of his insecurities and frustration back to the surface. It had been too much to handle, the feeling of helplessness as they fought and the guilt for knowing that he'd played a significant role in the Logans' shame. To top it all off, he was scheduled to leave on his mission in two months' time to teach the people of Chile that true peace and happiness came from changing their lives and accepting the gospel of Jesus Christ. Missing that same peace that had eluded his own family for so long, Gage had not accepted the call.

Pierce hadn't fared much better. Jared and Sarah's divorce became final when Pierce was almost ready to come home from his mission. Even though he stuck it out, he'd had a few hang-ups to work through before marrying Noelle five years ago. He'd been afraid to take a chance on love. Fortunately, Noelle had shown him that through faith and commitment, their relationship would work out.

Pierce and Noelle quietly cleared the table and packed the extra food away. Eric stayed by Sarah's side, a forlorn expression making his face appear longer.

Gage's stomach clenched. His mom wouldn't even look at him. "Mom?" he asked tentatively.

She shook her head and sniffled. "I'm sorry. I can't have this discussion with you right now. Please excuse me." She stood and abruptly left the room.

Gage couldn't blame her. He wished he could run away from himself too. Pierce took advantage of the lull to leave the room as well, telling Caleb to grab his soccer ball so they could go home. His jerky movements and rigid back spoke of his anger.

Gage's heartache at his mother's disappointment was coupled with the regret of watching father and son in perfect harmony as Caleb asked Pierce if they could kick the ball around for a few more minutes. Until that moment, Gage hadn't thought about all the things he'd missed out on with Zach.

Noelle shrugged apologetically. "I'm sorry, Gage. You'll have to excuse Pierce. He's always been very protective of your mother. Your news is going to take some getting used to." She wrote a phone number on a piece of paper and handed it to him. "This is my dad's number. He'll be happy to help you."

"Thanks, Noelle." Gage pocketed the slip of paper. "I'm sorry, Eric. I don't know what to say. I've screwed up big time."

Eyeing Gage sympathetically, Eric said, "Give your mother some time. She'll come around. In the meantime, I suggest that you come up with a workable plan on how to become a real father to this boy. That's going to take a major sacrifice on your part, considering that you've come and gone as you pleased through the years. You'd better decide if you're in this for real or if it would be better to let someone else take care of him."

"As far as I'm concerned, there is no one else. I'm in this for real."

Eric nodded sagely. "Glad to hear it. Bring him by next weekend, if you can. We'd love to meet him."

Gage couldn't help thinking that it should have been his own father saying the words, but he appreciated his stepfather's offer nonetheless. "I'll see if I can. Thanks." Knowing that he'd worn out his welcome, he stood to put his plate and utensils in the dishwasher. "I think I'd better go. Tell Mom I love her and that I'm sorry. I'll call her in a few days."

Once he was in his car, Gage released the breath he'd been holding. He rubbed his tired eyes and then ran his hand through his hair, missing the longer thickness. At times like this, he wished he could grab it and yank.

Gage growled in frustration. April wasn't the only one who needed to put her life back together. He needed to make some serious changes as well.

Valerie momentarily stopped scrubbing the smudges of makeup off the walls to watch her brother-in-law, Brent, run the steam cleaner back and forth with precision. As the powerful machine picked up the residue of the gooey substance, Valerie began to hope that the carpet hadn't been ruined. Her oldest sister, Chloe, was in the living room reading bedtime stories to Whitney and Justin after brushing their teeth and helping them find their pajamas. Thankfully, Brent and Chloe's children were now old enough to stay home by themselves.

Brent turned off the steam cleaner, indicating the area where her liquid foundation had formed a puddle in the carpet. "I've gone over the floor twice but that makeup went down pretty deep in this spot and we're almost out of cleaning solution."

Valerie nodded. "I used some when Justin smashed a banana into the living room carpet last week."

Brent shook his head. "You're going to have to do something about that kid."

Valerie chuckled even though his comment rankled. "Like what? Institutionalize him?"

"No. I just meant that you're going to have to keep a closer eye on him. Otherwise, you're going to have to pay to replace your grandparents' things before they get home."

He had a point. Still, Valerie turned away in irritation and left the room, not bothering to tell her no-nonsense brother-in-law that she'd stored her makeup case on the top shelf of her closet and that Justin must have climbed up to get it. He wouldn't understand, anyway.

When she entered the living room, Chloe was just finishing reading the last book. Whitney was nodding off. Justin's yawn told Valerie that he wasn't too far behind. She gently lifted Whitney's shoulders off the couch, prodding her to stand up. "Tell Aunt Chloe thank you."

"Thank you, Aunt Chloe." Whitney gave her aunt a hug.

Chloe returned the embrace. "Sure thing, sweetie. Be a good girl for your mom, okay? You're her number one helper."

"I know. What would she do without me?" That earned a chuckle from the adults, who knew that Whitney was simply repeating Valerie's oft-repeated accolade.

Valerie pulled Whitney into her arms, loving the feel of her soft body. "Sweet dreams. Run along to bed. I love you."

"I love you, too, Mommy."

Valerie watched her go and turned to Chloe hesitantly. "Thanks for coming so quickly. I'm sure that's what saved the carpet from being ruined. And thanks again for the clothes." Chloe had brought over a garbage sack filled with clothing her children had outgrown after Valerie had spilled the whole sordid story to her over the phone.

"No problem, Valerie. I'm glad we could help."

"We've run out of cleaning solution. I'm going to make a quick run to the store for more."

"Since when is running to the store a quick trip?" Chloe quipped before adding with a sigh, "Hurry. It's getting late and we need to get home to our own kids soon."

"I know. Thanks, Chloe." She got into her car and drove off as much to calm her nerves as to get the cleaning solution.

Gage passed a department store on his way home and pulled into the parking lot at the last second. He should make a list of all the things that Zach would need, but for now, Gage figured a few odds and ends to get through the weekend were in order.

He wheeled his shopping cart into the kids' section, knowing from his visits that Zach liked dinosaurs and cars and trucks and basically anything with wheels. He grabbed toys and books, then headed over to the housewares aisle to pick up a few extra sheets and a blanket for the bed he'd recently purchased for the spare bedroom. Not that he'd anticipated needing to use it so soon. Zach had never been to Gage's place before. Now he wondered if his subconscious had been trying to tell him something.

What else did he need? *Night-lights? Toothbrushes? A dog? Hmm. Maybe I should think about getting a dog.*

Remembering that he also needed a few basic items like paper towels and garbage bags, Gage headed in that direction next. His mind was so focused on whether or not Zach would like a Minion pillow or the Incredible Hulk one he'd seen, Gage absentmindedly looked at the woman with the pixie-like face and blonde hair approaching him from the opposite direction, barely registering her slight nod as she passed. A memory clicked into place, making him stop in his tracks.

He turned and looked back, surprise hitting him in the gut when he realized she'd done the same thing. She looked the same but different. More grown up. Gage looked her up and down. Heat suffused his face when he remembered how he'd embarrassed her upon hearing through her best friend that she was harboring a crush for his older brother. He'd been a jerk back then. Come to think of it, Gage thought with chagrin, that hadn't changed. He offered her a reluctant smile. "Valerie Levington, is that you?"

Valerie's heart began hammering in her rib cage. That deep voice could only belong to one person. Gage Logan, the boy who'd teased her mercilessly at church when they were teenagers. Gage always knew how to rile her when she was feeling particularly shy among the fourteen-year-old loudmouths in their Sunday School class and hadn't let her forget the one time she mentioned to her friend that she had a crush on Pierce. Valerie's cheeks still burned at the memory of him bringing the adolescent changes of her body to the attention of the other boys in their class. She'd hated him ever since.

She hadn't seen him since the summer she'd graduated from high school and found Nick. Her mother had mentioned that he'd straightened himself out and received a mission call to Chile years ago. She'd even heard that he backed out of the call and became inactive soon after. No surprise there. But then she'd become engrossed in bottles and diapers and Gage had fallen off her radar.

She took a fortifying breath. "Actually, I'm Valerie Hall now. Hi, Gage."

As he came closer, Valerie could see that Gage had matured and become quite good-looking. His hair had always been dark, but now it was shorter than she'd ever seen it. His face was fuller, his build slightly stockier. Fine lines were starting to form at the corners of his eyes, probably from too much sun. Though his brown eyes still held a hint of flirtation, they had dimmed over time. A slight hesitation had replaced his usual confidant air. "It's been a long time, Valerie."

"How are you?"

His smile slipped a little before he put it back in place. "I'm all right. How about yourself?"

Valerie found it increasingly difficult to hold her easy-going stance in front of this man who'd somehow been able to see what none of the other kids had—her anxieties and fears—and enjoyed getting a rise from her. Valerie remembered her mother's admonition. "He'll keep teasing you as long as you let him, honey. If you want him to stop, you need to quit reacting so negatively to it."

Swallowing past the unpleasant memories, Valerie shrugged. "I'm okay. What brings you to this part of town?"

"I actually live nearby. I decided to make a quick stop on my way home from my mom's place. She moved to Tempe after marrying my stepdad."

"I heard that she got married again. I'm glad for her. So," she said to fill in the silence that followed, "what have you been up to?"

"Working mostly."

"Where do you work?"

When he mentioned that he worked for the Diamondbacks ball club, Valerie was impressed. She listened as he gave her an overview of the responsibilities of his job. "So what's going on in your life?"

"Nothing much," she answered, suddenly feeling tongue-tied. She held up the plastic container of steam cleaner solution and chuckled to ease the tension. "I'm trying to be a magician by making things disappear. Messes, in particular. My son is good at making them." Valerie offered him a half-smile.

Gage responded with one of his own. "So, I knew that you'd gotten married, but I didn't realize you were living in Mesa."

Valerie hesitated for a split second before blurting out the fact that she was divorced.

Gage's eyes sharpened at this news, immediately zeroing in on her ring-less finger. "How long ago did that happen?"

"It's been a few years," she said softly. "I'm staying in my grandparents' home until they return from their mission."

The grim line of Gage's mouth told her all she needed to know about how he felt about missions. *He obviously hasn't come back into the Church*, she thought sadly. He was one against the world, a feeling she was very familiar with lately. For some strange reason, the thought made Valerie want to wrap her arms around him.

Which, of course, she would never do. Her tendency to shy away from people kept her from forming deep relationships. Initiating physical contact with someone she wasn't close to wasn't her style. *But this is Gage*, a little voice told her. *You've known him for most of your life.*

But that didn't mean she'd ever appreciated who he was or how he'd treated her. Instead, she should be running from him as far and fast as she could go. Why, then, did Valerie feel so compelled to comfort him in a moment of weakness? "Gage," she began haltingly. "I heard that you—well, that things didn't exactly work out for you after your parents divorced. I'm sorry."

"Sorry for what? It isn't your fault."

"No. I just meant that I'm sorry for the disappointment you must have felt. Life has a way of turning everything on its side just when we think we have it figured out."

Gage studied her intently for a moment before agreeing. "Yeah. I've taken my share of bumps lately. But things will work out. At least, that's what I keep telling myself."

Valerie furrowed her brows. "What's wrong, Gage?"

He shrugged as if whatever was bothering him was of no consequence, but Valerie recognized the signs of someone in distress—the averted gaze and loud swallowing. The jawline that was tight enough to crack his teeth.

And although he was obviously trying for a light tone, Valerie didn't miss the strain in his voice. "I'm just trying to figure a few things out. Mainly, I've decided that I need to file for custody of my four-year-old son, but the logistics of that change will be difficult to work around, especially where my job is concerned."

She hadn't known that he'd gotten married. No sooner had that thought come than when another followed, which formed a sick feeling in her stomach. What if he *hadn't* married her? It was quite a common thing in today's world. Impulsively backing up, she bumped into a display of household cleaning supplies and accidentally knocked a few down. "Well, good luck with that. I, um, I'd better get home. My sister is watching my kids and I promised her that I wouldn't take too long. It was good to see you, Gage."

Picking two containers of Clorox wipes up and setting them back on the display, Gage gave her a cool smile. "Yeah. It's good to see you too. Take care."

She spun around and headed down to the frozen foods section. This kind of a day called for some serious ice cream. Chocolate chip cookie dough was just the thing.

G age was getting tired of this commute. He'd made it spo- radically for the past three years, depending on his job schedule. Pulling his black Chevy Camaro into Oracle Foothills Estates in Tucson, Gage took the familiar turns until he came to the impressive adobe-style home that belonged to April's parents, Keith and Madeline Westbrook. Keith was a well-respected oral surgeon and Madeline the owner of a prestigious art gallery. April had called at the last minute and told Gage to pick up Zach at his grandparents' house, leaving Gage with the sneaking suspicion that April had already snuck out of town with her boyfriend.

He parked the car and wiped his sweaty palms on the denim fabric of his jeans before exiting the vehicle. What was it about April's parents that turned Gage into a nervous wreck every time he saw them? They were rich, but they weren't snobbish. Yet they'd been a little cool toward him since the divorce, making Gage feel like he'd disappointed them somehow.

He rang the doorbell and waited for the housekeeper to appear. Within moments, Gage saw the impish grin of Zach through the glass, and heard his excited chatter muted by the massive oak door. Gage grinned back.

The door opened and Zach darted out like a bullet, slamming into Gage's legs with such force that he had a hard time staying upright. "Daddy! Daddy!"

"Hey, Zach. How's it going?"

The housekeeper nodded shortly before ushering him inside and bidding Gage to wait in the formal parlor for April's parents. "Daddy, look what Grandma and Grandpa gave me." He ran out of the room and came back holding an electronic tablet up for Gage's inspection. "Cool, huh?"

Lifting one brow, Gage met Zach's excited gaze and replied, "Yeah." The few times Gage had allowed Zach to play games on his smartphone, the four-year-old had impressed him with his knowledge and dexterity. But he'd also noticed how habit-forming these small devices could be, even for himself. He'd be talking to April about this as soon as she got back from Vegas.

Gage stood when Madeline Westbrook rounded the corner, wearing a paisley scarf with a stark white tailored pantsuit that accentuated her thin face and dainty frame. Her auburn hair was pulled back into a loose bun. Pulling her glasses down the length of her nose, she peered at her grandson. "Now remember, young man. That is to be kept here at Grandma's house so that you'll have it to play with the next time you visit."

"Okay, Grandma." Gage's irritation eased a little with those words.

"Hello, Gage. This is quite a momentous occasion for you, taking Zachary for an entire weekend. Are you sure you'll be able to handle him for that long?" Her skeptical look rankled as nothing else would have.

"We'll be fine," he said evenly.

She studied him for a moment before adding, "Keith would like to speak with you first."

Gage kept his features carefully under control. It wouldn't do to let April's mother to see the doubts he was harboring about his parenting abilities. "Sure."

She left to summon her husband. Gage only half-listened to Zach's excited chatter concerning the "trip" he was taking with his dad. He would need to tell Zach at some point that this wasn't going to be as fun as he was imagining it would be. Up to this point, Gage's visits had consisted of trips to the zoo or the children's museum where he and Zach loved to participate in the science-based activities together. But this time, Gage would mostly be tied up at work. He would take Zach to someplace fun today. He just wasn't sure where yet.

"Gage, good to see you," Keith Westbrook said when he and Madeline entered the room, stretching his hand out for a hand-shake. His grip was firm, his smile tight. His eyes were like steel.

"Hi, Keith."

"Have a seat." April's father indicated the stiff settee Gage had been sitting on only moments before. Gage clamped his mouth shut in an effort to keep from blurting out that he'd already waited long enough and would rather be on his way.

"Now, then," Keith said in a falsely amiable voice, "Madeline and I want to be sure that we're on the same page with you. I'm not sure how much April has told you, but we are concerned about the fact that she has this new boyfriend living with her. They've been leaving Zachary with us quite often lately to go off to who knows where."

"That or they always have a whole horde of other adults at their place," Madeline said, "like they're indulging in one endless party. I'm having difficulty finding a moment to talk to April alone."

That came as no surprise. "She's been asking me to watch Zach more often as well."

Looking at his wife solemnly for a moment, Keith continued, "We can't seem to get it through April's head that she needs to stop acting like a teenager and take care of her son. Madeline and I have decided that it's time to take some course of action, namely seeking custody of Zachary, so that he will have a stable home and more positive learning environment."

Along with a set of grandparents who will spoil him rotten like they did with his mom, Gage thought sourly.

"I don't know if you are aware of this, but things don't seem quite right with April lately. Whenever we take care of Zachary, he devours his food before asking for seconds."

"He's a growing boy," Gage said, although he had a feeling that Keith was leading up to something more serious.

"That's true, but this isn't our only concern. Zachary has nearly grown out of his clothes, yet when Madeline asked April when she was going to buy him some new outfits, April only gave vague excuses. We'll gladly help out with expenses if necessary but Madeline and I are wondering if you are keeping up on your child support payments."

"Of course I am." Gage gritted his teeth to keep from shouting. "She obviously isn't using it for Zach's care."

Keith appeared thoughtful. "Well, it isn't right or fair to make Zachary suffer the consequences of April's poor choices."

"Are you saying that the only time Zach gets a decent meal is when he's at day care or when he's with you?" Gage growled, becoming angrier by the second.

Keith's mouth twisted into a grimace. "The situation needs to change soon," he said, neither validating nor assuaging Gage's alarm.

Gage couldn't agree more. He decided to lay it to him straight. "Keith, you don't need to worry about filing for custody of Zach. I'm already planning to do that."

Keith studied him shrewdly before agreeing. "I've always felt that I could trust you, Gage. When April met you, we had high hopes that you could help her turn her life back around. However, she was already a party girl by that time. You may not believe this, but she really did love you, even though she wasn't a good wife for you."

Gage quirked an eyebrow. "Are you sure about that? It seems to me that keeping the news of Zach's birth from me points to the exact opposite." The fact that April's parents finally convinced her to do the right thing was the only reason Gage was working so willingly with them now.

"She was afraid you'd take him away from her. We're sorry,

Gage. Instead of protecting April, we should have allowed the two of you to work things out for yourselves."

"Well," Gage said tightly, shrugging off his apology, "the good news is that we can at least help Zach now. It sounds like we want the same thing for him."

"Absolutely. But my question is, how are you going to take care of him, being a single father? Relocating him will take quite a bit of adjustment on both your parts. Maybe it would be best if Zachary stays with us, after all."

Not a chance, he inwardly seethed. This family had cost him enough already. In a neutral tone, he replied, "Let me worry about those details. At least we both agree that April shouldn't be his main caregiver anymore."

Keith sighed. "No. Zachary needs you right now. But are you sure that you are ready for this responsibility? Kids aren't easy to haul around. You have to carefully choose your activities with them. What about your penchant for weekly cocktail hours or your Cardinals football games?"

Gage's face grew hot with Keith's interrogation. So what if he went out with his co-workers once in a while after a long week and attended the NFL games more religiously than church? His life wouldn't change all that much. There was no reason that Gage couldn't take Zach along with him to the Cardinals' games during the Diamondbacks' off-season.

An inner voice pierced his conscience. *Would your way of raising Zach be much better than the Westbrooks'?* Gage squelched the thought immediately. He wasn't a bad guy just because his lifestyle differed from that of his parents. Unlike April, at least Gage had a sense of responsibility where a kid was concerned. It wasn't like he kept whiskey in his home. In fact, Gage had given up drinking alcohol a long time ago. When he went out with his friends, he opted for a cola because he was the designated driver.

The Westbrooks weren't members of the Church and had never condemned Gage for his indulgences. If Gage was honest with himself, he'd admit that he'd be hard-pressed to find a willing babysitter for those visits to the bars and clubs. Neither Noelle nor his mother would put up with that.

Gage groaned, accepting the inevitable. His life was about to change in a big way. How he'd manage, he didn't know.

Sarah Nielsen slammed the trunk of her car down with a little more force than necessary after loading her groceries. Rounding the car, she turned the key in the engine and waited for the hot air blowing from the vent to cool. Or maybe it was her own vent that needed to cool. Because of Gage's shocking revelation from the night before, Sarah was having difficulty putting one foot in front of the other today.

Gage? A father? Something he'd known for several years and had refrained from telling his family? *Oh, Gage. Where did I go wrong with you?*

If only things had been different while raising her boys. She and her ex-husband, Jared, shared the blame. But enough time should have passed since those difficult years for Gage to recover from her and Jared's neglect and become a responsible and trustworthy man, right?

Her cell phone chimed. Sarah's oldest son's number illuminated the screen. With a shaky voice, she answered. "Hi, Craig."

Craig, who normally thought everything through before acting, blurted, "Is it true?"

Which meant he could only be speaking about Gage.

Sarah sighed. "Yes. How did you find out?"

"Through Pierce. He called late last night with some half-baked story about Gage and April having a four-year-old son. Did he really just tell you about him last night?"

Sarah rubbed the spot where a headache had badgered her since this confusion began. "I'm afraid so, Craig. I knew that Gage was traveling back and forth to Tucson for the past few years but he wouldn't tell me what was going on, only that it was something that I didn't need to worry about. I don't understand why he excluded us."

"He's probably embarrassed about it."

Sarah found herself nodding even though Craig couldn't see her. "Yes. Gage mentioned that last night." But Sarah knew that couldn't be all. Something else must have held her youngest son back, in spite of the unconditional love they'd shown.

"So what's going to happen to this boy now?" Craig asked.

"Gage says that April's behavior is becoming more erratic lately. He's decided to file for custody of his son, but he's unsure if he can pull it off with his tough job schedule."

"Hmm. Maybe we could all fast for Gage."

A tiny seed of hope loosened the tightness in Sarah's chest at his suggestion. "Yes. Let's do that. It isn't just Gage who needs the Lord's help, Craig. This is threatening to divide our family."

Craig gave a low whistle. "You're not kidding. Pierce was still pretty upset when he told me. He was grumbling about Noelle having to watch Zach for a couple days. Said something about not letting Gage pawn his kid off on her any longer than that."

"I confess I want to throttle Gage too." She smiled at Craig's chuckle. Then she grew serious. "But Gage has been struggling for a long time. Now we at least know where he's coming from. No matter how tempting it is to stay angry with him, we need to show him our support."

"I agree. Have you already talked to Dad about this?"

"No, I haven't."

"Would you like for me to call him instead?"

Craig had always been a pillar of strength in their unhappy home. Now, as a school counselor, listening to others and helping them understand and work through their difficulties was his specialty. Even though Sarah appreciated his willingness to ease her burden, she declined. "This is something I need to do. Why don't you call Pierce back, though, and let him know about the fast? And if you feel a lecture about treating his younger brother kindly coming on, I won't stand in your way."

Craig guffawed. "Will do. Keep me in the loop."

"Okay. Love you."

"Love you too."

Ending the call, Sarah brought up Jared's number in her list of contacts. Taking one more deep breath, she pushed the call button and waited. Two rings later, Jared Logan answered. "Hi, Jared. It's me."

"What do you need, Sarah?" His voice sounded mildly surprised.

"I, um, need to talk to you. About Gage."

In the awkward pause that followed, Jared asked, "What about him?"

In halting sentences, Sarah explained the situation, noting Jared's sharp intake of breath. "Are you serious?"

"Yes. The boy's name is Zachary. Zach for short."

"What can I do to help?"

Releasing a pent-up breath she hadn't realized she'd been holding, Sarah presented Craig's idea of the family fast. "Sure, we'll do that," he said easily, referring to his current wife, Tamara. "Sarah, I feel that Gage will pull through this in time. He's a smart guy. He'll figure it out."

"Hopefully before anything else happens." She hated to sound pessimistic, but nothing had come of the many times she'd tried to help their youngest son. "It seems to me that Gage should have figured out by now that he can't do this on his own."

"He's tenacious, which can be a good thing in the business world. But in personal relationships, as you know, that characteristic presents a challenge. I'm afraid he may have picked that up from me."

A seemingly random memory came to Sarah. "Do you recall when the boys were little and they would get into little arguments? At times, they had more energy than they knew what to do with."

"That was when you would take them to the park or set them up with a project to do."

"Anything to change their focus. If we can get Gage to focus his efforts on more spiritual matters, he could be a great asset to the Church."

"You're right," Jared said, considering. "But he's not going to come back into the Church until he's ready. God is the only one who can bring Gage back. We can't force the issue. I have a feeling that we haven't seen the worst of this situation yet."

"What do you mean?"

"Sometimes a guy's situation has to get really bad before he's ready to listen and make big changes in his life." They both knew he was speaking from experience.

Sarah's mouth tightened, recalling Jared's shrill voice several years ago when he discovered that his employee had embezzled a hefty sum of money from his business. In the heat of the moment, without thinking his actions through, and because she had initially talked Jared into hiring the man, the yelling had been directed at her. She supposed that losing his business altogether after they divorced had been a pivotal moment for him. "So you don't think that Gage has reached the breaking point yet?"

Jared said, "Trust me. This is only the first phase. Of course, we don't want to see our children suffer, but if Gage truly reaches the point where he's ready to ask the Lord for help, he will most likely receive it."

Sarah's heart nearly stopped at the pronouncement. Surely the Lord would be merciful to their son. "Well, in the meantime, what can we do to help him and this new grandson of ours? I worry about how April's negative influence will affect Zach through the years."

Jared's sigh spoke volumes. "It won't be easy, but we've got to include him in the family. Get to know him and let him get to know us."

"Exactly. And somehow introduce the gospel to him in small ways. Let him feel the Spirit."

"Which is going to be hard to do if Gage doesn't allow it."

"He gave Pierce and Noelle permission to take him to a baby blessing, at least."

After Sarah filled him in on the rest, Jared agreed. "That's a start. Things like that will make a difference. Let's pray that Gage wins custody of Zach."

"I'll keep you posted on the situation."

"Sounds good. Thanks." After ending the call, Sarah shifted the gear into drive, hoping that her perishable groceries didn't completely melt before she got home.

G age loved his little boy.
He really did.

They'd had a fun day together, going to an indoor recreational park called Amazing Jake's after they'd driven into Mesa. But now it was almost nine p.m. and Zach's constant chatter still hadn't waned, which grated on his nerves. He was used to coming home to an empty house near midnight and crashing in the early morning hours, then lazing around a bit until late morning. Gage wondered if Zach would ever slow down.

"Hey, Dad. I liked the bumper cars and the laser tag game and the—"

"Yeah, I did too, buddy." Cutting his son off may not be the best way to handle his developing headache, but Gage couldn't take anymore. "But you know I have to work tomorrow and you're going to meet your cousin Caleb along with Uncle Pierce and Aunt Noelle. We need to close our eyes and get some sleep." They were lying on their backs on Zach's bed looking up at—well, nothing. The ceiling, like the walls, were perfectly white.

Perfectly boring.

Maybe he ought to decorate Zach's bedroom. Visions of brightly painted dinosaurs amid Jurassic period scenery came to life in his mind's eye. Or maybe Zach would prefer a racetrack with cars whizzing by.

After helping his son brush his teeth and reading him his favorite bedtime story for the third time, Gage had given in to the urge to stretch his long frame out on Zach's bed, saying that it felt more comfortable than his. Thankfully, Zach had taken the bait and stretched his little body out too. If Zach didn't settle down soon, Gage just might be desperate enough to try a nighttime prayer with him.

He closed his eyes, listening to the pounding inside his head, while Zach chattered on. Gradually, Zach's speech slowed and his breathing became even. Cocking one eye open, Gage breathed a sigh of relief. This parenting business was a little tougher than taking a kid to an amusement park for an afternoon of fun. Gage soon fell asleep in his own bed.

The next morning, Gage awoke with a start when he turned over and bumped into a warm little body. What? Oh, yeah. Gage felt guilty for not hearing Zach come in. The aspirin he'd taken for his headache had knocked him out.

He quickly got up and headed toward the shower. Twenty minutes later, he was standing in his kitchen, dressed in shorts and a T-shirt and brewing some coffee when Zach wandered in appearing groggy. As soon as he saw Gage, his eyes brightened and he ran toward him. "Hi, Daddy!"

"Morning, Zach." Gage caught him and lifted him up in his arms, loving the feel of the little guy's weight along with his chubby arms wrapped around his neck. Gently setting him down, he asked, "Are you ready for breakfast?"

"Yep. I'm hungry."

"All right. What'll it be?" He named the variety of kids' cereal he'd bought when he'd run into Valerie the other night.

His mind conjured the image of her standing there with her grocery cart. It had been such an unexpected encounter. How ironic that amid all the upheaval of that day, a familiar and welcome diversion had come in the form of Valerie Levington. *Hall,* he reminded himself, inexplicably hating the sound of it. Had Gage imagined it or had she understood and even empathized with the stress he was going through? For a split second, her eyes had regarded him with compassion even after looking unhappy to see him. Seeing her had grounded *him*, however, and calmed his nerves.

Gage's eyes gradually refocused on Zach's face staring up at him. As if coming out of a trance, he realized that Zach's mouth was moving but that he hadn't heard any sound. And Zach didn't look too pleased. "Daddy! Did you hear me?"

Feeling chagrined at being caught daydreaming, he said, "Sorry, Zach. What were you saying?"

Zach told him what kind of cereal he wanted—and didn't want—then Gage poured some into a bowl. "Promise me that you won't be picky about food tonight at Uncle Pierce's house." Zach's eyebrows slashed together as his expression grew stormy. "What's wrong?"

"Do I *hafta* go to somebody else's house today? I wanna stay here with you."

Gage sat down at the table next to his son. "I'm sorry, Zach. Your mom didn't give me enough time to rearrange my work schedule. I promise you'll like Caleb. The two of you will be best friends by the end of the day."

"*Pleeeze*, Daddy?" he asked again, his voice going up an octave. "I don't want you to leave me too."

Gage's heart dropped to his stomach. He'd suspected that this wouldn't go off smoothly, but he'd had no idea how much his little boy was hurting. Even at his young age, Zach knew that he wasn't wanted by his own mother. Gage didn't know what to say.

Zach stared up at him with a mixture of pleading and childlike trust. Gage swallowed the lump in his throat. "Listen, Zach. There's a difference between why your mom leaves you at day care or with your Grandma and Grandpa Westbrook and why I have to tonight. If I stayed home with you, my boss wouldn't be very happy and then I wouldn't have a job. I'm sorry, but that's the way things work in the real world." *Something your mom knows nothing about,* he wanted to add.

The dejected look on Zach's face undid Gage like nothing else would have. "Hey, buddy. What if I take you to McDonald's for lunch?" That would fit nicely into his schedule before heading over to Pierce and Noelle's house. "Will that be okay?"

Zach's face brightened and he gave Gage an exuberant hug. "Yeah. I love McDonald's."

Gage already knew that, which was why he'd bribed him with it. Taking a swig of his coffee, he smiled at his son. One meltdown averted.

Gage slowed his Camaro down to park in front of Pierce and Noelle's house. Holding his breath, Gage nervously rang the doorbell, hoping that Pierce had had a chance to cool down for Zach's sake.

Noelle opened the door and welcomed them inside. Bending down as far as she could go to look Zach in the eyes, she smiled at him and stuck out her hand. "You must be Zachary. I'm your Aunt Noelle. And this is your Uncle Pierce."

Gage looked up to see Pierce approaching. Looking at Pierce in wonder, Zach said, "You look like my daddy, but kinda different too."

Smiling, Pierce answered, "That's because your dad and I are brothers."

Zach then turned to Gage and exclaimed, "Cool! I wanted a brother, but Mommy said I couldn't have one." He said it like it was as easy as buying one at the store.

Zach might have had a younger brother if things with April had worked out differently. Then again, there would be much more to argue with her over. Squeezing his shoulder to catch his attention, Noelle told Zach lightly, "You have a cousin. And that's almost as good as having a brother."

"Is there a baby in your tummy?" Zach blurted.

Noelle chuckled. Crouching down beside him, Pierce said, "Yep. Looks like you're going to have another cousin soon. This one is a girl."

Zach's face scrunched up. "Eeww." Looking up at Noelle again, he asked, "How did the baby get in there?"

Pierce straightened, sporting a huge grin. "I'll let your dad explain that to you."

Gage shook his head in exasperation and with monumental effort, clamped his mouth shut.

Pierce noticed and asked, "Something bothering you, little brother?"

"Nope," he muttered, ignoring him and turning to Noelle. "Where's Caleb?"

"He's feeding the dog." She took Zach's hand and led him toward the kitchen. "Come on. I bet you'll like our dog. She's a chocolate lab named Midnight."

"Very original," Gage said drily.

Noelle shrugged. "Caleb named her." Gage watched Zach go with apprehension, wondering if he'd be okay here with people he didn't know. Added to the fact that Gage would pick him up late tonight when the Diamondbacks' game was over and then bring Zach back here early tomorrow before the midday game, he wondered if this was such a good idea after all. Yet what else could he have done? He hadn't volunteered for this weekend duty.

Pierce's voice brought him back to attention. "Cute kid. Doesn't look like you, though."

Gage's eyes narrowed. He was well aware of the fact that Zach favored his mother with his blond hair and blue eyes. "Look, I get the fact that you disapprove of my lifestyle and maybe I haven't made the best choices through the years, but don't think for one minute that I'm going to let you drag Zach into this. He already has enough to deal with. So I'd appreciate you keeping your comments to yourself."

Pierce held up his hands in surrender. "Wait a minute. I'm not trying to pick a fight—"

"Well, it seems like it."

"Believe it or not, I realize that things weren't going well for you with April. But we would have rallied around you had we been given the opportunity. And to not know about you having a son really hurts, man. We used to be close."

Gage's eyes shut tightly as the memories collided inside his brain—the accusations and constant yelling. What good was a marriage when neither partner could stand to be in the same room with the other? Had it ever been good with April? Except for their elopement and honeymoon in Las Vegas when they were blissfully beyond worries (and common sense), once they'd sobered up, the futility of their marriage had come crashing in on them. "Some things are better left in the past. I was just trying to cope." Gage swallowed hard and looked away.

He felt a hand on his shoulder. Finally meeting Pierce's gaze, Gage was startled to see remorse in his eyes. "Sorry, Gage. I wish I had been there for you."

He smiled to lighten the mood. "You and Noelle had just gotten married. I thought I had found someone to share my hopes and dreams with too. Just because April wasn't the woman I thought she was didn't mean that I wanted to advertise it to the rest of the family."

Studying Gage closely, Pierce said, "If I'm not mistaken, you're still not over her."

Gage opened his mouth to protest. He was definitely over April. But the failure of his marriage was another matter. "I'm all right," he stammered. "I have a few things to work out, but life is good."

"Life could be even better with help." Pierce paused. "Ours and the Lord's."

Not this same discussion again. How many times had he told his family members that he wasn't interested in talking about this? Gage shook his head. "Thanks, anyway."

"Gage." Pierce's voice was stern. Gage looked at him sharply. "Come to church with us. You might find that you've actually missed it after all this time."

He laughed humorlessly. "Really, Pierce? Who would want me there after all I've done?"

Slowly, Pierce's eyebrows untangled themselves as he met Gage's eyes squarely. "We would."

Abruptly, Gage turned and headed toward the door. "I'd better get to work. Thanks again for taking care of Zach. Call me if something comes up."

"He'll be fine. It's you I'm not so sure about."

Gage whirled on him with a force that shook him. "Stop acting like you have all the answers. Going to church might make you feel like you're some sort of saint, but I've had it with your self-righteous attitude."

"Come on, Gage. I wasn't—"

But Gage didn't wait long enough to find out what Pierce was refuting. He slammed the door behind him and stalked off to his car. Turning the ignition, he gunned the engine and tore out of the driveway.

The only problem was, while he could outrun his brother, he couldn't outrun his tumultuous thoughts or ignore the jagged ripping of his heart. He had learned early in life that things rarely turned out the way he wanted them to. He'd grown up singing "I Love to See the Temple" and "Families Are Forever." He'd loved and trusted his parents until he gradually became aware of their arguments behind closed doors. When Gage's mom faithfully attended church week after week without his dad and he realized that their marriage was just a sham, he'd tried to fill the emptiness he felt inside with parties and beer.

The sheer heartache of it all came crashing down on him as he drove into Phoenix. When his parents' divorce became final, Gage knew that he could never go back to being that pre-missionary teenager believing in eternal families. Nothing anybody said or did could have altered the chain of events that occurred like a stack of dominoes falling. He'd crossed over an invisible line, wearing his devil-may-care attitude like protective armor.

Arriving at Chase Field, Gage parked the car in the garage there and took several deep breaths. It wouldn't be wise to go in breathing fire. Moments later, feeling reasonably calmer, he entered his office. Sitting at his desk and pulling up his email, Gage ran a hand through his hair before the thought hit him.

Families were nice to belong to but not always easy to get along with. And that was the crux of the problem.

T he next day in church, Valerie shushed her children, sending them a stern look.

"Justin won't share the crayons." Whitney's long-suffering sigh prompted Valerie to suggest that she look at a book instead. "No. I want to color!"

"Whitney!" This came out in the loudest whisper that she dared. "Please cooperate. Give him a turn first, and when he's finished, you can use them." Justin was still in the everything-is-mine mode that most children had outgrown by this age. Valerie figured they needed to be patient with him a little longer. In time, he would outgrow it, too, she hoped.

When Whitney's mouth tightened and her brows scrunched together dramatically, Valerie resisted the urge to roll her eyes at her daughter's antics. "Why does he always get what he wants?" she demanded.

Surprised by the venom in her daughter's voice, Valerie placed her hand on her shoulder. "You make a lot of concessions for your brother and I appreciate it. Now Uncle Kurt is almost ready to bless little Hope. You can help me to keep Justin quiet by being happy."

They were visiting her brother and sister-in-law's ward in Queen Creek, a large community that had mushroomed in the farmland southeast of Mesa and Gilbert in the last decade or so. Whitney frowned at Valerie but opened her book. Valerie sighed in relief just as her brother Kurt stood with his infant daughter, who looked like a little angel in her billowy white gown, and made his way to the front of the chapel.

Justin looked up as the blessing concluded and Kurt walked proudly back to his little family. "There's Hope!" he blurted loudly. "Hi, Hope!" He stood on the bench and waved his arm back and forth, causing Valerie to freeze. Feeling others' eyes on her and Justin, she forced herself to remain still. This was nothing new. Her own ward members were used to Justin's outbursts by now. The silver lining on this particular cloud was the unlikelihood of her seeing these people again.

Valerie's younger brother, Luke, and his wife were also there with their children from Texas. "Hi, Val," Luke said jovially after the closing prayer. "How's it going?"

"Good. I'm glad you could make it."

"Uncle Luke! Guess what?" Whitney smiled up at him, her amber-colored locks swaying when she hugged him.

"What, squirt?"

"Mommy said we could go to the beach this summer if we saved enough money, and we now almost have enough to go!"

"You're not going to come see us?" Luke's teasing eyes held hers for another second, then focused on Valerie. "I'm hurt."

Valerie chuckled. "We're actually going the other direction," Valerie replied. "To California."

"Disneyland too?"

She hesitated. Taking her kids to Disneyland was something she'd always wanted to do, but Valerie could never afford it. Not only that, she didn't even want to attempt it alone with Justin's unpredictable behavior. His tendency to storm off without warning when he became upset at insignificant things meant she had to always be alert. "Not this time. But we'll still have fun doing other things."

"You work hard, sis. You deserve a vacation."

Her smile was fleeting. "Thanks." She had spent this year scrimping and saving every penny she had earned from working as a waitress to plan something fun for her kids.

The Levingtons, who were a close-knit clan, gathered around to take a few pictures of Kurt and his wife with their darling daughters. Two-year-old Sonja seemed to be enamored by her baby sister, Hope.

Two parents, two babies. All appeared right in their world. Remembering when she had posed for the camera after Justin's baby blessing, Valerie couldn't help but compare the happy couple before her to her own troubled marriage. Until that point, Valerie had ignored the misgivings that had pervaded her marital bliss. Justin's arrival had upset the precarious balance on that scale.

She turned away to hide her melancholy and came face-to-face with Pierce Logan. As distracted with her kids as she'd been during sacrament meeting, Valerie had only glanced at him as he approached the priesthood circle for Hope's blessing. Now she realized that Pierce and his wife looked like the perfect little family with their two boys.

"Oh, hi, Valerie. How are you?"

"Fine, thanks. How are you?"

"Good." He smiled. "This is my wife, Noelle. Sweetheart, this is Valerie Levington, Kurt's sister." An awkward pause followed. "I'm sorry. I don't know your married name."

"Hall," she supplied. "And this is my son, Justin. My daughter is around here somewhere. Probably with her cousins."

"No husband?"

Why did it still hurt to hear it that way? "No. I'm divorced."

"Oh."

Oh, yeah, *that* was why. As soon as she said the word *divorced*, the person she was talking to suddenly clammed up, leaving Valerie feeling like she was some sort of misfit.

To Pierce's credit, he offered, "I'm sorry to hear that."

She smiled to cover her discomfort. "So you have two little boys?" And a third one on the way, from what it looked like. Valerie unsuccessfully fought the encroaching feeling of envy. She'd always wanted a large family, maybe not as large as her parents' but definitely more than two.

"No, actually. This is our son, Caleb, and our nephew, Zach," Noelle said, indicating each one in turn.

Pierce and Noelle's son looked to be about three years old and had his father's dark eyes and delightful dimples. Zach was blond and blue-eyed and looked like he would fit right in with the four-year-olds she taught in Primary.

"You remember Gage, right?" Pierce asked. "We're watching his son for him today."

Valerie gave Zach a second look. "Really? He doesn't look much like him."

"He takes after his mother, Gage's ex-wife. Drop-dead gorgeous but nothing underneath."

"So he married her after all," she murmured to herself, remembering her doubt and how she'd practically ran away from Gage at the store.

"Excuse me?"

"Oh, it's nothing." Valerie's cheeks burned as she came out of her trance. "I wasn't sure if . . . well, when Gage mentioned his custody issue with his son, I wondered . . . about her," she finished lamely.

Pierce peered at her speculatively. "I didn't realize that you've kept in contact with Gage."

"I haven't," she admitted. "We ran into each other while shopping the other night. Until then, I hadn't seen him in several years."

"That's interesting. He didn't mention anything. Then again, he rarely does anymore," he muttered under his breath.

"Maybe that's because you hound him to death when he does," Noelle said pointedly.

Valerie looked from one to the other, noting Pierce's defensive posture. "I was only trying to help, okay?" he told his wife.

"Does Gage know that?"

"If he doesn't, then that's his problem."

This sounded like a conversation that she shouldn't be hearing. "Well, it was nice to see you again, Pierce. And I'm glad to meet you, Noelle."

"You're coming to the house for dinner, right?" Valerie heard Kurt's voice behind her just before his hand landed on her shoulder. "Val? Pierce and Noelle?" He looked at them expectantly.

"Yeah, we're coming."

"Great." Kurt continued talking to his friends while Valerie slipped away with Justin. Within minutes, she found Whitney and led them to her beat-up car. Looking at the sad excuse for transportation, she decided that she wouldn't risk taking it on their vacation. She'd ask her parents if she could borrow their vehicle instead.

Driving an extra thirty minutes past his house in east Mesa to pick up his son normally wouldn't have been a big deal to Gage. But now that he'd finished working his second shift in the past thirty hours, he was ready to call it a day. Learning from Pierce a few minutes ago that they were still at Kurt Levington's house in Queen Creek and that it'd be another few hours until he could crash in his bed made him feel that much crankier.

Or was it because he knew he'd have to show his face to the Levington family again after all this time? John Levington was probably the one person in Gage's ward while growing up who hadn't given up on the Logan brothers after their father slipped off the ward's radar. Gage wondered what kind of a reception he'd receive from him now.

After taking the turnoff to Queen Creek, memories of Gage's college days stretched out much like the long road he was driving on. The weekend frat parties at Arizona State University became the only thing he'd looked forward to. Considering the daze he'd been in each Monday morning, it was a miracle he'd been able to pull off decent grades.

He'd been blessed with many talents, not in the least of which was an ability to read people with innate accuracy and tailor each sales pitch to their particular interests. For that reason alone, Gage couldn't understand how he'd been duped so blindly by April Westbrook. He'd met her after graduating from ASU and finding employment as a marketing strategist at the University of Arizona in Tucson. Her beauty pageant looks had enhanced her down-to-earth persona.

April had been a student that summer, making up a class that she'd failed earlier in the spring semester. April's inability to pass her classes should have been a red flag. But she was so fun to hang out with. When she and Gage traveled together with a group to Las Vegas, talking and laughing the whole way, Gage fell for April—hard. Amid the parties and drinking, they exchanged marriage vows in a cheap wedding chapel.

Back in Tucson, Gage learned that his new wife was an utter fake. Gage found himself at home alone nearly every night, needing to sleep so he could go to work the next morning, while April went clubbing with their friends. The stories he heard of April's flirtations with other men vexed him. She'd left the club a few times with a new guy and not returned until the early hours of the morning. April's hateful words when Gage confronted her about it still echoed inside his head. "All you really were to me was my ticket out of school, Gage. I was sick of always trying to please my parents." With a sneer, she'd added, "It's too bad you weren't the rich, naïve kid I thought you were." He'd been naïve, all right. Gage still felt like the world's biggest fool for being reeled in by the cold, calculating woman whose sweet, innocent, and almost shy looks she'd passed his way.

Perhaps the biggest irony in their marriage came in the form of an unplanned pregnancy. How April managed to conceive Zach when she was using preventative measures, Gage didn't know. But Zach's arrival had unwittingly done what Gage had tried so hard to do—pin his wife down for a time. Only by then, she'd become his ex-wife.

Gage turned the radio on in an effort to dislodge his gloomy thoughts. A reporter, his voice sounding a little harried, grabbed his attention. "We interrupt this program to inform listeners of a multi-car pileup along I-10 near Casa Grande, due to low visibility caused by a sandstorm." Gage cringed at the graphic scene and growing number of fatalities the reporter listed. His mind immediately went to Zach. Gage was glad to know that his little boy was safe and sound at Kurt Levington's house.

G age parked his Camaro farther down the street from the
many cars that flanked Kurt's house. As he approached the
door, it burst opened and a screaming little boy with dark wavy
hair darted out, heading straight for the street. His instincts kicking in, Gage immediately ran to his left to catch up with him.
A few seconds later, he caught the boy around the arms. "Whoa,
buddy. Where are you going?"

The boy didn't stop screaming or trying to dislodge Gage's hold
on him. Pinning him against his legs, Gage looked up in time to
see Valerie Hall rush toward them.

"Justin, come back here." When she saw him holding the boy,
her mouth dropped open. "Gage!" She disentangled the boy from
Gage's grasp and lifted him up, putting her head on his to stop
his tantrum. However, the boy kept pummeling her chest and
screaming.

Valerie spent a few more minutes shushing him and rocking
back and forth on her feet. Breathing hard, Gage waited until he
felt that she would be able to hear him over the noise of the boy's
tantrum before he spoke.

"I'm sorry, Valerie. I saw him running away and I just reacted.
I hope I didn't hurt him."

She raised wide eyes to him, her lips trembling—whether from shock or fear, Gage didn't know. "No. Thank you, Gage. You saved him from getting hit by a car."

Gage tore his gaze from her to study Justin more closely. This scrappy kid had run with amazing speed. He was still struggling with Valerie, though he had stopped screaming. "If I had pulled up a few minutes later, it would have been mine." The enormity of the situation hit him hard, especially after just hearing the horrific news on the radio. "I'm glad he's okay. Why did he run away?"

Her lips pressed together in a straight line. Gage tried not to notice how full and soft they looked. "Justin was upset with one of his cousins over a toy they were playing with. Something trivial."

If it was so trivial, then why did the disagreement cause such a strong reaction? "It was important enough for him to cry over it."

She lifted one shoulder indifferently. "With Justin, it's hard to know what is important and what isn't."

That didn't make sense. What kind of mother didn't know what was important or unimportant to her child?

Valerie set Justin down and knelt to his level, disregarding the fact that her ankle-length dress was dusting the ground. Looking at Justin with compassion, she told him firmly, "Remember what I've told you, kiddo. If something happens that you don't like, you can come tell me. Please don't scream in front of everybody else. They are here to enjoy each other's company and have a good time."

Gage watched the interaction between mother and son. Valerie was an odd mixture of lace and steel. Her voice softened to a near whisper before asking, "Can you do that for me, little man?"

Justin didn't answer, looking at his feet instead. With a firm but gentle touch, Valerie lifted his chin. "Look at me," she commanded. When, after another long pause, he still hadn't responded, she prodded with a little more gusto, "Justin!" The stormy look he sent her shocked Gage. He'd never seen such a belligerent child. "We'll go home in a little while. But first I would like for you to go tell Paisley that you're sorry."

"No. I don't want to!"

"Please?"

"NO!"

Time stood still for Gage. Valerie and her son glared at each other in a standoff that left Gage feeling like he was watching an old Western on television. Who would back down first?

Valerie heaved a sigh and stood, walking with Justin back to the porch and sitting on the porch swing. Feeling totally out of his element but too curious for his own good, Gage slowly followed.

Valerie smiled wanly. "You can go inside, if you'd like. We're going to be here for a while."

Leaning against a post and crossing his arms like he had all the time in the world, Gage replied, "No, I'm good." The truth was, he was concerned about Valerie. A few seconds ago, she'd given the impression that she was indifferent to her child's needs. Upon closer inspection, however, she appeared to be on the verge of tears.

"Please, Gage? I need a few minutes alone with my son."

Yep. Her voice was definitely shaky. Pushing himself off against the post, he came closer and crouched down in front of her. "Is there anything I can do to help?" he asked softly.

She shook her head, keeping her gaze down. Something about the way she rubbed Justin's back while simultaneously cradling his head in her arms touched a place in Gage's heart that had long been dead.

"Valerie," he said softly.

She lifted her eyes to him. Gage's heart constricted at the sorrow he found there. Who would have imagined when they were young that they'd both be single parents? He'd always teased her so that he could see a flare of indignation light her gaze. That fire had apparently been extinguished a long time ago.

He'd have to see if he could reignite it.

Taking a deep breath, Valerie looked up at Gage. He was still crouched down, wearing a surprising expression of tenderness that nearly knocked her off balance. "How can I help you?" he implored gently once again.

She took a deep breath before answering. "It's time for us to leave. It would be best if Justin stays out here. Would you mind sitting with him while I run inside to find my daughter?"

Gage turned his gaze onto Justin, who'd hunched his shoulders at her suggestion. His silence indicated that while he might not like having Gage sit with him, at least he wouldn't throw another fit.

Because of Justin's disorder, they were all living on intense emotions far too often than was healthy. She knew that medications were a lifetime commitment. If she could find a way to stabilize his emotional state without the use of medications, so much the better.

Gage nodded. "I could do that."

"Thank you. I'll only be a few minutes." She stood and turned Justin around so that he was facing her. "Justin, this is my friend Gage. Can you stay with him for a few minutes while I get Whitney? And then we'll go home."

Justin scowled at Valerie. "All right."

Valerie ruffled his hair affectionately. "Okay. I'll be just a minute."

She entered the house and found Kurt and Ashley, congratulating them again on Hope's blessing. When she reached for her handbag, her mother asked, "Going so soon, honey?"

Valerie looked up at the circle of faces that were watching her. Her dad, who stood close to her mom as they talked with Pierce and Noelle, paused to hear her answer. "Yes, I think Justin has had all the stimulation he can handle for one day. But it's been good to see you all." She smiled brightly to mask her disappointment in always having to leave family functions early for this reason.

Her mother's face showed compassion. "I'll find Whitney and tell her you're ready to leave." She excused herself and left the room.

"Pierce, Gage is here to collect his son. He's waiting outside."

"He is?" John Levington said jovially. "Bring him in here. I haven't seen that boy in ages." Valerie's dad had been the Scoutmaster in their ward for several years while Valerie was growing up, and as a result, many of his formers Boy Scouts remained close to him.

"He's sitting with Justin on the porch swing right now," Valerie said quietly. "I'd better go. Please tell Jake that I'm sorry for the way Justin behaved toward Paisley. We'll try to make it up to her next time." Paisley was the youngest daughter of Valerie's oldest brother.

Valerie noticed Pierce and Noelle gazing at her speculatively. They must have sensed her discomfort because they didn't ask any questions. Whitney soon joined the group. With a sigh of relief, Valerie herded her daughter out the door.

"Hi, Justin. I'm Gage."

Gage held out his hand for the boy to shake, but instead of responding, he lowered his eyes to the ground. Gage slowly lowered his hand. Okay, so he'd been a little stressed out lately, but most people usually responded positively to his upbeat personality.

He decided to try again. "How old are you?"

A long minute passed before Gage heard him say quietly, "Five."

"Really? That's great. I have a little boy named Zach. He's four. Did you see him inside the house?"

After another pause, Justin gave a quick nod. "He showed me his cars."

"Yeah, Zach likes cars. What about you, Justin? What do you like?"

No response.

Gage was starting to wonder if he'd said the wrong thing. "Well, Zach likes dinosaurs too. Do you like dinosaurs, Justin?"

Another quick nod followed while keeping his gaze down. Gage didn't know much about children, but even he could see that this wasn't a typical five-year-old. Some kids were shy, but this one seemed to be extremely so.

"What are some of your favorites?"

"T. Rex and triceratops."

"Yeah, those are some of Zach's favorites too."

Just then, the door opened and Valerie exited with a cute little girl in tow. "Thank you, Gage." Leaning slightly to one side so that she could balance her bag on her shoulder while reaching for Justin's hand, she said, "Okay, let's go."

Gage held out his hand to Justin. "I've got him."

Valerie looked startled when her son placed his little hand into Gage's large one. Turning, she led them to a car that had obviously seen better days. Gage wondered about Valerie's ex-husband and what had happened in their marriage.

Whatever kind of man he was, Gage knew one thing about him. He was out of his mind for letting Valerie go.

Valerie's daughter peered up at Gage quizzically. "Who are you?"

"A friend of your mom's."

She studied him closely before turning back to Valerie. "Mom, is he your boyfriend?"

Though the words startled him, Gage was amused to see Valerie blush. "Whitney," she said sternly, "you know better than to ask a question like that." Whitney stared at Gage for a full five seconds before looking at her feet.

"Will you be all right?" Gage asked after Valerie had buckled the kids in her car.

Her back stiffened and she raised her chin, meeting his gaze straight on. "We'll be fine."

The determination in her voice was hard to miss. Obviously, Valerie wasn't comfortable with accepting help from other people beyond her own family members. Gage smiled to show his support.

She smiled back, offering a truce. "We've had two chance meetings now. What are the odds of that? Maybe next time you'll let me in on what's going on between you and Pierce."

If there was a next time.

Gage coughed. "Just a little family matter. I'm sure it'll blow over soon." He hoped.

She seemed to accept the fact that he didn't want to talk about it. "We all have our little spats from time to time."

Exactly.

Gage entered Kurt's home, determined to ignore the feeling of being out of place. Aside from the Levington family, the place was packed with lots of people he didn't know. Amid the chatter, Gage heard Zach's voice as it carried from down the hallway. "Daddy!" He was followed by Caleb and a bunch of miniature Levington-ites.

Zach looked like a different kid altogether in his borrowed church clothes, with his hair slicked down. Fleetingly, Gage wondered what his son had thought of his church experience. He'd probably been confused by it all. "Hey, buddy," he greeted, lifting Zach up to him. "Looks like you're having fun."

"Yeah. There are lots of kids here to play with!"

Gage chuckled and set him down. Zach frowned up at him. "Is it time to go already?"

"Almost. How about five more minutes?"

"Ten, please?"

Gage shook his head. "We've been in the Levingtons' way long enough."

"*Pleeeze*, Daddy? I don't wanna go yet." While Zach's scrunched-up face was kind of cute, Gage knew exactly whom he'd perfected that ploy from. Another reason to put some distance between Zach and his mother.

"We'll see."

"Gage." John Levington's booming voice interrupted his train of thought. His old Scoutmaster had given him a good start in Scouting before Gage's interest had gradually waned. He didn't seem to hold a grudge, however, as he pumped Gage's arm up and down enthusiastically. "It's good to see you, son."

"Thanks, John. It's good to see you too," he said, noticing the sparseness of hair on his head. His kind eyes and friendly smile were still the same, though, making Gage feel that old but familiar connection.

Valerie's mother, Brande, walked up to him and enveloped him in a loving embrace. "The prodigal son returns," she teased.

Gage grimaced. While not intended to be offensive, the pun had hit its mark. Judging by the chagrined looks on everyone's faces, they knew it too. *There's nothing better than being put on the spot,* Gage thought morosely.

"I've been watching that adorable son of yours," Brande continued. "He's a fireball of energy, isn't he?"

"Typical four-year-old, I'd guess." He was beginning to learn that Zach had two speeds, fast and zoom.

"True enough. Come into the kitchen and fix yourself a plate."

While Gage ate heartily and listened to the others chatting, he took note of the closeness the Levington family still shared. Valerie wasn't the only member who had changed. Her oldest brother, Jake, and sister, Chloe, were showing tinges of gray. Even more compelling than that, Valerie's younger brother, Luke, had grown taller than Gage and was married with a baby, making Gage feel old.

One by one, the Levington siblings departed with their families, promising to get together again soon. Kurt's wife left the group to say good-bye to her family as well. All that remained were Kurt, John and Brande, and Pierce and Noelle.

"So, Gage," John said, "what have you been up to these days?"

At Pierce's look of warning, Gage decided to answer with caution, giving the same watered-down answer he'd given Valerie a few days before. "Working, mostly, and trying to stay out of trouble."

"Are you succeeding?" John asked, catching Gage off guard.

"Beg your pardon?"

"Staying out of trouble, I meant. Are you succeeding?"

A corner of Gage's mouth lifted up. "Not very well."

Pierce arched his brows. Gage ignored him. John chuckled, turning to his wife. "You need a good wife to keep you out of trouble. Doesn't he, Brande?"

And that was the problem, wasn't it? Gage tried not to squirm under John's all-knowing gaze.

Noelle must have sensed Gage's discomfort because she said, "He has a good job and a really great son. Two out of three aren't bad."

"Marriage is a tricky proposition these days. Most of our children have found wonderful spouses. It's comforting to know they are taken care of," Brande said.

"Except for Valerie," Kurt blurted. Gage wondered if he realized how insensitive he sounded, mentioning his sister's difficult situation when she wasn't here. "What will she do once Grandma and Grandpa come home from their mission?"

John and Brande looked at each other uncertainly. "She doesn't know yet," Brande answered. "She's worried about having to increase her hours at work so that she can pay rent on an apartment."

"She can't be away from her kids all day," Kurt said.

"I agree." John's smile faded.

Gage cleared his throat. "Pardon me for asking, but I noticed that her son has some difficulties. What's the story there?"

In the awkward pause that followed, Gage wished that he'd never opened his mouth. But his curiosity had gotten the better of him. Ah, well, it seemed that he and Kurt were in good company.

Kurt answered, "He's been diagnosed with mild autism. But just because he's high-functioning doesn't mean that he's easy to deal with."

So that was it. Autism. Interesting. The Diamondbacks Foundation, in conjunction with their affiliated radio station, conducted an annual fund-raiser for autism research and educational programs for children and teenagers who fell on the spectrum. And throughout the year, various school groups came to the gates at Chase Field for guided tours. Once in a while, when a group of special needs children was brought in, extra personnel was secured to handle them. Their excitement at being at the ballpark was contagious.

Although Gage had heard a few co-workers talking about autism, he didn't know much about the disorder itself. Warren, an older gentleman at work, had a teenager with Asperger's while Rhonda, a mother of three, was dealing with her youngest child's recent diagnosis. It had been rough going for a time, but now she seemed to be adjusting. "Of course not."

Brande regarded Gage compassionately. "Valerie is a very dedicated mother. Unfortunately, she has received some negative reactions to her son. When she lived with us for a short time after her divorce, the members of our ward had a difficult time accepting her because Justin kept disrupting sacrament meeting with his tantrums. Because of this, she is more sensitive to what she construes as criticism."

Hmm. So that was why Valerie had acted so put out when Gage had first offered to help her. But his persistence had paid off and she'd visibly softened toward him. "I'm sure it's not easy. I admire her for her fortitude. Let's hope that Justin continues to improve." Gage held his hand out to John. "It was nice to see you again. But it's time for me to take my son home. He goes back to his mother tomorrow."

Pierce eyed Gage speculatively without commenting.

"Thanks for letting us barge in on your family time. Sorry for the imposition."

"Gage," Brande reassured him, "it wasn't an imposition in the least. We're very glad to see you again." She gave him another warm hug. "You take care of yourself, all right? And tell your mother I said hello."

"Uh, thanks. I will." He still hadn't reconciled with his mom. He decided to call her as soon as he dropped Zach off at April's place.

As it turned out, there was no need for Gage to call his mother when he and Zach arrived home. Through the glare of the setting sun, he spied her silver Jetta off to the side of the driveway. Gage pulled in and parked his Camaro, taking a deep breath before stepping out to meet her. Sarah Nielsen, looking a bit anxious, stepped out of her vehicle as well and approached him slowly.

Gage tried to maintain a calm, controlled air as he greeted her. "Hi, Mom."

She offered him a stiff smile. "Hello."

"Been here long?"

"About fifteen minutes or so. I had almost lost my nerve and decided to leave when you pulled up."

"I assume that you're here to meet Zach," he said tentatively.

Sarah pinched the seams of the dress she'd worn to church in a nervous gesture. In all his years of growing up, Gage had never seen his mother like this. She'd always been so poised. Even when she and his dad had gone through so much strife, she'd kept the greater part of it from her sons.

"Yes. Eric wanted to come, too, but I needed to do this alone— you know, with Zach being my grandson. Mine and your father's."

She cleared her throat and stepped forward. "I'm sorry for the way I ran out of the dining room. It was very rude of me."

Gage scoffed. "Mom, if anybody should be apologizing, it's me. I've been such a jerk. You've loved me and supported me even with all the stupid things I've done. I should have come to you when April told me about Zach. But I didn't want you to know that I was such a loser not to even know about having a son."

"Believe it or not, I understand. Having two older know-it-all brothers and an absentee father did a number on you."

Gage stared at her, stunned by her keen observation. He'd never told anyone about his insecurities. Craig and Pierce had both earned top grades in school, served missions, and married nice Mormon girls. Gage had earned decent grades through the years, but that was as far as the similarities went. And his dad's indifference during that time hadn't helped matters.

"Zach fell asleep on the ride home." He backed up and opened the passenger door. "Let's see if I can get him out without waking him."

"Gage, you're avoiding the subject. You can't hide from the past forever."

Lifting a sleeping Zach to his shoulder, he met her gaze head-on. "I know that."

"Do you? Or are you just saying that to appease me?"

As he considered his answer, all of the old doubts and fears came soaring over him, taking him back in time to when he was just a kid. He'd sensed, if not understood, that his parents' relationship was strained. He'd felt the tension but had somehow known not to ask anyone about it, not even his older brothers.

Then, for some reason that he couldn't define even to this day, Gage had put the blame on himself. He wasn't good enough for his dad anymore. He wasn't smart like Craig or a go-getter like Pierce. He wasn't able to separate his anxieties from his actions and had slipped off the proverbial cliff, looking for acceptance with a group of friends that dragged him down with them. That old pain crept up inside him, the pain he'd worked so hard to block out through the years. "Let's go inside where we'll be more comfortable."

He led her inside through the kitchen to the front room where he deposited Zach on the couch. Sarah sat on the other end, looking longingly at her grandson. "He's beautiful."

"You're the only person who'll be allowed to say that about my son."

She chuckled. "When is his birthday?"

Gage answered that he'd just had one, saddened by the knowledge that he'd deprived his mom of loving Zach. She hadn't been able to shower him with gifts or give him the mushy hugs that little boys outwardly loathed but secretly craved. In that moment, the guilt piled on Gage as he realized the full extent to which he'd hurt his family to protect his pride.

It seemed as if Sarah could read his mind. "I wonder if by not telling us about Zach, you were trying to cover up a guilty conscience of your past behavior."

Gage was silent for a long time before admitting, "I feel guilty about a lot of things."

She waited patiently for him to explain. When Gage realized she wasn't going anywhere until he did, he began, albeit a little defensively, "I feel guilty about marrying April. Guilty about backing out of my mission. For all the hurt I've caused in the family. I mean, hey, if it wasn't for me, everyone's life would have run a lot more smoothly, don't you think?"

"Gage," she admonished, her tone letting him know she meant business.

He sighed, releasing the tension he was feeling. "Okay, fine, Mom. When I was little, I got a lot of the attention from you and Dad because I was the youngest—and cutest, I was told."

She nodded.

"But then it all suddenly stopped. I was too young to understand what was going on between you and Dad and why he stopped going to church. All I knew was that everything was broken. Craig and Pierce seemed to handle it just fine, and Dad was always telling us to 'man up,' so I didn't push it. I kept hoping that whatever happened would eventually get better."

"Instead of getting better, it got worse." At his mom's stricken face, Gage swallowed hard. Maybe it was better to just keep these memories buried. Really, what good did it do to dredge up the past?

He shrugged. "I may not have been as sensitive to your moods as Pierce was, but even I knew when you were upset. I didn't understand why I had to wait to get baptized so Dad could do it. Later on, when he became inactive again and couldn't ordain me to the Aaronic Priesthood, I saw just how important I was to him at that point." Gage couldn't quite keep the sarcasm from his voice. "I had to find friends who would make me feel good about myself. At least then I would be important to somebody."

"You were important to me."

"I know that now. But back then you were almost never home."

"Now it's my turn to confess that I felt guilty for being gone all the time. I quit my job in the hope that spending more time with you would curtail your disruptive behavior. But I was too late, wasn't I?"

"I feel guilty about that too. You wouldn't have needed to quit working for Dad if I hadn't been pulling stupid pranks with my so-called friends. And later, Dad's business fell apart because that jerk he hired in your place embezzled Dad's funds."

Gage offered her a tiny smile. "But I got excited when I sent my mission application in and kept telling Dad all about the things I was learning in the mission prep classes. He just told me to quit preaching to him. I had hoped to open my call with the two of you, but he told me that he was with a client and that he would be home late. He couldn't even set work aside long enough to be with me for that."

Gage hated seeing the tears that formed in his mom's eyes.

He lifted his shoulder in what he hoped would be a show of indifference. "But it doesn't matter much now. I knew that I had no business telling people that families can be together forever when mine was falling apart."

Sarah grabbed a tissue from a nearby box. "Gage, it has hurt so much to see how this has affected you. Please understand that you weren't at fault for my decision to quit working for your dad. I think we were all emotionally drained from that time. You were looking for peace, too, just not in the best places. I wish you would come back to church."

Where Gage had yelled at Pierce for suggesting the same thing, there was no way he would do that to his mom. Still, he needed to be firm. "I've made some mistakes and I want to be the kind of dad to Zach that Dad wasn't for me, but I just don't know if I can believe in that stuff anymore."

"Meaning the teachings of the gospel."

He nodded, his heart pounding in his chest. "Yeah. We've been told that Christ overcame the sins of the world. He suffered for us so that we wouldn't have to. But people suffer all the time. Look at Valerie Hall."

Sarah squinted as if trying to conjure a mental image. "Who?"

"Levington," he clarified. "She's divorced now with two kids to raise. Her youngest is autistic. Where's the fairness in that?"

Sarah reached over and patted Zach's when he shifted in his sleep. "I didn't realize that you knew what was going on in Valerie's life."

"We've reconnected," he replied simply.

Her eyebrows shot up in surprise. "Well, I haven't heard much about her lately, but from what I understand, her husband was a charmer who didn't know how to deal with an autistic child. He couldn't put up with the disruptions it caused in their home life."

Gage's eyes narrowed. As far as he was concerned, Valerie shouldn't have had to put up with her husband.

Reigning in his errant thoughts, he trained his ear once again on what his mom was saying. "Believing that your life will go smoothly just because you live the commandments is incorrect. Part of the gospel plan is for us to be tested. But because of Christ's Atonement, whatever sorrow we suffer in this life will be made up for in the next."

"How can you be sure of that, Mom?"

Her gray eyes softened as she responded, "I know because when I almost lost hope of ever being happy again after your father and I split up, the Lord lifted that burden. I was reminded that He still loved me. Through the Spirit, I was guided to seek others who had been through similar situations. And in time, I knew that the Lord had prepared me for something better. He never left me alone."

Her testimony pierced Gage's heart so directly that if he didn't know better, he'd think it was bleeding.

Suddenly, a memory surfaced of him standing in his dad's mansion in San Diego, California, five years earlier when he and his brothers met their new stepmother, Tamara. After dinner, when Tamara had asked the three Logan brothers to clear the dishes, she'd stood at the kitchen island and addressed the pain that their father had inflicted on them. Alluding to her own abusive marriage, she stated boldly that if they wanted to forgive their father, which would allow them to establish a closer relationship with him, they needed to let go of the pain.

Gage recalled telling her that it wasn't as easy as she was implying and she'd instantly declared, "Oh, I know it won't be easy for any of you. But that's what you've got to do."

Let go of the pain.

But how? Five years later, he was still trying to figure out the answer to that question.

Sarah must have read his thoughts because she asked Gage, "Have you prayed at all since receiving your mission call?"

That had been nine years ago. Almost a decade. Gage was shocked to realize that he'd wasted so much of his time looking for solace in all the wrong places.

"Not much," he said honestly. Most of his prayers, when he'd rarely uttered one, had been desperate pleas for help out of the current jam he'd gotten himself into.

Sarah placed her hand on his arm. "We held a family fast for you today."

He was so shocked, he didn't know what to say. "You did?"

Nodding, she replied, "We feel that you need the Lord's help right now more than ever."

For Gage, fasting had simply meant going hungry for two meals. He'd never experienced any benefit from doing it. But inexplicably, he was touched beyond measure that his family would do that for him. He felt a sudden sting of tears in his eyes and blinked rapidly to drive them away. "Thanks, Mom."

"Gage, I want to see all three of my sons in the temple someday soon. I want to challenge you to *sincerely* ask Heavenly Father what he wants you to do. You know the principles of the gospel, but you've lost the Spirit. If you really want your life to change for the better, you need to be willing to change as well."

Gage felt a long-forsaken but not forgotten warmth spread through his chest.

Sarah stood and made her way to the front door. Before turning the knob, she paused to smile at him. "Please, Gage. I love you very much and I want to see you happy. Do this, not for us, but for yourself." With that, she kissed his cheek and quietly let herself out, leaving Gage standing as still as a statue.

The next morning after Gage and Zach had finished breakfast and were putting their dishes in the sink, Gage's phone buzzed. It was Keith Westbrook. What would he be calling about? Gage and Zach were scheduled to leave for Tucson in just a few minutes. "Hello?"

"Gage." A keen note of distress hit Gage's ear as Keith began the conversation. "I'm calling about April."

"What is it?" he asked in alarm.

"April and Ryker were caught in a multi-car accident on I-10 yesterday afternoon. The police have informed us that they both died." His voice cracked with the admission.

Gage nearly dropped his phone. *"What?"*

A lengthy pause followed with muffled sounds of heavy breathing punctuated by tearful moans. When Keith came back on the phone, Gage quickly accepted his strangled apology. He wanted to know more. "Madeline and I are on our way to the coroner's office right now. They've asked us to identify the body. . ." Keith could no longer go on. Gage could hear Madeline sobbing in the background.

Gage felt like his stomach had dropped to the ground. He couldn't believe it. April was gone? His ex-wife? The mother of his son? He couldn't help but think of their last phone call and all the rude things he'd said. He could never take it back now. . . . "I'll hold on to Zach for now," he said hoarsely.

"We'll let you know when we find out more information," Keith said, his voice still filled with anguish. "The police did tell us that an autopsy has been scheduled. Witnesses testified that their car didn't slow down even in the swirling dust. They rammed another vehicle from behind."

Gage groaned at the mental image of Keith's description. *Oh, April*, his heart cried. Why? Had it been a result of inebriation or a simple lack of clear vision?

Then another thought struck just as forcefully. How was he going to tell Zach that his mother was dead? His heart beat an uneven pattern as he approached Zach, who was stuffing his toy cars into his backpack. His world was about to change drastically. And Gage was the lucky guy who had to break the news to the poor kid.

After asking Keith to keep him posted, Gage ended the call. It was going to be a heck of a day.

Two days later, Gage and Zach headed to Tucson to retrieve Zach's belongings. Having taken a week's worth of vacation time to be there for Zach, Gage decided that Zach needed to see his grandparents and they needed to see him.

April's funeral was scheduled for Friday. Exhausted from the sleepless nights of holding and comforting his distraught son, Gage reassured Zach that he loved him and that his mother loved and missed him too.

Sarah and Jared both expressed their condolences and pledged their support when Gage shared the news over the phone. Gage thanked them and told them that his first concern at the moment was his son. He wanted to make the transition from living with his mother to living with him as smooth as possible.

"Mommy's in heaven now, right?" Zach asked Gage. "That's what Grandma told me on the phone."

Gage hesitated, knowing that it was a little more complicated than that. But how to tell a four-year-old the intricacies of the afterlife, especially when he himself wasn't even sure about all of it anymore?

If the goal was to live with Heavenly Father again, then Gage wasn't feeling so sure about April's chances.

And what about him? What was going to happen to him after he died? He grunted impatiently, mad at himself for getting worked up over it. He hadn't given much thought for his salvation in a very long time, so why start now? Suppositions were totally useless in the real world.

Zach ran straight into his grandmother's arms as soon as his feet hit the ground. Gage watched Madeline Westbrook stoop down to hug him for all she was worth, a bittersweet feeling enveloping him at the sight of their reunion. If Gage was being honest with himself, he'd admit that he was a little jealous of their loving relationship. He wanted Zach to feel that way about him someday.

Gage approached them slowly, lamenting their red eyes and long faces. "She's dead," Madeline whispered as she gathered Gage into her embrace. "I can't believe my precious girl is gone."

"I'm sorry." His words felt inadequate, yet Gage could offer no more consolation than that.

He looked past her shoulder to see Keith wiping a tear from his eyes. "We did everything we could to get her to change her ways. We tried to make her understand that she was ruining her life, but she wouldn't listen to us."

April hadn't listened to him, either. What good did it do to be incredibly beautiful and have lots of money if you didn't use those gifts in the right way?

April's funeral was held at a non-denominational church in Oro Valley near Tucson. Gage helped Zach into a suit that he'd purchased at the mall. Zach had been silent for the past three days, crying quietly at unexpected times. Gage hurt for the little boy, but his detachment to April made it nearly impossible for him to keep his impatience with Zach's sorrow in check. Gage had to remind himself that it was all right for Zach to grieve for his mother, even if he couldn't do it.

After parking his car outside the church and leaning on the steering wheel, memories of April's smiling face assaulted him. She really had been a stunning woman. But she'd been heartless and deceitful too. He wasn't sure how he was going to endure sitting through her funeral. He certainly didn't want to listen to her family members carry on about what a wonderful person she'd been. He was still mad at her for all the heartache she'd caused him, but somehow it didn't feel right to condemn a dead person.

Gage did a double take when he and Zach walked up to the church building. His parents and their spouses, Craig and Marissa, and Pierce and Noelle were all waiting for him on the front lawn. With a lighter heart, he squeezed Zach's shoulder. "Look, Zach. Remember Uncle Pierce and Aunt Noelle?"

"Yeah."

"Well, there they are with your Uncle Craig and Aunt Marissa and your other grandparents," he said, gesturing toward them. "Come on."

Upon approaching them, Gage shook his head in disbelief. "Hey, y'all," he intoned for the benefit of his stepmother, Tamara, who hailed from North Carolina. She sent him a wide grin in return. "I can't believe you're all here."

"We wanted to be here for you, Gage. You shouldn't have to go through this alone." His father, Jared Logan, stepped forward and embraced his youngest son. It still felt strange to give his dad a hug. It was ironic, really, that Gage hadn't been able to help bring his dad back into the Church when he was preparing for his mission. Then his dad suddenly turned a new leaf, embracing the gospel again after Gage had discarded it. He knew that his father's marriage to Tamara had a lot to do with the change.

"Thanks, Dad."

Hugging his dad was just a precursor to the gigantic one he knew he'd have to endure from Tamara. "Hello, sugar." He braced himself before she nearly squeezed the breath out of him. Just when he thought he might pass out, she let go. "Gage, we haven't seen you for so long. You're looking a little run-down, honey. Is there anything we can do to help?"

Mustering every ounce of strength he had left, he flashed her a brilliant smile. "Now that you're all here, I'm doing much better." Turning to Zach, who was looking at this bunch of people like the strangers they were, he said, "I want you all to meet my son, Zach." Lifting him up, he introduced him to each of his parents and their spouses, followed by Craig and Marissa. Zach looked at Gage in awe. "You have *two* brothers?"

"Yep." He nodded. "Uncle Craig is the oldest."

"And the smartest," Craig quipped.

"And the best looking, although your dad comes in a close second," Marissa put in with a wink. Craig shared a loving smile with his wife, ignoring Pierce's good-natured protest. In that moment, Gage knew that he'd never felt that kind of connection with April and wished that he could find a woman who was meant just for him, one whom he could laugh with and share his dreams with.

The group headed inside and Gage reluctantly pulled Zach away from his family to take him to April's parents.

To say that the funeral service for April Westbrook Logan was very different than any funeral Gage had ever attended was a huge understatement. The minister prayed for her soul but spoke very little of an afterlife. "Ashes to ashes, dust to dust . . ." Was this all there was to look forward to? Surely God in all His glory had prepared a better place for His children after this life. As choices went, April had made several stupid ones. But surely all was not lost, especially since April had never received the gospel message, thanks to him.

What am I thinking? Gage asked himself silently. He'd already decided that he didn't believe in that nonsense anymore.

How can you be sure? He'd asked his mother that question just last week right before all of this headache began. Her answer came back to him. *The Lord still loved me. He never left me alone.*

But how could any person know with certainty, with an undying conviction?

Just then, a soft whisper came to his heart. *You know it's true.*

Tuning out the words of the minister's misguided sermon, Gage's mind went back to the first time he'd read the account of Alma the Younger as a teenager. His chest had felt like it was on fire. Tears had come to his eyes and he knew that Alma had relied on the mercy of Christ, knowing without a doubt that his sins had been forgiven.

Last Sunday, his mother had told him that he knew the gospel backward and forward but no longer felt the Spirit. Maybe she was right.

Maybe the Holy Ghost was speaking to him right now.

And maybe it was time to listen.

Standing next to her husband, Eric, on the grass outside the church building, Sarah Nielsen watched her ex-husband exit the building with his wife, Tamara. She bore no ill feelings toward him. Hers and Jared's lives had turned out surprisingly well after the trials they'd gone through during their twenty-five years of marriage. Still, she felt a pang for causing their sons to suffer. Craig and Pierce had recovered well with the help of their beautiful wives. But who did Gage have?

She squeezed Eric's arm. "I need to talk to Jared for a moment." Eric smiled at her. She really was fortunate to have found such a wonderful man.

Sarah's palms became damp as she approached the happy couple. Although she had no qualms about talking to her ex-husband, talking to his wife always put her on edge. Shrugging off her discomfort, she lightly touched Tamara's shoulder. "Do you mind if I steal a moment of Jared's time? There is something we need to discuss."

Looking mildly surprised, Tamara glanced at her husband, whose brows knitted together. "Not at all, sugar," she said in her Southern drawl, her drawn features conveying her curiosity.

"Thank you." Without looking to see if he followed, she walked to a nearby tree. Jared joined her shortly.

"What's this about, Sarah?"

Sarah scrutinized her ex-husband's face, unsure of what exactly she was searching for. The pride he'd carried like a shield for so long was gone. Deeper lines had appeared on his face, perhaps etched in time by the tremendous stress of his job through the years. When he'd lost his business, he'd had to build a new one along with a new relationship with his sons. He'd made a valiant effort. However, Sarah's conversation with Gage the other night confirmed her suspicions that all was not right between Jared and their youngest son.

"I talked to Gage a few nights ago after meeting Zach for the first time. He was more open with me than he's been in a very long time. I suspect it was due to the stress he has experienced lately. He's finally starting to realize that he needs help."

Noting a bit of impatience on Jared's face, Sarah came right to the point.

"Gage is still hurting, Jared. He told me himself that he regrets all the wild things he's done. But he also mentioned the time when he received his mission call. He remembers you pushing him away when he was learning so much about the gospel. I could be wrong, but Gage made it sound like your negative reaction cut more deeply than he first let on."

A look of remorse replaced Jared's impatience. "I was harsh with him, wasn't I? Why didn't he say something to me?"

"I don't know. You might want to talk to him about it."

He nodded thoughtfully. "I will."

She smiled wanly. "Thank you. I'm worried about him, Jared. I think he knows what he's missing by staying away from the Church and us, but he's afraid to come back."

"It's hard to take the first step." Jared Logan, with his coal-black eyes and chiseled face, was still a handsome man. She'd known that she couldn't make any demands. However, she wanted to make sure that he understood her concern. If the pained expression on his face was any indication, he did.

"So what did you think of that sermon?" Pierce asked Gage as they left the church grounds.

Gage grimaced, glancing back to where he had left Zach standing with his grandparents, who would keep him for the next week. "It was . . . different. Kind of missed the mark, didn't it?"

"By a mile," Pierce replied, shrugging. "Then again, I learned from my mission that there are a lot of people out there who believe that this is the end."

"Then what gives them hope for the next life?"

"I have yet to figure that one out, bro." He regarded Gage thoughtfully. "Now that you'll have Zach full-time, are you going to raise him to believe there's nothing to look forward to?"

"No." Gage looked down at the ground and then back up at him. "But if you're asking if I'm ready to take him to the LDS Church, I'm not sure about that, either." That was as close as he'd come to admitting that he'd had an epiphany a few moments ago.

"Who's going to take care of him while you're at work?" Pierce asked. "If you're planning on asking Noelle, the answer is no."

Gage shook his head in consternation. His actions of late might not have been stellar, but even he knew that Noelle was not a candidate for the position. "I haven't had much time to think about this problem. Zach will be staying with April's parents for a week or so until I can make arrangements for full-time care."

"As in day care?"

Gage nodded. "At least part of the time." But he wasn't sure how that would work with his crazy schedule. And deep down, he knew that day care wasn't the right answer. Gage wanted to find someone who could give his son the care he really needed. Sure, Zach's teachers at day care might praise and encourage him. But Zach needed a motherly type who would speak to him softly in place of April's shrill voice. A woman who would take the time to really listen to him.

"Wait a minute!" he exclaimed, snapping his fingers. "Would you be willing to get Valerie Hall's phone number from Kurt?"

Pierce quickly connected the dots. "You want to ask Valerie to babysit Zach?"

Brother and Sister Levington had mentioned that Valerie was struggling financially. This might be a deal both of them needed. "It's worth a try."

"She already has a job. And she's a single parent. What makes you think she'd want to take on your little squirt?" Pierce grinned to soften his words.

"Maybe if I offer her more money than she's earning now, she'll agree."

"What about her autistic son? Do you think Zach can handle being around him?"

"Zach dealt with an incompetent mother for the first four years of his life. He's sensitive to others who aren't fully capable of handling themselves. I think he'll be fine with Justin."

Pierce pulled his phone out of his pocket. "It might work. I'll call Kurt right now."

"Thanks, Chloe. I sure am glad my kids have a good place to go to every day after school. See you tomorrow."

"You're welcome. Take it easy, sister. You look beat."

Valerie nodded wearily. Chloe had her pegged. Waitressing wasn't a fun job. Most days, Valerie was able to placate her customers with an easy-going smile and cheerful word. But today, she was weighed down with decisions that needed to be made soon.

Justin's preschool teacher was preparing the necessary paperwork for Justin's next IEP meeting and needed to know Valerie's decision on where to place him for the next school year. On the one hand, Justin was in a good situation where he was but Valerie wanted him to progress at the same rate as other kids his age, although that would entail finding a teacher who would minimize his tantrums through patience and understanding and allow him to work at his own pace. Teachers like this were rare gems. Valerie had been praying for a decision.

Once in the car, Whitney piped up, "Mom, I'm so glad that summer is almost here. I'm tired of school."

"I'm thankful too, sweetie." Though how she was going to manage to work with them being home was a mystery. Last summer, Valerie's mom had filled in as much as she could because there was no way that Valerie could afford full-time child care. But now her time was largely spent on her new calling as the Relief Society president in her ward.

Forty-five minutes later, the phone was ringing as she walked inside from the backyard. Her arms were laden with zucchini squash, red ripe tomatoes, and green peppers from the garden for the salad she'd decided would go nicely with her chicken casserole. In this regard, Valerie was a lot like her grandmother, Molly Skylar, whose gardening talents rivaled that of a pro. Because the extreme heat of central Arizona's summers zapped the plants in early summer, Valerie had planted her "summer" garden in a raised bed of soil in early February. The tomato vines were already showing signs of heat-related stress.

Dumping the vegetables on the nearest countertop, Valerie answered on the third ring. "Hello?"

A deep male voice greeted her, sending shivers up her arm. "Hey, Valerie. This is Gage Logan. How are you?"

"Gage?" she asked, wondering why he would be calling her and how he'd gotten her number. "I'm fine. And you?"

A pause followed before Gage admitted, "Things haven't been going so great lately. I hope you don't mind that I got your number through Kurt. I have a dilemma—a business proposition, really—that I'm hoping you might consider."

That sounded intriguing. What could Gage possibly need from her? It wasn't like Valerie had had a chance to develop many business skills through the years. "I'm listening."

"I would rather explain it in person. Would you mind if I dropped by your place in a little while?"

Mentally, she reviewed the condition of the house. If the three of them quickly picked up the toys in the living room, they could make it look presentable. And she had plenty of food to share. That wasn't the problem.

The problem was that Gage Logan had a habit of making her feel nervous. And the other problem was that Valerie almost never invited company over. She'd learned from past experience that outside influences were better off left . . . well, *outside*, as far as Justin was concerned.

But her mouth didn't want to obey what her instincts were telling her. "I'm making dinner right now. Why don't you come on over and eat with us?"

"That sounds great. Meet you in thirty minutes?"

Was it her imagination or did he sound relieved? "Sure."

After giving him her address, she hung up and whipped around the corner to the living room, frantically calling for her kids to help her straighten up the place. Justin immediately balked at Valerie's request. Before she could address his grievances, Whitney looked at her mother curiously. "Who's coming over?"

Although it irked Valerie that her daughter assumed that they were cleaning up just because someone was coming over, this time her guess was right on the money. "My friend, Gage Logan. Hurry and help me, okay? And when you finish picking up this floor, will you wash your hands and come help me in the kitchen, please?"

The fact that Whitney was looking at her as if she'd lost her head didn't escape Valerie's notice. But now there were more important things to worry about. She raced around the house, picking up stray clothing, backpacks, and books before heading to her bedroom to change out of her work clothes and don a loosely fitting blouse and comfortable jeans. Then she quickly ran a brush through her hair and dabbed on some lip gloss before heading back into the kitchen to rinse the vegetables.

Whitney had just finished washing her hands. "Can I slice the cucumbers, Mom?"

"Sure. And I'll shred the lettuce and grate a few carrots."

"Okay." Whitney loved using the plastic serrated knife that was specially made for children.

The doorbell rang far too soon. Taking a deep breath and squaring her shoulders, she pasted a welcoming smile on her face and opened the door. Gage stood alone on her front porch, looking as handsome as ever, in a dark red dress shirt, striped tie, and black dress pants. Valerie's heartbeat zinged into overtime as she inanely blurted, "Hey, it's good to see you again, although it's a little unexpected."

Instead of the flirtatious grin she expected in return, one side of his mouth dipped down self-consciously. "I'm a little surprised to be here myself. But considering everything that's happened this week, I'm glad you agreed to meet with me."

Valerie studied him thoughtfully, thinking back to the days when he'd been cool and confident. Arrogant and even harsh in his teasing, which had bordered on insulting.

Interestingly enough, he appeared to have lost that persona. She was sure that his confident demeanor still lie dormant some-where and would resurface soon. After all, what would Gage want with a simple woman like her? He was probably used to spending his time with more sophisticated women. But it seemed that life had recently kicked him in the shins.

Hmm. Well, she would find out what he wanted and then turn him away right after she fed him dinner.

"Come in." Valerie's words snapped Gage out of the trance he'd fallen into after seeing her again. Her lightly made-up face and easy smile shouldn't have been anything to make his heart thump rapidly. Gage was used to being around beautiful women. But he'd never forgotten Valerie's openness and natural beauty.

"Thanks."

With only a nod of acknowledgment, she turned and walked back into the house, leaving him no choice but to follow. The house was beautiful. It had that nostalgic feeling like it had been in the family for generations. The rustic lines were softened by the rose-colored drapes on the windows and the muted brown tones of the couch and lampshades. Sepia-colored photographs from genera-tions of family members graced the walls.

Stopping to gaze at each one, Gage was quickly able to pick out the Levington family. There was Valerie, standing in front of her brothers Kurt, Jake, and Luke. Seeing her youth immortalized like this, with her hair in ringlets and her freckles uncovered by makeup, caught him off-guard. He wished that they could go back to those years before they'd become enemies and form the friendship that he should have cultivated when he'd had the chance.

Her son was lying on his stomach on the floor, driving his cars around on a play mat. *Wow*, Gage thought, *a kid who still plays with cars instead of electronics.* He leaned down to look at Justin. "Hi, Justin. Remember me? I'm Gage."

Justin looked up at him briefly before his eyes flicked down again. "Hi," he said in a low voice.

Gage glanced up at Valerie quizzically. "Don't be offended. He avoids eye contact with most people."

Gage decided to try again, sitting cross-legged on the shaggy carpet beside him. "Whatcha got, Justin? Let's see your cars."

To his surprise, Justin held as many of them as he could in his hands out for Gage's inspection. Gage bent over, exclaiming over each one and at the same time, keeping a respectful space between the two of them. Carefully taking a red car off the floor, he made a revving engine sound with his lips and made it zoom around the play mat, stopping at the police station and then the house.

Suddenly, Justin's excited voice boomed, "I'll race you."

Gage grinned. They raced their cars around the play mat for a few minutes, stopping at the bank, the farm, and the lake before Valerie's soft voice broke into their interplay.

"So where is Zach tonight?"

Gage met her gaze. "Zach is spending the rest of the week with his grandparents in Tucson." Raising his eyebrows, he ventured, "Actually, that is what I'd like to talk to you about."

"Dinner is almost ready. Should we eat first?"

"Sure. Anything I can do to help?"

Handing him a bucket, she said, "Maybe you could encourage Justin to put his toys away while I help Whitney set the table."

When she left the room, Gage held the bucket out to Justin. "Hey, Justin. Your mom says it's time to clean up your toys. Wanna help me put the cars in the bucket?"

Justin kept driving his cars around in obvious reluctance. Gage figured he could allow Justin a few more minutes to finish playing.

Soon he held the bucket out again. "It's time for dinner. If we hurry and pick up your toys, we'll be able to eat that much sooner. And your mom will be really proud of you."

It almost seemed as if the boy hadn't heard him.

Finally, after a third prompting from Gage, Justin picked up a silver car and placed it along the edge of the play mat. Gage watched, fascinated, as Justin lined the rest of his cars parallel to the first, arranging them by color and size. Then, one by one, he picked them up and dropped them into the bucket. Although Gage's instincts were screaming for him to hurry, Justin continued in agonizing precision.

When the last one landed in the bucket with a plunk, Justin grinned up at Gage and held his hands up, fingers spread apart, and shook them back and forth briskly in some sort of sign language. "All done." He clapped happily.

Gage swallowed. "Well done, Justin," he said huskily at the same moment Valerie reentered the living room. The meaningful look she sent Gage lit a lightbulb inside his brain. She'd given him a test. At this point, he wondered if he'd passed or failed.

Dinner was a simple affair, consisting of chicken casserole, a garden salad, and buttered rolls Valerie had pulled from the freezer. She asked her daughter to bless the food and then they began passing the dishes around the table.

Gage inhaled appreciatively. "Smells delicious." Most of his meals came from boxes. Or the ballpark.

"It's nothing fancy. Most of my dinners are one-dish meals. Clean-up is a lot easier." Lowering her voice into a stage whisper, Valerie added, "Plus, I can sneak more vegetables into their diet that way."

"I heard that!" Whitney exclaimed.

Valerie sent her daughter a mock horrified look, making Whitney break out into giggles.

Gage grinned. He was seeing a different side to Valerie. She was the perfect choice for Zach, who could also benefit from the lively interaction of a real family. Gage's conscience pricked when he remembered his first impression of Valerie as an uncaring parent. His judgment had been way off base.

After dinner was over, Valerie asked her children to place their dishes in the sink while Gage helped her to clear the table. When they were finished, she thanked him and invited him back to the living room.

"You were saying something about a business proposition?" Valerie asked after they were seated comfortably and the kids went off to their rooms.

Taking a fortifying breath, Gage answered with a question of his own, hoping to appeal to her natural mothering instincts. "If you were given the choice between being a stay-at-home mom or having a great career, which would you choose?"

She took a moment to consider. "That's a hard question to answer. Ideally, I would love to be home for my kids while they're still young. But since I need to work, the next best option would be a job that works around their schedule. Unfortunately, that isn't the way the world works."

"Have you thought about going back to school?"

"I would like to someday, but the time has never seemed right."

Gage was intrigued by the fact that she felt torn between the two worlds. He wondered if most women felt that way at times.

"Why do you want to know?"

"I wanted to check on your availability and long-term goals before presenting my offer, which would allow you to stay home with your kids and still earn enough to make a living, if you're interested."

"I'm interested but I don't think that's possible."

"It is, but it would require some unconventional hours. The upside to it is that for some of those of hours, you'd be asleep."

"Sleeping while I'm earning money?" she asked incredulously. "I'm not following."

"Do you remember me telling you that I was going to file for full custody of Zach when we ran into each other at the store?"

Valerie nodded.

"Well, April, my ex-wife, was in a fatal car accident ten days ago. I no longer need to file the claim. I've become my son's only living parent overnight and I'm trying to figure out how to make everything work."

She gasped. "Oh, Gage. I'm sorry to hear that. How is Zach taking his mother's death?"

He sighed. "Not very well, which is to be expected. It will take time for him to adjust to April being gone."

"That's so sad, Gage. Is there anything I can do to help?"

Now was his chance. So why was he hesitating with the next phase of his request? Would she reject him outright or seriously consider doing it? "Yes, actually. I'm in need of a full-time care-giver for Zach immediately. I work late hours during the baseball season and day care isn't really an option. Zach stayed with Pierce and Noelle for a few days, but she is almost ready to have a baby and I can't rely on them. I'm wondering if you would be interested in taking the job. The money I paid April for child support could be allocated to you." When he named the sum, Valerie's mouth fell open.

"Gage, that's too much. My children already receive child sup-port from their father. I'd feel like I was stealing your money."

In April's case, Gage felt that she really had been. The money she'd squandered on countless parties and trips left a bitter taste in his mouth. But with Valerie, he knew the money would be put to good use. "No, Valerie. I want to pay you that much. Anyone can see that you take good care of your kids. I know that Zach would be in good hands."

Valerie studied him thoughtfully while little beads of sweat broke out on his forehead. What if she said no?

"The fact of the matter is that I'm required to work during the Diamondbacks' home games. I don't get off work until after the games end, which is around ten o'clock or sometimes later, depending on if they go into extra innings. Then I have to finish my reports for the night before I can come home. I was think-ing that Zach could just spend the night with you and I could pick him up in the morning. And then we'd be back on your doorstep again at one o'clock in the afternoon so that I can be at work by two."

Then, afraid that he might be asking too much of her, he added, "You can take some time to think it over, if you'd like. I know this will be a big change for Justin, and if you think it would cause too many disruptions to have another child in your home, I understand."

"I don't have a problem with that," Valerie countered. "But how do you feel about Zach being with my rowdy bunch? Justin isn't the easiest kid to get along with. Neither is Whitney, for that matter."

"They're just kids, Valerie," he reminded her. "Seriously, I think it would be good for Zach to be around them. He's been in day care part-time and he's normally an easy-going kid, but losing April has thrown him off. I'm worried about him. He could really use a friend or two right now." Truth be told, Gage could too.

"I'm assuming that you'll need a babysitter for Zach on Sundays?"

"For every Sunday when the D-Backs play a home game. Baseball season is hectic for me. But since Sunday games are played in the afternoon, I get off at a decent hour."

"Would you mind if I take Zach to church with us on the Sundays when I have him? I would be his Primary teacher. And I insist that you allow me to take him to Primary even on the Sundays when you're home." Her infectious smile was back.

"And if I don't agree?" he asked mischievously.

"Then no deal," she answered cheekily.

He chuckled. "You drive a hard bargain. And I'm fine with that as long as you don't tell Pierce I gave in so easily."

"Do I sense a sibling rivalry going on here? You and Pierce always seemed to have a great relationship."

Gage shrugged. "We did until recently."

"What happened?"

Now it was Gage's turn to become silent. Could he really tell her without lowering her opinion of him? Then, figuring that Valerie's opinion of him probably wasn't very high to begin with, Gage decided that he really had nothing to lose.

He began by telling her about meeting April at the University of Arizona, their short marriage, and the subsequent events after their divorce. Noting the initial shock on Valerie's face, he lowered his head in shame. "My family didn't know about Zach.

I—couldn't tell them. It was just too hard to admit that I made so many mistakes."

"It's not easy to admit that to yourself, let alone anyone else," Valerie said softly. "I'm sorry that you've had to deal with that all on your own."

"That's the thing. I didn't have to." Gage swallowed thickly. "I should have told my family a long time ago. They were pretty upset with me too. But we're working it out." He was still amazed over the way his family members had pulled together for him during April's funeral.

"I hope things will get better for you. You can only move forward from here."

Gage smiled at her. "Thanks. Now that you've agreed to watch Zach, I feel like I've already taken a step in the right direction. I have a feeling that you and I will make a great team."

Valerie smiled back. Their gazes connected for a moment and time froze. It was almost like the years had melted away and he and Valerie had made a silent pact to put aside their differences for their children. In essence, that was what he hoped to accomplish.

Then Valerie's smile faded. "Maybe because we've gone through so much of the same heartache—divorce and knowing that we're the black sheep of the family."

"You feel that way too?" Gage asked, surprised.

"Oh, yes."

"But what happened to you wasn't your fault, at least from what I heard your family say after the baby blessing."

Valerie lifted her bangs out of her eyes, moving her fingers toward the back of her head and grabbing a fistful of hair. Apparently, he wasn't the only one who did that.

"When you are the only divorcee in a strong Mormon family, it's hard to avoid everyone's pity. Don't get me wrong, Gage. My family loves me and they are very supportive. But I know deep down that I've disappointed my parents. When I recall the way I envisioned living my life, I'm disappointed in myself. I should have known better."

Better than what? But at that moment, Whitney and Justin came running into the room in their pajamas, claiming that their teeth were brushed and they were ready for scripture time.

Gage took that as his cue to leave. He wasn't retreating, he told himself after telling them good-bye with a promise to call the next day. He was simply giving Valerie the time she needed to help her children get ready for bed. Family scripture study had never been a regular part of the Logan family's routine, so there was no reason to stick around as Valerie gathered her children close to her side now. Gage shut the door with a decisive click on his way out.

Zach was elated to learn that he was going to live with his dad from now on but not as much when Gage told him that he'd be spending his afternoons and evenings with Valerie and her children. "Do I have to?" became his favorite phrase.

"Yes," Gage asserted sternly. Then, softening his words, he added, "Give it a try. I'm sure you'll like them." Zach seemed to respond better to his entreaty.

But once they arrived at Valerie's, Zach's scowl was back in place. Whitney, the outgoing sibling, broke the ice by ushering him and Justin down the hallway to show him where the toys were.

Gage and Valerie exchanged a meaningful look. She grinned at his sigh of relief. "You look like you've been through a major battle."

"Yeah," he agreed. "I can take it as long as he behaves himself for you."

"I'm sure he'll be fine. It takes a little time to adjust to a new situation."

His hands flexed nervously. He knew he should go or he'd be late for work. But leaving Zach was tougher than he'd imagined it would be.

"He'll be fine, Gage. You'll see."

Looking into her eyes, Gage noticed how peaceful Valerie

seemed. She was in her element. "Your boss didn't give you too much grief about quitting?"

"Nope. It worked out perfectly. One of the college students who was working weekends wanted more hours with summer approaching and took over my shift."

"I'm glad." Coming out of his trance, he said, "All right then. Thanks again. Tell Zach I love him and I'll see him tomorrow morning."

"I will."

Sitting in his Camaro with his hand on the ignition, Gage looked at the beautiful old house with the wide porch surrounded by sunflowers and closed his eyes, uttering the first prayer he could remember saying in a very long time. "Dear Father in Heaven, please watch over Valerie and the kids. Please bless Zach to be all right." He closed the prayer reverently and waited. Nothing physically happened, but somehow Gage felt lighter and ready to face his day.

Okay, so maybe this was a little more than I bargained for, Valerie thought rashly as she scurried from one child to the next. Justin pulled on her leg, mumbling about his lost pajamas as Valerie helped Zach reach the sink to finish brushing his teeth. Frantically, she called to Whitney, who was in the bathtub, to turn the water off before it overflowed. What had she been thinking to agree to take on the responsibility of another child? While Valerie was glad to see Zach's outgoing personality engage Justin's introverted one, now she really wished that she had kicked Gage out the door when she'd had the chance.

Yesterday, her parents had come over to help her dismantle one of the beds from the guest bedroom and move it into Justin's room. Valerie's mom had asked her point blank if she was sure about agreeing to this arrangement. "Although we like Gage, he has been inactive for quite some time. And he's hurt you in the past."

Valerie swallowed in light of the fact that her mother's concerns were her own. But she couldn't deny the warm feeling she'd felt when she'd prayed about it. "I'm not dating Gage, Mom. I'm just babysitting his little boy. Getting involved with him again was an unforeseen turn of events, but this is an answer to my prayers."

Now, however, with the bedtime routine deteriorating before her eyes, Valerie was seriously questioning her sanity. Family scripture time was a disaster. When Zach asked for the zillionth time why they needed to read them, she muttered, "It's just something we do." Before she could ask him to kneel, she had to intervene in a brief argument between her children. Finally they were all ready for prayer.

Then Zach asked her what a prayer was. Sorely tempted to skip the ordeal altogether, she told him, "We pray to our Father in Heaven at the beginning and end of each day. We love Him and He loves us."

Zach gazed up at her in confusion. "Huh?"

"Never mind." She sighed. "You'll catch on in time. Fold your arms and kneel down like this."

The next morning, Gage rang Valerie's doorbell. When she opened it, he asked anxiously, "How did it go last night?"

Was it his imagination or did her smile seem forced? "It went all right. The boys became buddies in a short time. The only glitch we experienced came at bedtime."

"Zach was hard to put down for the night, wasn't he?"

Her slight hesitation confirmed his suspicion.

"You can level with me, Valerie. I've had a hard time putting Zach to bed too. Any time you have trouble with Zach, please let me know. I'll do what I can to fix the problem."

"We can't fix every problem, Gage. Give Zach time to adjust. Some things just take longer to work themselves out. And others, well . . . if they don't work out, then you're the one who has to adjust."

"Like you've had to do with Justin's autism," he replied automatically.

She nodded reluctantly.

"That's got to be tough, dealing with it every day."

"Yes," she said quietly. "There are days when I have to remind myself that Justin will be made perfect someday. But for right now, I have to endure. I get really excited when I see the tiniest improvement in him. And it will be the same for you with Zach."

"I hope so."

"As soon as he realizes that this is his new norm, he'll settle down." Spoken like a true mother. He was never so happy to know he had made the right choice.

"Next Tuesday at ten o'clock," Valerie confirmed later that afternoon as she wrote down the information her friend had given her. "Thanks a lot, Kiera. I'll see you then." Valerie ended the call with a smile. Because of Gage's job offer, she could now afford to place Justin in swimming lessons. His motor skills were coming along. Valerie had taught him enough basic skills to prevent him from drowning, which had been a necessity due to his undeviating fascination with water since he was a toddler. But Justin had never actually become proficient at swimming. Whitney would be taking intermediate lessons as well.

That evening, she passed the information on to Gage. "I've just signed my kids up for swim lessons with two sisters in my ward who teach them privately. They have one more opening, if you're interested in having Zach take lessons too. Does he know how to swim?"

Gage frowned. "I haven't really spent enough time with Zach to know if he does or doesn't."

"Even if he does, a refresher course wouldn't hurt. My kids love spending time at the pool during the summer."

"Yeah, I guess I'd better look into that. Thanks."

"Swim lessons start a week from today." She handed him the slip of paper with Kiera's phone number, ignoring the zing that raced up her arm when his hand brushed hers. Valerie didn't need any complications in her life. But she wouldn't mind if they finally became friends.

"Hand me the crayons, Justin," Whitney said harshly after having already asked for them once before. Valerie prayed for patience, not realizing until recently that her daughter resented the extra responsibilities that had been placed upon her due to Justin's disorder. She'd need to tread lightly with Whitney, who was playing the "I'm the oldest so you have to do what I say" card quite heavily lately. This was quickly becoming a sore spot with Justin.

For this being Zach's first time in sacrament meeting, he was behaving fairly well. He colored with Justin or looked at books and responded to Valerie's reminders to whisper. Amazingly, he and Justin had established an instant rapport. It was like they had always known each other. Zach seemed to anticipate Justin's needs. And while Valerie's mind stumbled over the fact that Zach was younger than Justin but was more physically able to do most things than he could, her heart took comfort in knowing that her son had found a true friend.

When the meeting was over, Valerie asked the children to quickly gather the array of books, paper, and crayons before turning to hustle them to Primary. She was waylaid, however, by Sister Ashcroft, a widow, who slowly walked up the aisle. "Valerie," she said jovially, "who is this handsome young man you have with you today?"

"Hi, Sister Ashcroft. This is Zachary, the son of a friend of mine. He'll be attending church with us from now on."

Sister Ashcroft answered in a quivering voice, "Wonderful!" She peered down at Zach, not needing to bend over as her back was curved almost horizontally with age. "Hello, my young friend. Thank you for sharing the books so nicely with Justin. What a thoughtful boy you are!"

She held her gnarled hand out for Zach to shake it. Zach hesitated, his expression a mixture of awe and fear. Valerie gently placed her hand on top of his little one, lifting it up to grasp Sister Ashcroft's. "Tell her thank you," she whispered in his ear.

"Thank you," Zach whispered solemnly. Valerie hid a smile. Maybe she should tell him that he didn't need to *always* whisper in church.

Straightening her body, Valerie cupped her hand on the elderly woman's shoulder and said, "Thank you, Sister Ashcroft. We're off to Primary now, but I'll drop in later this week with some cinnamon rolls, if you'd like."

"Oh, my. That would be a lovely treat. Anytime, Valerie. Come and visit anytime."

The next three weeks were an adjustment for everyone in the Hall household as the school year came to a close. Valerie had almost decided to go through with her decision to place Justin in the local elementary school when Justin threw two major tantrums at preschool. Justin's tendency to frequently lash out at other students, coupled with his teacher's training in dealing with this kind of behavior, prompted Valerie to change her mind. Her mother was right. Justin really could use one more year at this school to help him develop the proper social skills that he would need to rely on. When she informed the staff of her decision and they met to go over Justin's IEP, she felt as if a huge weight had lifted from her shoulders.

Now that summer was here, the days were long and hot. Valerie took the children outside to the garden early in the mornings to weed and harvest the vegetables that were ready for picking. The garden had almost grown itself out before Valerie and her sister, Chloe, had managed to preserve a good amount of vegetables last week. In another week's time, the plants would be completely scorched.

Gage's knack for picking Zach up just as Valerie and the kids were completing their work outdoors dismayed her. The first time this happened, Gage lifted a sardonic brow at the picture they all made—Valerie, with her wide-brimmed hat and sweat-stained clothing, and the kids who were smudged from head to toe. "Playing in the dirt, I see. Having fun?"

She shrugged self-consciously. "I wasn't about to turn down their offers to 'help.' I hope you don't mind Zach getting dirty."

Gage's gaze softened even while holding a hint of admiration. "Dirt washes away. The important thing is that he's happy."

Usually after Gage took a washed-up Zach home, Valerie and her children enjoyed some free time before Gage brought him back to her place in the afternoons. On Tuesdays and Thursdays, she took Justin and Whitney to swim lessons at Kiera Erickson's house. Gage brought Zach as well. Valerie didn't know if she was more pleased that Gage had signed Zach up for the sake of him learning to swim or for the opportunity to spend more time with him.

During that time, she learned a lot about his job, including the fact that Gage had earned a master's degree online in sports management while working at the University of Arizona and shortly after he had hired on with the D-Backs. She also learned that his job wasn't as glamorous as it sounded. Gage spent a lot of time on the phone, talking with potential clients, before meeting them in person to give them a firsthand look at their package deal. He also researched buying trends from their fan base through strategic marketing analytics before sending his reports to upper management.

Gage didn't interact with the Diamondbacks players too much except when they occasionally crossed paths at Chase Field or when the marketing team was putting on a special promotion. Under the shade of the canopy by the pool, watching the kids' progress with their instructors, Valerie posed a question. "So of all the Diamondbacks players you've encountered, who are the easiest to work with?"

"Miguel Santiago and Brody Renford are fan favorites, of course. They're pretty easygoing. One of the suites we rent out coincides with Steve Hunsaker's uniform number. Now that he's a member of management, we've struck a deal with him, which in essence, ensures that he'll make an appearance to the group who rents his suite at their request."

"Everyone loves him," Valerie agreed. "Who would you say are the most difficult players to work with?"

"I shouldn't divulge any names," he hedged. "But some of the players have more brusque personalities than others. They're very focused on doing their jobs well and don't get too caught up in the fan hoopla. Of course, all the players are under contract to make occasional public appearances. Some of them take it in stride while others get a little testy."

"So you're saying that your job is a little more stressful than you'd like?"

He answered carefully. "It's a fun job for the most part, but sometimes it's tough to draw people to the ballpark when you're competing with various forms of media and a losing streak. Even our die-hard fans occasionally need a little coaxing."

Valerie would never admit it aloud, but she missed the times when Gage brought Zach to swimming lessons and they could chat. When the D-Backs were on a road trip, Gage worked more normal hours, leaving Zach with Valerie for most of the day before picking him up just before dinnertime.

As the swim lessons progressed, Gage and Valerie would end each of their chats by analyzing the latest D-Backs' game. Gage seemed impressed with Valerie's knowledge of the players' stats. "You must watch their games often to know most of that stuff," he told her during one swim lesson in late June.

She blushed. "No. I just listen to my brother Kurt. He's a walking sports encyclopedia."

"You wouldn't let him talk your ear off about it if you weren't a big fan," he persisted.

"Well, it is kind of hard to make him shut up." Gage chuckled at her attempt at humor. "But, yes, I do watch the games sometimes."

"If you'd like, I could get you a good deal on some great seats for Saturday's game."

"Thanks for the offer," Valerie replied hesitantly, "but attending a game at Chase Field isn't really an option for us."

Gage's eyes widened and he gave her his full attention. "Are you serious? Who can resist a day at the diamond, eating hot dogs and cheering their favorite team on?"

Valerie's gaze slid to the children with their swim instructors, but she wasn't really seeing them. "It wouldn't be good for Justin to be around so many people."

He leaned over to stare her down. "Says who?"

"Says me," she said evenly.

"Have you tried it yet?"

"No. And I don't want to, either."

"Why not?"

"Because Justin gets too agitated around a large group of people, as you saw for yourself at the baby blessing. It's hard on him and me," she admitted tersely.

He lifted an imperious brow. "So you're going to keep him in a cage all his life? Pardon me for saying so, but I don't see how that's going to help. He's got to learn to function in society eventually."

"Just drop it, Gage. You know nothing about this." Her jaw clenched. "You haven't had to put your life on hold to help your developmentally delayed child outgrow his toddler years. You haven't had to stay up all night with a kid who couldn't turn his hyperactive brain off long enough to fall asleep. You've never had a complete stranger ask what is wrong with your child or tell you how to 'fix' the problem. And you certainly haven't had to deal with a husband who blamed the dirty dishes, the laundry stacked to the ceiling, the fussy kid—everything—on you, when you were doing your best to hold it all together. You might be Zach's father, but your ex-wife did more for your son than you realize. Who stayed up with him when he was sick or changed his dirty diapers for the first two or three years of his life? It wasn't you!"

Valerie almost flinched as Gage's eyes darkened like the onset of a coming storm. "I might have if April had given me the choice. Thanks to her selfishness—or maybe she felt that she knew better than me—we'll never know, will we? Tell me that you at least gave your ex-husband the chance to know his kids."

She stood and began pacing. "I did and he threw it away— at least with Justin! Whitney is his favorite. But Nick was always spending time on the golf course, schmoozing with clients. I never knew when he'd be home, yet the minute he walked in the door, I had to be at his beck and call." Valerie bit down on her lip to keep it from trembling.

Gage quickly jumped up and stepped in front of her, effectively stopping her in her tracks. "Maybe you should have explained to Nick that you were feeling overwhelmed and needed help."

With a humorless laugh, Valerie tried to step around him. "And opened myself up for more criticism? I was barely holding onto my sanity as it was."

Gage turned his body, blocking not only her retreat but her ability to see the kids at the other end of the pool as well. "Then you know how it was for me. According to April, the only thing she ever did wrong was marrying me. I hate to break it to you, Valerie, but when a guy spends all his time at work, it's usually to get away from a bad situation at home. It was probably more stressful than he was able to deal with."

"Oh, so now you're pinning the blame for Nick's defection on me?" Her voice rose in sync with the tremors that were running through her body. "Thanks a lot!"

Having been pushed beyond reason, Valerie fought an uncontrollable urge to push back. Before rationality could prevail, and with a force she hardly recognized as her own, Valerie shoved at his chest. Gage's eyes registered shock just before tumbling backward, his feet catching on a pair of flip-flops. Valerie winced as Gage hit the water with a huge splash.

Loud screams erupted as Kiera and Deb frantically reached for their charges. Gage quickly pulled himself out of the water, coughing and swiping his hand through his hair. Wordlessly, he yanked his wallet, keys, and phone from his pockets and tossed them onto the concrete where they landed at her feet.

Oh no! What have I done? Valerie backed away.

"Dad! Are you all right?" Zach cried as he rounded the corner and hurled himself against his father's leg.

He coughed again and patted Zach's back. "Yeah. I'm okay."

Horrified, Valerie could only think of escaping. She quickly gathered shirts, towels, and shoes and herded Whitney and Justin along the stone path that led to the backyard gate, all the while ignoring Gage calling her name and the other parents' outraged faces.

"Mom, why did you push Gage in?" Justin asked loudly.

As from a fog, Valerie mumbled an inane response while fumbling with the latch. Too bad her fingers had suddenly become all thumbs.

Maybe Gage hadn't changed all that much. By presenting her perspective, along with a little of his ex-wife's, Valerie had hoped to help him see the whole picture. But if his responses were any indication, he'd missed the point entirely. She couldn't get out of there fast enough.

Still dripping from the aftermath of Valerie's fiery outburst, Gage growled in frustration. His idea to set that fire ablaze in her eyes again had just started to get interesting, but this went way beyond what he'd imagined. "Valerie!" Not even sure of what he wanted to say, he followed after her. But if he'd expected her to turn around and apologize, then he'd been kidding himself.

Yet he couldn't deny that she was right. Nor could he fathom the struggles Valerie had been through. Gage was just as guilty of treating his ex-wife as Valerie's ex was in the way he'd treated her. He had blamed April for everything that was wrong with their marriage. While most of his finger-pointing had been on target, maybe he should have used softer gloves in their shouting matches. Her claim that he was trying to control her had rankled and he'd slung several cutting remarks of his own her way in retaliation.

As hard as Gage tried, he couldn't let the thought go that his life should have been different. It would have been if he had never left the Church. He took a deep breath in an effort to calm himself. One thing Gage did know was that the once-extinguished embers in Valerie's eyes had smoldered back to life in her defiant glare.

He now knew what he wanted, which was the same thing he'd wanted all those years ago. He wanted her to look at him and really see the person he was inside. His pride had gotten in the way of him being the person he should have been before. But Gage wasn't the same jerk she'd known back then. Now, more than ever, he wanted her to know that he was an honorable man, one worth knowing and possibly even loving.

After several attempts, Valerie was finally able to unlatch the gate. She increased her speed when she heard Gage call her a second time.

"Valerie!" He was closer now. Her heart started pounding, but worse, tears threatened to fall. Humiliation over losing her control after bearing the brunt of his censure drove Valerie to quickly herd her children into the car. She thought she'd gained a narrow escape just when Gage and Zach caught up to her.

She sighed, knowing that she couldn't avoid him any longer. With reluctance, she told her kids to wait for her by the car. Gage bid Zach to follow them.

"Valerie." The urgency in Gage's voice hadn't diminished though the volume had. He came around and tugged on her arm entreatingly, pulling her into an embrace. His cold, wet shirt against her skin was a shock to her face. It had been such a long time since she'd been wrapped in strong arms against a solid chest. His heart was racing at the speed of hers. Though the sensation was discomfiting at first, it brought a keen awareness of the man she'd thought she'd known.

Valerie had never considered Gage a romantic interest. He was always the pest that kept disturbing her life. But Valerie was seeing a different side to him lately and she wasn't sure what to think about it.

Keeping his arms loosely around her, Gage backed up. "I'm sorry," he said softly. "I didn't mean to hurt your feelings. You've said yourself that you're looking forward to the day when Justin will be made perfect. But you've got a really great kid right now. Sure, he has some flaws, but we all do. The more you work with him to help him achieve success in life, the better he'll feel about himself and the more he'll achieve. Don't let fear of what others think hold him back."

She huffed in exasperation. "I don't. Everywhere I go, I face a new critic who thinks they know more than I do on how to handle my son. Then I lived with my husband's rejection over *our flawed son*. I go to church each week not knowing if Justin will throw a fit for the entire ward to see. And what should be a simple trip to the grocery store is nowhere close to one if I don't give him plenty of advance notice. Taking my kids to a Diamondbacks game is a *really big deal*. The fact that I can't predict what will happen scares the heck out of me."

The tears had fallen, probably creating wet streaks along her cheeks. "I know," Gage said gently. "I'll take a personal day and Zach and I will go with you. I'm sure I could procure some extra tickets."

Valerie's jaw dropped. "No, Gage. You don't need to do that for us. Really."

"I want to take you." His hands lowered to her shoulders while his voice softened. "What do you say? I'll be with you if anything goes wrong."

The offer was tempting, but Valerie wanted to make sure that all her bases were covered, so to speak. "And we could leave in the middle of the game if we needed to?"

Gage's eyes flickered with uncertainty. "Let's just try it and see how it goes, all right?"

Looking away, Valerie spied the telltale ink markings of a

tattoo peeking out from under the short sleeve of Gage's shirt. Intrigued, she lifted his sleeve to reveal the image of the Arizona State University mascot, Sparky the Sun Devil.

"Uh," Gage said, crossing his arm over to tug his sleeve down. "I see you found the evidence of my stupidity."

There was a story behind that, Valerie felt certain. However, she didn't have time to delve into the matter. The temperature outside had already reached the century mark.

"Will you tell me about it if we go to the D-Backs' game with you?" she asked boldly.

His face registered shock before his mouth split into a grin. "I told you that you drive a hard bargain. You've got yourself a deal."

She turned to leave when he spoke her name again, even more softly than before. "Valerie." She was beginning to like hearing him say it.

"Yes?"

His eyes, which had turned warm with compassion, held a hint of sorrow. "I'm sorry for teasing you all those years ago. It was wrong of me and I need to ask your forgiveness."

Feeling brave, she responded, "Why did you do it?"

His eyes dipped down briefly before coming back up to meet hers. "Partly because I was an annoying teenager, always seeking attention from the other guys, and partly because I heard that you liked Pierce." He paused. "I might have wished it was me."

Nothing could have prepared her for his confession. "Really?"

He shrugged as if it didn't matter. "Yeah."

"I hated you back then, Gage. I wanted to fit in with the other girls in my class. But now I realize that the Lord was preparing me for my future trials. I've had to learn to stand up for myself. Please don't feel badly about it anymore."

"If anything, you've managed to make me feel worse."

Lightly placing her hand on his arm, she said with a teasing grin, "Your conscience is starting to bug you. That's probably a good thing."

"Yeah, probably."

"So, are we good now?"

"Nope."

His lip twisted into a wry grin, and before Valerie could decipher his meaning, Gage took hold of her waist and bent down to kiss her.

66 I s Gage your boyfriend, Mommy?"

Valerie turned onto Greenfield Road, watching traffic carefully through her rearview mirror. Already feeling shaken after her confrontation with Gage, his kiss had rendered her senseless. The fact that Gage actually appeared to be as shocked as she'd been was little consolation.

Taking a calming breath, she deliberately raised her voice an octave. "Boyfriend? Are you kidding me? Boys are gross."

Valerie hoped her falsetto voice would bring a smile to Whitney's face. Instead, her puckered brow denoted the fact that her silly attempt had failed.

In a normal tone, she said, "You already asked me about Gage, remember? And I told you that he's just a friend."

"But he kissed you."

Valerie's heart skipped a beat. Yes, he had. Valerie couldn't very well shrug it off, saying that it was just a kiss, either, or she'd be sending the wrong message to her daughter about her standards of dating.

"Gage and I were just talking, honey. I'm taking care of Zach while Gage is at work. He appreciates my help. Remember, we've known each other for a very long time."

"No, Mom. I think he likes you. You know, like how a boy likes a girl? Like Daddy liked you?"

Whitney's anxiety seemed to intensify tenfold the deeper they dug into this conversation. She couldn't possibly remember her parents showing affection for each other but was probably wishing for what once had been. Nick's adoration of Valerie had drastically changed when Justin came along. But despite Nick Hall's flaws, he loved his daughter. The feeling was mutual. Despite Justin never visiting Nick in his own home, Whitney alternated weekends between her parents.

After Valerie had pulled into her grandparents' driveway and turned off the car, she asked Whitney, "If that is true, then how do you feel about it?" She might as well get her daughter's opinion before any further developments occurred.

"I don't know. I like Gage. But I like Daddy too."

Valerie got out of the car and placed her hands on Whitney's shoulders. "Well, sweetie, that's one thing you don't need to worry about right now because I am not interested in going on a date with Gage. He stopped going to church a long time ago and if I ever get married again, I would want that person to have a strong testimony of the gospel." Not that there was much chance for her to remarry as long as she was taking care of Justin. But she was fine with that.

Yet she did get a little lonely sometimes. Valerie missed being able to share the events of her day with someone. And if she was honest with herself, she'd admit that Gage's kiss had been surprisingly pleasant. Heat suffused her face. Okay, fine. Earth-shattering was more like it.

She wouldn't mind having someone with which to share the responsibilities of taking care of her children. Maybe when they were older, she might think about dating again. It was too soon to be thinking along those lines, wasn't it? If Whitney had misgivings about her dating another man, then Justin's reaction would definitely be a deterrent.

Oh, good grief! Who was she kidding? Gage's easy-going smile and warm brown eyes were etched in her memory, as was his kiss. She couldn't believe he'd done that! Her anger simmered. She didn't date all that much nor was she a casual kisser. If he thought that he could get away with that foolishness, then their babysitting agreement was over!

But it had been a really nice kiss.

Valerie growled. It was so irritating when her head and her heart said two different things.

"So why are we going to a baseball game with Gage?" Whitney asked.

While arguing with herself, Valerie had almost forgotten that Whitney was still standing beside her. "He wants to take us so that we can help Justin adjust to being around more people."

"Okay. Just checking." With that enigmatic response, she turned toward the house, leaving Valerie staring after her in bewilderment.

"The Diamondbacks beat the Rockies yesterday three to one. But today's pitchers are more evenly matched."

"It will be exciting to see what happens," Valerie replied as they rode in Gage's Camaro to Chase Field. Seeing Gage over the past few days when he dropped Zach off and picked him up had been difficult for her. Neither of them had mentioned the kiss. It was almost like it had never happened.

Now, as she sat next to Gage in his Camaro on their way to the Diamondbacks game, she was feeling decidedly nervous. She'd told Whitney that this wasn't a date. She'd be lying, though, if she didn't admit to herself that she wished it was.

She glanced back at the kids, who were squished in the back but looking thrilled to be attending a Diamondbacks game. "I've always loved being out there, smelling the popcorn and hearing the bat when it connects with the ball."

Gage looked at her speculatively. "So you have been to a few of their games, after all."

It was more of a question than a statement. "Nick and I went every so often for the first few years we were together." *Before Justin came along*. But she wasn't about to say it aloud with her son sitting in the backseat.

Gage must have caught her backward glance at Justin because his jaw tightened. Evidently, he wanted to say more but restrained himself. Valerie appreciated his sensitivity to her children's feelings.

He had arranged for them to take a pre-game tour of Chase Field. When the tour was over, they were among the first groups of fans in line to collect autographs from the players. Valerie watched with interest as Gage casually walked up to Brody Renford. "Gage?" the left fielder said, flipping his shades up to double check.

Gage held out his hand to him. "Hey, Renford. How's it going?"

"Hey, man. Whatcha doin' on that side of the fence?"

"I took a day off to bring my son and our friends to the game." Gage gestured toward them. Nate Dorman, a pitcher who wasn't on the rotation due to an injury, joined them. Valerie took in the appraisal of the three men before Gage turned back to the players. They lowered their voices so that Valerie could no longer hear what they were saying. At one point, Renford lifted his eyes to assess her and then turned back toward Gage. A few seconds later, Gage shifted his stance awkwardly, flexing his fingers down at his side. An all-too-familiar sinking feeling settled in the pit of her stomach. She knew they were talking about her.

Finally, it was their turn to get autographs. As Gage performed the introductions, she shook each player's hand. Her smile, which had only been a polite gesture before, became genuine when each of them gave the kids a high five, greeting them with a kind word. The five of them then went in search of their seats.

Gage pulled his phone out of his pocket and was scrolling through it. The memory of her shoving Gage into the water hit her again. She cleared her throat. "So . . . I'm assuming you had to get a new phone because of my thoughtless actions from the other day?"

Gage's face was unreadable. "Afraid so, along with a new key fob for my Camaro. I was stuck at Kiera's house for a few hours afterward."

Heat stole into her cheeks as mortification set in. "Oh, Gage. I'm so sorry. Maybe you should dock the cost from my pay?"

Gage paused in consideration. "Hmm. That's an idea. But then again, the price to pay for that kiss was worth it, wouldn't you agree?"

Was it possible to feel any more humiliated than at this moment? She decided to change the subject. "What did you say about me to the players?"

"That is classified information, Ms. Hall."

"Mm-hmm," she replied, unconvinced. "I think I have a right to know, since you were talking about me. Weren't you?" she pressed uncertainly.

After a moment of studying her intently, Gage sighed. "Brody Renford liked your girl-next-door looks a little too much for my peace of mind. He has a tendency to overlook the total package, as most ballplayers do."

Instinctively, she knew that Gage was giving her the G-rated version. She'd wondered why Gage had been flexing his fingers. He'd probably been itching to give the guy a piece of his mind. "So you told him that we're just friends?"

"Nope. I let him think we are an item."

She scoffed. "So now you're turning into one of my overprotective brothers?"

His eyes darkened as they bore into hers. "What do you think?"

What did she think? She thought the best-looking guy she'd hung out with in a long time was looking at her in a way that was anything but brotherly. And at that moment, what she was feeling for him was scaring her more than the idea of coming to the game had. Her mouth felt like she'd swallowed a bunch of cotton candy. "I think . . . that they're announcing the starting lineups so we should really get our minds on the game."

His slow grin let her know that he wasn't fooled by her blasé answer. "Nice save, Ms. Hall. You're very good at evading tough questions. But this conversation isn't over yet." With that enigmatic response, he turned his attention to the players on the field. Blowing out a relieved breath, she settled back to do the same.

Chase Field was one of the best fields in the National League, as far as Valerie was concerned. She and Nick had once attended a party put on by his father's company at the pool that was located just beyond right-center field. Chase Field also boasted a retractable roof, which was closed today with respect to the scorching heat. The announcers were loud, but Justin had never seemed to be bothered by loud noises as much as some autistic children were.

Gage was in his element, pointing out the awesome things for the kids to look at and thumbing through their programs to find the players' stats. He obviously loved this place. His face was alight with pleasure at seeing the kids' wonder as he answered all of their questions with ease and patience.

Valerie wasn't sure if she had more fun watching him or the children. Although they had really good seats along the third base line, Whitney's gaze was continually drawn upward to the huge screen that showed the replays. Justin's eyes darted up and down between it and the action on the field. Valerie wasn't even sure how much of it he understood.

Zach, however, was enraptured with every little detail, talking to his dad at a speed that could have competed for the Indy 500. Valerie was amazed at the four-year-old's scope of knowledge. He and his dad shared a bond that made her feel both happy for them and a little envious for Justin's sake.

"Look, Justin!" Zach yelled as Brody Renford smashed a ball down the first base line, the fielder's glove missing it by only a few inches.

The fans cheered while he rounded first base and headed toward second. Justin belatedly followed the direction of Zach's finger pointing to the ball. When Zach motioned for him to watch Brody's safe slide at second base for a double, Justin turned a few seconds too late, essentially missing the play altogether. Valerie's heart constricted from wondering whether he noticed or what he internalized in different situations.

"Who's hungry? How about popcorn for everybody?" Gage asked as a vendor made his way past them, calling out his wares.

"Justin? Zach? Whitney?" They all answered with a boisterous yes. "Valerie?" His smile, which had always been engaging, seemed especially flirtatious at that moment.

Valerie's heart was on a roller coaster. Really, did he have to break out that killer smile right now when she was feeling so vulnerable? "None for me, thanks." Her voice sounded flat even to her own ears.

Gage's eyes narrowed slightly. He paid for the popcorn and then hailed a guy selling lemonade. "Thirsty?" Gage asked warily as he handed her a cold plastic cup.

"Yes, thank you." Hoping to make amends, she accepted it gratefully.

Then, before she knew what happened, Justin yelped and started wailing loudly. Gage and Valerie both turned to him in alarm. Leaning closer to him, she asked in a calm and steady voice, "What's wrong, Justin?"

"That guy hit me!" he cried, turning around and yelling at a man who was moving down the aisle behind them with his beer in hand, oblivious to Justin's outrage.

The man and woman seated directly in back of them looked at Valerie sympathetically. "He was bumped in the back of the head while the guy was moving down the aisle," the woman said.

Valerie smiled and thanked her. After trying a few diversionary tactics with nothing working, she pulled Justin up by the arm. "I'm just going to take him for a walk," she told Gage. "That usually calms him down. Do you mind staying with the other two?"

Gage nodded. "Sure. You have your phone in case you need anything, right?"

"Yes. We'll be fine. It's time for a restroom break, anyway."

Once she hustled Justin out of the stands toward the concessions, the incredible-smelling food made Valerie's stomach growl. She was hungry and the kids probably were too. Not knowing what Gage had planned, she decided that splurging for food would go a long way toward placating some hungry munchkins.

But first she had to help Justin calm down. She pasted a wooden smile on her face for the people who were sending them strange looks, all the while wishing that Justin would stop crying. As soon as they found the restroom, she led him to a corner and looked him straight in the eyes. "Justin!" she said quietly. "Remember what we talked about? We're here to have fun and we can't do that if you are doing this. You're going to have to be a big boy and stop crying."

Her words only made him wail louder. "He's a mean man! I hate him! I'm gonna hit him back!" he screeched.

Valerie sucked in her breath and let it out forcefully. "No, you aren't," she replied firmly. "Listen, Justin. I know it hurt when that guy bumped you on the head, but it was an accident. He didn't mean to do it. Crying about it won't make it feel better."

Unfortunately, Justin's reasoning skills were zilch and Valerie knew it. She could deal with the tantrums in the privacy of their own home when he cried it out in his bedroom. But in public settings such as this, the more Justin lost his control, the more Valerie struggled to hold onto hers. At this point, the only thing she could do was pray. Desperately, she pleaded for Heavenly Father to help Justin calm down. An idea flashed through her mind. "Justin, let's sing. Which song shall we sing? 'Popcorn Popping' or 'I Am a Child of God'?"

Justin chose the latter, so they sang the first verse of "I Am A Child of God," paying no attention to the people who had stopped what they were doing to listen. Instead, Valerie watched as a gradual transformation came over Justin. He loved music, especially Primary songs.

When his tears had subsided, Valerie took him to a sink to wash his face and dry it with a paper towel. A little girl wearing a pink top and denim ruffled shorts was running her hands under the water faucet next to them. The girl's mother looked at them curiously, giving her a compassionate smile. When Justin had sufficiently calmed down, Valerie took him to stand in line to use the facilities.

Emerging from the restroom almost fifteen minutes later, they stood in another long line of people while waiting their turn to buy the expensive hot dogs. Silently, Valerie willed the line of people to move faster, desperately hoping that Justin wouldn't break out in tears again. Waiting was another of his weaknesses.

This time, he surprised her when he held up his hand. "Look, Mommy. I can sign my name. J-U-S-T-I-N. That spells *Justin*."

"You're right. Now can you sign Whitney's?"

Moving inch by agonizing inch, they finger-spelled Zach's name in ASL next, followed by hers and Gage's. Then they signed the names of objects they saw. By the time they finished, the line had moved up considerably. Valerie breathed a sigh of relief.

Justin helped her carry their food back to their seats. "Hot dogs, anyone?" she asked brightly as she held out her bounty. Two small pairs of hands reached out and grabbed one.

Gage looked up from his phone, glancing at Justin. "Everything okay?"

"Yep." Valerie hated the overly bright voice she had to use so much of the time. "We're okay now."

Gage eyed her dubiously before seeming to accept her answer. Ignoring his silence, she grabbed a handful of napkins and passed them out, efficiently helping the kids with their hot dogs. Valerie looked up to offer one to Gage only to find him staring at her. Suddenly feeling self-conscious, she shoved a chunk of hair behind her ear. "What?"

A secretive smile graced his face. "Nothing."

Gage couldn't have taken his gaze from Valerie if someone had forced him. She had a natural charm and grace that couldn't be replicated. Why hadn't he been able to tell the difference between April's beauty, which had only been on the surface, and a woman like Valerie who hadn't been blessed with April's stunning looks but whose inner beauty transcended that of his ex-wife's? Her mothering instincts were right on target. Not only did she seem to have it all together, but she didn't have a deceitful bone in her body. When Gage thought about the way April had laughed and joked with him, making him feel like he was the only one on her radar, his cheeks burned in humiliation. How could he have been so wrong?

But now, seeing Valerie laughing and joking with their kids, the light in her eyes as she reveled in their excitement of the sights and sounds of the game, he knew without a doubt that Valerie was the real deal. April had only been a cheap substitute.

"You know, I was planning on buying some food for us soon," he said, indicating the hot dogs. "Did you know that you can place an order at Chase Field using your smartphone?"

A faint blush settled in her cheeks. "I don't own a smartphone. But that's okay. The diversion of standing in line came in handy."

"I meant to pay for them."

"I work for you, so in essence, you did."

"Not the same thing," he insisted. "The money I pay you for watching Zach should be used on you and your kids, not Zach and me."

A scowl crossed her face. "Drop it, Logan. You already paid for the tickets and the drinks. I can afford to buy lunch."

"Valerie, this was my treat."

When she arched one brow at him, he knew he was in trouble. Then she inclined her head toward the scoreboard. "Maybe we should buy one of those to keep track of who wins each argument? The way I see it, we're here to have fun, right?"

She had a point. But it was fun to see her get riled. However, that saucy glint in her eyes told him that he'd better drop the subject before she became angry.

"I just want to make sure you have what you need for your upcoming moving expenses."

Her mouth dropped open. "You know about that?"

"Yeah," he answered, failing to see what the big deal was. "Your parents told me."

She sat so still that Gage instantly knew he'd said the wrong thing. Fortunately, the couple who were sitting behind them tapped Justin on the shoulder, drawing Valerie's attention away from Gage.

"Hi, there. My name's Joy. What's yours?"

Justin immediately scanned the concrete at his feet. He said quietly, "Justin."

"Well, Justin, it's nice to meet you. This is Chad."

"Hey, Justin," her husband chimed in, "it's a great day for a ball game, isn't it? It's too bad our D-Backs are losing, though. Let's hope they score soon because it's almost the seventh inning."

He nodded even though he was still avoiding eye contact with them.

"Who's your favorite player, Justin?"

Gage doubted that Justin would be able to answer that question. But to his surprise, however, Justin replied, "Brody

Renford and Nate Dorman." Interesting. Had Justin named those players just because they had signed his baseball before the game started?

Chad and Joy chatted with Justin for several more minutes, not seeming to mind that most of his responses were one word or less.

"So what do you think the D-Backs should do to win this game, Justin?" Chad asked.

Amazingly, Zach and Whitney kept quiet, seeming to sense that Justin should be given time to come up with the answer. Gage held his breath, looking at Valerie. Her apprehension over this line of questioning was palpable.

"Hit a home run."

"I think so too. Let's cheer for our D-Backs together, okay?" Joy said enthusiastically, shaking an oversized plastic red and black rattler's rattle back and forth before handing it to him. "Here. Would you like to try it out?"

Justin shook the rattle, repeating the motion with a huge smile on his face. Turning to Valerie, he said, "Look, Mom. I'm cheering for the D-Backs."

Valerie ruffled his hair affectionately. "You sure are, little man. Keep it up."

When Gage caught Valerie's attention again, he lifted his eyebrow as if to say, *See? I told you he'd be fine.* She quickly looked away.

Now that his recent explosion had subsided, Justin was having the time of his life even though the Diamondbacks were trailing the Rockies by a score of seven to six. It didn't even seem to matter to him that they were losing.

Before they knew it, it was time for the seventh inning stretch. Joy and Chad encouraged Justin to sing the classic song, "Take Me Out to the Ball Game" while teaching him the lyrics. Then a familiar song blasted over the sound system and the crowd immediately launched into performing the actions to "YMCA."

"Hey, Justin!" Joy shouted at Justin in an attempt to be heard over the loud music. "Come on up here and do the YMCA song with us. We'll teach it to you."

Justin's arm motions were a bit uncoordinated, but he got the hang of it before too long. Whitney and Zach got into the rhythm of the song and started dancing. Valerie laughed at their antics. She wasn't one to go all crazy like that, dancing with gusto in front of complete strangers, but she enjoyed watching the kids having so much fun. Once again, she caught Gage's eye, but this time, she didn't look away.

Three tired children slumped over each other as they drove east on Loop 202 toward Mesa. Gage was pleased with how well the day had turned out, although there had been some tense moments when he wasn't sure how Valerie or Justin would react, such as the one they endured as they were packing up their stuff to go when the game ended. After shaking hands with Chad and Joy and expressing their appreciation for making the day special for Justin, Joy commented on their beautiful family, further embarrassing Valerie by remarking that Zach looked just like his mother and Justin looked like his dad. Valerie had gasped and quickly looked at Gage before looking away.

Gage and Valerie each grabbed one of the boy's hands and walked toward the exit with Whitney in between. The crowds thinned as they made their way up several blocks to Gage's car. Suddenly, a little girl with ribbons in her ponytails, wearing a pink shirt with ruffled denim shorts, pointed to Justin and said, "Look, Mommy. There's the boy who was crying in the bathroom."

Her mother immediately hushed her, telling her to mind her manners. The woman looked at Gage apologetically. Gage smiled in return to convey the message *no harm done* when in reality, he didn't know if that was true or not. Glancing at Valerie, he noticed two red spots on her cheeks, which could be a result from too much sun, but he seriously doubted it. The retractable roof had been closed during the game and she was studiously ignoring the mother and her daughter.

A sick feeling settled in the pit of his stomach. What had happened in the restroom? He'd smirked at Valerie to let her know that Justin was fine, just as he'd said he would be, and she hadn't refuted him. Had she deliberately downplayed a more serious situation?

Now as they drove toward Valerie's home, Gage made a snap decision. "Hey," he said, looking at the kids from the mirror, "Zach and I have some ice cream in our freezer. How do you feel about going to our place for sundaes? Maybe we can find a movie to watch."

Valerie's sharp gaze seared him.

Or not. He almost capitulated, but then a strange thing happened. The same instinct in his gut that told him to take Zach the weekend April died was telling him to not let this go. He knew he needed to do this.

"The kids are tired, Gage, and we have church tomorrow. I'd really rather have you take us home so that we can shower and get ready for bed."

Pouring all the urgency he could into his gaze, he reached for her hand and squeezed it. "We need to talk." When she hesitated, he added persuasively, "A promise is a promise. I never told you about the tattoo."

That did the trick as he'd hoped it would. "All right."

He made a quick detour off the freeway. Within minutes, he pulled into the garage of his sprawling white home with red brick trim and rolling green grass. Gage loved the landscaping, which was what had first caught his attention when he'd purchased the house a year and a half ago. Two orange trees and a lemon tree supplied more than enough Vitamin C for him and his neighbors.

He hadn't admitted it to Valerie when she and the kids came inside with dirt under their fingernails from tending her garden, but his hobbies weren't too different than hers. Earlier this spring, at the advice of a fellow gardener, he'd planted a couple of Baja fairy duster shrubs and some bird of paradise plants along the outer edges of the property, hoping they would survive the summer heat. So far, they looked promising.

Gage led them into the house through the garage, turning lights on as he went. They came directly into the kitchen, which boasted granite countertops and a wraparound bar. After bidding them to have a seat on the stools, he pulled some vanilla ice cream from the freezer to thaw. He noticed Valerie staring at his coffee-maker. His nerves became taut as he waited for her censure.

Surprisingly, it never came. Instead, she asked, "What can I do to help?"

Coming closer to tuck an errant strand of hair from her face, he smiled warmly. "Just sit back and relax. It's your turn to be waited on."

To his pleasure, she blushed. "Thanks," she said softly.

Gage was about to say something else when, out of the corner of his eye, he noticed Whitney scowling at him like a mountain lion eyeing its prey.

Fortunately, Zach broke the mood by finding his second wind. "Hey, guys! Want to see my bedroom?" Gage cringed, wishing that he could find time to paint the dinosaurs he and Zach had talked about. He promised himself he would get around to it on the team's next road trip. The kids raced through the dining area and adjoining family room before turning a corner that led to the stairs, leaving him and Valerie staring at each other.

Clearing her throat, she asked, "Kind of a big house for just two people, don't you think?"

Shrugging off his discomfort, he replied, "Yeah, but a realtor friend of mine told me about this place after it was foreclosed on and encouraged me to take a look. I'm not even sure why, but it called to me, you know? I can't explain it, but somehow it seemed familiar."

"I felt the same when I met an elderly sister in my ward. She's wonderful." As the silence stretched uncomfortably between them, Valerie ventured, "So you said we needed to talk?"

"Yeah. Can I offer you a drink?" He pulled two glasses from a cupboard and walked over to the refrigerator to fill them with ice from the ice dispenser.

"Ice water will be fine."

He motioned her into the family room where they sat diagonally across from one another on a comfortable couch. Gage took another swallow of his water to moisten his dry mouth before changing the subject. "Thanks for coming to the ball game with us today. I love watching the D-Backs play, but it was even better being there with all of you."

Her answering smile was fleeting. "I'm glad."

He wondered if she was still thinking about Joy's comment regarding their beautiful family. It kept replaying through his head. Deep down, Gage admitted to himself that he'd never completely forgotten that dream.

"Valerie, I want to know more about Justin's autism. You mentioned once that complete strangers have publicly accused you of mishandling your son. What happened?"

Her jaw tightened as she averted her gaze. He realized that he was entering dangerous territory. But he wanted to understand.

When she finally spoke, her voice sounded strained. "About a year ago, I took the kids to the grocery store for a few items I needed to make a dinner for a family in our ward. Justin saw a toy that was strategically displayed in the aisle and demanded that I buy it for him. When I told him no, he screamed so loudly that everyone around me began staring at me like I'd been beating my child. I was trying to think of what to do when a woman came up to me and asked me to let her try to calm Justin down. At first, I refused her."

"Why?"

"I don't normally allow random people to interact extensively with my children the way Chad and Joy did today. I prefer to handle Justin's tantrums myself. I told the woman that we'd be fine. But she persisted, saying that she'd been trained to deal with those kinds of situations. Finally, despite my misgivings, I stepped back to let her try."

"So then what happened?" His own voice now sounded strained.

"She couldn't calm him down. She tried to pick him up and he twisted around like a snake." She paused. "She almost dropped him. That's when she handed Justin to me and ran out of there." Valerie looked down. "It was so humiliating."

Gage's mouth dropped. "So what was already a stressful situation for you was made even more so by her. Did something like that happen today when you took him out at the end of the fourth inning?"

She told him about the tantrum in the restroom. "Even when he stops crying, that doesn't necessarily mean the end of the tantrum. Usually that's only round one. Each subsequent round is a little shorter. Gage, I could go on all night, telling you about Justin. The fact of the matter is that I've learned to leave other people out of my situation. It's just easier that way."

"But what about people like Chad and Joy who want to help and who seem to know how to work with autistic children?"

"What they did was commendable. Most people have good intentions, but sometimes it make things even harder for him."

"So, basically, you're saying that you would prefer for others to mind their own business."

"I just wish that the people who want to help me would be more sensitive to my needs."

"How does your ex fit into this picture?"

"He doesn't," she said flatly, her lips forming a hard, straight line. "Justin saw a neurologist while Nick and I were still married. Dr. Callahan prescribed an EKG as well as genetic testing, to determine the likelihood of autism and seizure activity. The results were normal, but Nick insisted that Justin's 'defect' came from me. He tried to convince me that I must have done something wrong during my pregnancy to jeopardize Justin's health."

"What did he accuse you of?" Gage said vehemently. "Pouring a gallon of gasoline down your throat to fry Justin's brain?"

"No. Nick was just venting about the fact that no one really knows what causes autism. There are so many conflicting theories out there ranging from immunizations to hybridized foods. It wasn't until after Nick and I divorced that Justin saw a developmental pediatrician who conducted the Childhood Autism Rating Scale or CARS test on him. At that time, Justin received his diagnosis."

Gage gritted his teeth. "So what convinced you that it wasn't your fault?"

"I asked my dad to give me a priesthood blessing in which I was given the knowledge that Heavenly Father gave Justin to us to help others learn tolerance and love."

"How ironic that your ex-husband couldn't figure that one out."

"Yes." Valerie nodded sadly. "Nick refuses to have anything to do with Justin."

"That's for the best."

Valerie nodded and folded her arms across her middle as if talking about her ex-husband brought a physical ailment to her body. "Gage, your job offer was a life saver for me. These tests aren't cheap. Neither are the specialists Justin sees."

"How do you do it, Valerie? You're always so calm." Then, remembering her uncharacteristic fit while shoving him into the water, he clarified, "Well, almost always."

"Please don't put me on a pedestal, Gage. I've taken my turn being very angry at God. At times, I watch other perfect mothers in my ward and wonder why they weren't given Justin instead. They could have cared for an autistic child better than I."

With a heavy heart, Gage stared at her, instinctively realizing how difficult it was for her to reveal this side of herself. He knew what it felt like when reality left a glaring hole in a person's idealistic dream.

Valerie took a deep breath while pulling her hand through her hair. "I also worry about Whitney with her visits with Nick every other weekend. When she comes home, I have to go through the process of undoing all the damage he's done in two short days."

"Damage?"

"She talks back to me. She thinks she doesn't have to do

anything I ask her to do. Nick makes sure our daughter knows that I am the one who broke up her family."

Gage could only shake his head in disgust. He'd thought his marriage had been miserable. "This guy took you to the temple and promised to love you and take care of you. How did you keep believing in all that after what he did?"

"I've gone through counseling. I was definitely a mess when my marriage fell apart, but my family was there to pick me up. My bishop was incredibly supportive. I spent a lot of time being angry, but I still know that Heavenly Father really does care about me. He always seems to place certain people in my path when I need them."

Like the way He'd placed Valerie in his path when Gage needed her?

Gage wondered how different their lives would have been had he been more of a friend straight from the beginning. She might have felt differently about him during their teenage years if he hadn't riled her so much. Would she have given him a second thought? If he had then served his mission, might she have possibly waited for him? And if so, would Justin have eventually become their son? Gage hated to wonder if he might have placed the same ridiculous blame on Valerie that her ex-husband had.

G age dished out vanilla ice cream. Zach and Whitney proceeded to see who could come up with the craziest combinations on their toppings, including strawberry syrup and sprinkles topped with gummy worms. *Gross!* Valerie thought.

Justin, of course, had been thrilled with the possibilities. When Valerie mentioned to Gage that his idea had been a winner for Justin, Gage quirked a brow. "How so?"

"I have found that Justin responds better to having choices, as long as there aren't too many to choose from at one time." He'd been a great reminder through the years that her parenting style needed to more closely match that of Heavenly Father's.

"Well, then," Gage said with a smile, holding out a dish filled with ice cream, "here's to brilliant solutions to life's challenges."

They each took a bite of their ice cream before Valerie ventured the question she'd been wanting to ask for so long. "So are you going to tell me about that tattoo or not?" She smiled to soften her words.

"You really want to hear the story?"

"Yep. Spill it, Logan. It's only fair since I spilled my guts to you."

When he hesitated, she couldn't resist teasing him by lifting his sleeve to take another peek at the cute but out-of-place Sun Devil.

"Is it symbolic of your devilish good looks or devil-may-care personality?"

He laughed sardonically. "You really don't have a very high opinion of me, do you?" She chuckled in return. This sense of camaraderie she was experiencing with Gage was something new and exciting, like nothing she'd ever felt before her. Somehow she felt freer and more alive than she had since she could remember.

The kids were just finishing their ice cream sundaes. Zach asked if they could play longer. Ruffling his hair, Valerie told them that they could play for five more minutes. Zach and the other two sprinted off.

Valerie looked up and found Gage staring at her with a glint in his eyes.

Raising her chin defiantly, she said, "Okay. I bought you five minutes. Be quick about it."

"Yes, ma'am. Actually, this story is so lame, I'll only need two." He took a deep breath. "My frat brothers at ASU were big-time jokesters and party-goers."

A wave of apprehension swept over Valerie. That was never a good combination.

"They made sure I was good and drunk and then dared me to go and get the tattoo of our mascot. I was too wasted to remember any of this at the time."

"Are you telling me that they took you to get a tattoo without your consent?"

"At least I didn't have to pay for it," he said self-deprecatingly.

She gasped, incensed over his humiliation. "Not with money, but with your dignity!"

"I guess I have been paying for it ever since," he replied soberly. "Especially when I went to work for the U of A and I met April. She saw the tattoo and taunted me about being a Sun Devil at heart. She became as much a challenge to me as I did to her. I guess in that way, we deserved each other. I may not have been the best husband to April, but at least I was faithful to her. She had no qualms about seeing other men while she was still married to me, though. She used me to keep the peace between herself and her parents."

Valerie's heart constricted. April had played Gage for the fool he'd been. "When I was going through counseling, the best piece of advice I received is to learn from the mistakes of our past and move on. Sure, you've made some, but you're trying to be a good father to Zach. And you've always provided for him. That's more than you can say about a lot of dads."

Gage's brow furrowed. "I skipped town when April told me about the baby. I hired on as a sales consultant for the Diamond-backs—anything to get away from that situation. Now I regret that I didn't see Zach's first steps or hear his first words. You were right when you accused me of not sharing any of the responsibilities of his early years."

Valerie laid her hand on his arm, willing him to stop being so hard on himself. "He's adjusting well. Given time, this will only be a small blip in his memory."

Gage's eyes widened. "He may never remember his mother."

"Keep a picture of her around. When he asks about her, let him know that she loved him the best way she knew how."

The appreciative smile he sent her way melted her heart. A special warmth spread throughout her body from knowing they had worked through some difficult things and found some common ground.

Gage sat on the steps of his patio much later that night, staring up at the bluish-black sky, mentally replaying the conversation he had earlier with Valerie. He needed to get some sleep soon because he'd be dropping Zach off at her house in the morning for church.

He couldn't believe it—his kid going to church. Gage grinned, recalling how easily Valerie had won that round. But like she'd said, they didn't really need to keep score. Parenting wasn't about who was right or wrong. It was about wanting what was best for the child.

So is marriage. Where had that thought come from? Maybe he was more tired than he thought. *Marriage is about unconditionally loving and wanting what's best for the other person.* He'd been a selfish jerk when he married April. Now he wished that he could at least tell her how sorry he was.

"Daddy?"

Zach's voice carrying from the kitchen broke through his thoughts. Gage quickly stood and made his way back inside to find Zach coming toward him where he'd left the back door open. "Hey, little man." Now he was starting to sound like Valerie. "You should be tired after the fun day we had. What's up?"

Picking Zach up, he carried his little boy to the couch where he'd talked to Valerie earlier that evening. "I had lots of fun with Justin and Whitney today," he said happily.

"I did too."

"And I like their mom a lot."

Gage's chest tingled as he smiled. He felt the same.

Then Zach's smile dimmed. "But . . . I miss Mommy." His voice became almost indistinctive with the sound of the crickets chirping outside.

"I know you do, Zach. You'll probably always miss her." If not April as a person, then the entity she represented. "Missing someone who has died is a hurt that never really goes away. But Heavenly Father makes up for it by sending other people in our lives to ease some of the pain." He didn't know if what he was saying made sense to Zach or not, but suddenly and with absolute clarity, he knew it was true.

"But will I see Mommy again?" Zach asked with all the urgency of a four-year-old.

"Well," he hesitated, searching for the right words. "If everything I learned at church when I was young is true, then yes, you will."

"You mean like the songs I'm learning in Primary? You learned them when you were a kid too?"

Gage had to smile at his son's awe. This was, without a doubt, the best form of hero worship he'd experienced in a very long time. "Yeah. Heavenly Father knows you and loves you, Zach. I'm sure He wants you to be happy and will do everything He can to help you if you do your part."

For the first time since he'd received his mission call, Gage felt like he could be given the same blessing, too, if he'd reach out for it. It was time to lay aside the selfishness and pettiness of the past and move forward. After sending Zach to bed with a hug, he walked over to a bookcase where a long-abandoned Book of Mormon lay. His mother had brought it over last year, claiming that she'd found his old set of scriptures among some books she'd stored away. Gage had shelved the volume with no real intention of ever looking at it again. Somehow it seemed disrespectful to throw it away.

Now he dusted off the cover and brought it to the couch, flipping it open to read the account of Alma the Younger once again. He continued reading into the night until he came to Alma 44 when the Nephites were fighting the Lamanites. Zerahemnah, the ferocious leader of the Lamanite army, tried to destroy the Nephite army, but the Nephites gained the advantage and warned him to back off. Zerahemnah failed to comply, which resulted in his gruesome scalping.

Gage pondered Zerahemnah's fate. Instead of listening to the Nephites' warning, he decided to proceed with his angry pursuit. At what point had it become too late for him to turn back? Where was the line drawn? Feeling certain that pride and anger motivated Zerahemnah's actions, Gage couldn't help but see the parallel in his own life. Letting go of those two emotions could change everything.

Valerie loved her little Primary class. There was Becca, who was sweet but shy, and Dylan, who was a little mischievous but impressed her with his brilliant answers. Braden told taller tales than anyone she'd ever heard and Isabelle didn't like to be the last in line for anything. Lindsey could try the patience of a saint with her dramatics but could also melt the coldest heart with her endearing smile. And then there was Zach who hadn't even known what Primary was, had never heard the words *prophets, scriptures,* or *baptism,* and who didn't know any of the songs until a few weeks ago.

Time was on her side, however. He had a lot of catching up to do, but he was quick like Dylan. When Valerie and the kids came home from church, she sat them down at the kitchen table to feed them lunch, asking Whitney and Justin to teach a few new songs to Zach. By the time they'd finished eating their grilled cheese sandwiches and carrot sticks, Zach had learned the words to "I'm Trying to Be Like Jesus" and "Book of Mormon Stories." Valerie's heart swelled with pride much like it had when Justin said his first words or Whitney learned to tie her shoes.

Wait a minute, she cautioned herself. *Zach is not your child. He is only in your care temporarily.* She needed to remind herself that Gage would have the final say on whether or not Zach would continue going to church once he no longer needed childcare. But she was determined to help him learn all she could.

When the Diamondbacks left for a ten-game road trip on Wednesday, Gage's work schedule changed, leaving Valerie to watch Zach from 8:00 a.m. till 6:00 p.m. when he arrived to pick him up. Valerie took all three children to Kiera's house for swim lessons on Thursday morning, then took them to the public swimming pool on Friday afternoon for more practice.

On Sunday, she drove to Gage's house to pick Zach up for church. Gage answered the door, looking like a man of leisure in his long shorts and rumpled T-shirt with his hair askew. "Growing your hair out?" She grinned at the dark strands that covered the tips of his ears.

"I haven't had time to get a haircut." He stepped aside to allow her to enter. "Zach's almost ready. I was just helping him with his shoes."

Just then, Zach came around the corner looking quite charming in his white shirt, black dress pants, and diagonally striped tie with his blond hair gelled to perfection. Gage had probably spent more time sprucing him up than Valerie had spent on her own appearance. Whitney and Justin had a tendency to monopolize her prep time on most Sunday mornings. Today, though, Whitney was with her father so Valerie had at least been able to put on a little makeup and twist her hair into a French knot.

"Hi, Zach," she said cheerfully, offering him her hand to grab ahold of. "Ready to go to church?"

"Yeah. Let's go."

"Okay." She took one step, lifting her head to say good-bye to Gage, when she caught the momentary look of longing on his face. Startled, she almost missed a step. "Gage, would you like to come with us?"

The second the words were out, she regretted them. His jaw tightened for a split second before he carefully schooled his features into an air of nonchalance. "No thanks. I've got some chores to catch up on here." Fingering his longish hair thoughtfully, he added, "Maybe I'll get that haircut now."

Swallowing her disappointment, she placed what she hoped was a nonthreatening smile on her face. "No problem. Enjoy your day off. I'll bring Zach home as soon as church ends."

The familiar strains of prelude music welcomed them as they entered the chapel and Valerie quickly found a seat near the back. When Valerie had first divorced Nick, she'd felt conspicuous coming to church as a single parent. She'd hated the feeling that everyone was staring at her. Over time, she'd learned that she wasn't the only single parent there and that she'd been foolish to let her insecurities impede her spiritual progress.

She'd cleared that hurdle only to face a new one every week while trying to keep her kids quiet enough to hear the speakers. Attending sacrament meeting could be a high-calorie-burning workout with little ones at times. Valerie was bending over to retie Justin's shoe when Zach accidentally spilled all the crayons from the box. As soon they finished picking them up, Zach announced rather loudly that he needed to use the restroom. Valerie sighed in chagrin. They hadn't even taken the sacrament yet.

Ten minutes later, with her attention still on Zach, who was choosing which crayon he wanted to use next—Valerie had decided to hold them in her hand so he wouldn't spill them again—her heart beat double time as Justin was suddenly lifted into the air by a pair of strong arms. Her gaze flew up in astonishment as Gage lowered his body next to hers, setting Justin on his lap. Zach looked up, smiling when he saw his dad.

What in heaven's name am I doing here? Gage wondered as he felt every eye turn his way while Justin looked up at him in glee. "Gage!" he said loudly, eliciting a chuckle from a few adults behind them along with a glare or two from people in front.

"Hey, Justin," he said lightly, pleased that Valerie's son had finally called him by name. He also acknowledged his own son before he glanced nervously in all directions, half-expecting someone to tell him he didn't belong here.

And he didn't. The only times Gage had been inside an LDS chapel in the past four years was for his niece's and nephews' baby blessings. Even while feeling a little out of place when every other male member of his family stood to join the circle, he'd managed to squelch his anxiety. His attendance had only been the fulfillment of a family obligation.

But this time was different. He'd chosen to come because of one beautiful female who'd captured his attention in his youth. If the stark look of sadness that had come over Valerie's face when he declined her invitation to church was designed to make him feel guilty, it had worked. He never wanted to see that look cross her face again. She'd already been rejected by her ex-husband. Gage wasn't about to be the cause of any more pain in Valerie's life.

Maybe that wasn't the best reason for attending sacrament meeting, but here he was. With his sweating palms, Gage turned to Valerie with a full-fledged smile. "Mind if I sit here?"

Valerie said nothing but only stared. Maybe coming to church hadn't been such a good idea after all.

But when her face broke out into a wide grin, all his doubts were swept away. Any discomfort he had to suffer through would be worth it to be the recipient of that beautiful smile. It wouldn't be the first time he'd encountered trouble in the form of a gorgeous blonde.

But this time, there was a lot more at stake. And if he wanted to win the prize, he'd have to spend some serious time on his knees.

"So you decided the haircut could wait?" Valerie asked as they exited the chapel with the boys. She was still recovering from the shock of seeing him there along with the strain of holding her head high amid the entire ward's stares.

Gage leaned forward, smiling nervously while managing to still look adorably handsome. "Yeah. Let's just say that my conscience has been giving me a hard time lately. Sorry I couldn't find a white shirt. Is that why everyone is staring at me?" His flirtatious wink gave him away.

She shook her head, not minding his teasing so much anymore. "No, it's because they're wondering if you're my newest love interest."

"Newest?" He caught onto that word. "As in more than one?"

Valerie groaned. "As in no one," she retorted. "Oh, look. Here comes the bishop. Hello, Bishop Gregory."

Valerie's bishop shook her hand, glancing quizzically at Gage. "Good morning, Sister Hall. I see you've brought a visitor today."

"Um, yes. This is my friend, Gage Logan. He's Zach's father," she said, identifying him with a sideways nod, "the boy I've been bringing to church for the past month."

"Ah, yes. Hello. I'm Bishop Gregory," he told Gage, extending his arm. "It's nice to meet you."

Gage returned the greeting and then turned to Valerie. "I'd better be going."

She wished he would stay. She kept her smile in place even as a feeling of disappointment slid over her once again. "Okay. Thanks for coming. The boys were happy to see you."

Gage arched his brows at her as if to ask, *Just the boys?*

Okay, so she'd been happy too. Thrilled, actually. Valerie backed away from his scrutiny, claiming truthfully that she was going to be late for Primary. Gage released his grip on Justin's hand to allow her to escort both boys down the hall.

"I'll see you at home," he called out to her.

Her cheeks burned as she turned an icy glare on him. Gage must not have realized how domestic he sounded, and right in front of the bishop too! "All right," she hissed, albeit sweetly. "We'll bring Zach to *your* home as soon as we're finished."

She groaned in frustration. She hadn't missed Bishop Gregory's speculative gaze on her as she turned away.

Fire and ice. When they came from a woman, they were one and the same. How could something that had sounded so right to Gage's ears come out sounding so wrong to Valerie's? Her quick intake of breath and glacial glare had been the tip of the iceberg, letting him know that his careless comment rattled her. Before she could escape, Gage caught her arm and leaned over to whisper in her ear. "So am I?"

"Are you what?" she whispered back impatiently.

"Your newest love interest."

Yep, the glacial glare she'd given him had, in fact, only been a tiny icicle compared with the frigid storm he now saw brewing in her blue depths. "In your dreams, Logan!" she ground out before turning away.

Gage grinned. The mind-numbing kiss he'd stolen from her not too long ago had plagued him ever since, especially since he could swear she'd kissed him back. They had chemistry, all right. If only Valerie was brave enough to acknowledge it, life would be good.

Slowly, he became aware of Valerie's bishop still standing there, watching him very carefully. Suddenly, his collar felt too tight. Realizing that he'd better clear her name, he hurried to explain.

"Valerie is my son's babysitter. We've known each other since childhood. She's been helping me a lot lately."

Bishop Gregory, with his tall build, graying hair, and angular face, could have passed for a defensive end ready to smash him, the opposing quarterback, had it not been for the smile that slid onto his face. "Care to visit with me in my office and enlighten me further?"

No, he didn't care to do that at all. But he was the one who'd opened his big mouth. When would he ever learn? "I'm sure you have your ward members to take care of right now."

"I have excellent counselors, Brother Logan. Delegation is a wonderful thing."

Brother Logan? It had been a long time since anyone called him that. It sounded strangely comforting to Gage. "I wouldn't want to take up too much of your time." Not that he really felt a pressing need to confess his sins to this man, but he'd said it with the hope of putting him off.

Bishop Gregory's smile stayed. "We can schedule another visit if needed. Valerie Hall has been through many trials in her young life, as I'm sure you are aware. She lives close to the Spirit. If you are truly her friend, then I feel certain she is praying for you."

Gage's breath quickened with the possibility. Was she really? Suddenly, he felt embarrassingly close to tears. He couldn't believe the next few sentences that came out of his mouth. "Thanks. I just might take you up on your offer. Our conversation would remain confidential, right?" Gage knew that each bishop was obligated to keep confidentiality, but he was just testing him to be sure.

Bishop Gregory never flinched. "Of course."

"What about Valerie? Would she know that I talked to you?"

"She'll never hear it from me," the bishop said easily. "My office is open. Right now is as good a time as any."

Gage took a deep breath, sensing that he stood on that same precipice of time as Zerahemnah, suspended between the choice of continuing on the debilitating path he'd followed for almost a decade or turning his life to Christ once again. Taking a closer look at the bishop's warm and friendly eyes, he decided. "All right."

Valerie was relieved to drop Zach off at Gage's house. Her Primary class had been so rambunctious that she was out of energy. While driving home, Valerie was startled to hear Justin's voice from the backseat. "Mom?"

"Yes, honey?"

"Gage will be my new dad."

The car almost swerved off the road with his pronouncement. *What?* Where had that come from? Struggling to right the car before sideswiping another vehicle, Valerie pulled into the parking lot of a convenience store and cut the engine, ignoring the blast from the other driver's horn.

"Justin," she heaved, turning toward her son. "What did you say?"

"My dad doesn't like me," he said quietly.

Valerie's heart constricted. Despite Justin's lack of social skills, he was an incredibly intuitive child. How could she defend Nick when his actions spoke so plainly of his intolerance for their son?

Before she could think of a reply, Justin repeated, "Gage will be my new dad."

Valerie opened her mouth to refute him when a soft, warm feeling overcame her. She sat still. "Are you sure?" She didn't know if she was asking Justin or the Lord.

"Yes, Mom. Gage will be my new dad. And Zach will be my brother."

His voice was so confident. Justin hadn't said that Gage *could* be his new dad or that he *would like* for Gage to become his new dad. The assurance came in his calm demeanor, which for Justin, was an unusual occurrence in itself.

But if the Lord wanted her and Gage to make a blended

family, a few miracles needed to occur, one involving Whitney's acceptance of Gage and another involving Gage's inactivity in the Church. In this, she wondered, would the Lord's justice or mercy win out?

"How was work today?" Sarah Nielsen asked Gage as he and Zach sat down to eat with her and Eric later that evening. Feeling restless over Bishop Gregory's encouragement to come to terms with his past, Gage had driven to their home to give Zach some time with them—and maybe himself some time to process everything that had happened today.

"I didn't go to work," he answered. "The team is playing in Atlanta this weekend."

"I can never remember your schedule." Sarah turned to her husband and asked, "Would you like another slice of cake, honey?"

Eric smiled back at her. "No, thank you, sweetheart." Scooting his chair back, he stood and kissed her cheek. "Dinner was delicious. Why don't you and Gage spend some time catching up while I load the dishwasher?"

Sarah beamed. "That sounds wonderful. Thank you, honey."

Resisting the urge to roll his eyes at their infernal sweetness, Gage stood to face Eric and his mother before he lost his nerve. "Wait, Eric. I wanted to talk to both of you." Eric slowly sat back down. Suddenly feeling nervous, Gage said without preamble, "I went to church with Valerie Hall today."

A prolonged silence hung in the air until Sarah whispered, "You did?"

"Yeah." Affecting an air of nonchalance, he grinned. "As you can see, I wasn't struck by lightning."

"That's great, Gage," Eric said. "What made you decide to go?"

Gage hesitated. "Mostly Valerie," he answered honestly. "We've been talking a lot about the things we're dealing with as parents. I didn't realize we had so much in common."

Sarah cocked her head. "Really?"

Gage nodded, giving her a brief summary of Valerie's struggles in raising her children while comparing them with his.

"So how are things going with Zach?"

Gage knew that she had deliberately waited until Zach had found his way to the kids' playroom before asking.

"He's adjusting fairly well. He still misses April, but he likes being around Valerie's kids."

"He gets along with Justin all right?"

"According to Valerie, they play well together most of the time. He seems to sense Justin's moods and knows when to back off."

Sarah stared at him in wonder. "That's amazing. I'm so glad that Zach can be a friend to him. They needed each other, didn't they?"

As always, Gage was impressed by her insight. "Yes. And he needed Valerie. I think she's filling a hole in Zach's life that neither April nor I could."

"And what about you?" she asked softly. "Is she filling the hole in your heart too?"

"What hole?" he said lightly, evading the question, though not very tactfully.

"Gage." When she spoke his name like that, softly with a bit of impatience mixed in, Gage always knew she meant business. "You know what I mean."

Of course he did, but he wasn't sure what to tell her. When he'd been quiet for too long, Sarah prodded, "I think you knew that April was the wrong woman for you before you married her, but life had become one cyclone after another up to that point. You were unsure of what you wanted."

"That's true," he admitted. "I went into that marriage simply looking for a good time."

"Every marriage has its good times and bad. A good marriage turns the bad times into good. But it takes the right partner to make that happen."

He hadn't had that kind of partner. Valerie definitely hadn't, either. They were both coming to a place in their lives where their focus was on raising good children—or in Valerie's case, righteous children. When all was said and done, would Zach be left behind?

If they merged their love for their children with a mutual friendship and respect for each other, could a more meaningful relationship develop in time? Or would they always be too afraid to admit that that was what they wanted? "I care about Valerie and I want to see her happy again."

There. He'd confessed his growing feelings for her. Gage swallowed, wondering what their reactions would be. As the bishop had pointed out, he and Valerie might have a great friendship, but where could a relationship for them lead? Nowhere until he was ready to change his life.

Much to his surprise, Sarah and Eric smiled. "I could hear your concern for Valerie in your voice when you spoke of her," she divulged.

"Nothing can come of it. She'll never go for a guy like me."

"How do you know?" Eric asked.

"Valerie's not going to settle for a Has-Been. Or Never Was. The best I can hope for is that she doesn't end up with another guy like her ex."

"So make the necessary changes in your life," Eric instructed, as if that was all there was to it. "Time is on your side. If she wants another temple marriage, she's going to have to get her sealing to her previous husband cancelled. You have time to work things out."

Gage thought on Eric's words. He was making changes, amazingly enough, a little at a time. He'd never thought that he would want to talk to another LDS bishop again, but Bishop Gregory had listened to Gage without judgment. Gage recalled his counsel to pray and read the scriptures to find out what Heavenly Father wanted him to do.

"One thing at a time," Sarah cautioned, placing her hand on Gage's shoulder. "Invite Valerie and her children to our family's Fourth of July celebration. We're holding it at Pierce and Noelle's home, unless she goes into labor before then, of course. And Craig and Marissa should be there, too, depending on their travel plans. I would love to become reacquainted with Valerie. She was always a lovely girl. I'm sure her children would have a good time."

Gage wasn't sure of that at all. Judging by Whitney's attitude toward Gage, she wasn't thrilled with his sudden interest in her mom. And Justin . . . well, he really was a wild card, just as Valerie had described.

Time was a precious commodity, Valerie had heard Grandma Skylar say many times over the years. Her counsel to use it wisely rang through Valerie's ears as if Grandma was standing right beside her. Grandma was always busy—if not in her garden, then in her kitchen canning the food she grew. If not cleaning the house, then washing the car. If not reading her scriptures, then preparing a lesson for church the following Sunday.

Despite the sage advice, Valerie sometimes wished the clock would reverse and she could do things over. Until recently, Whitney had always been a willing helper, but after visiting her dad, she was putting the brakes on whatever Valerie asked of her. She needed to get to the bottom of this now, especially since Whitney had just yelled at her over such a simple thing as being asked to help the boys pick up their toys.

Marching into Whitney's room and shutting the door behind her, Valerie shifted her weight onto one hip, folding her arms expectantly. "What is going on, Whitney?"

"I don't know," she said in a small voice.

"I think you do, honey. You've been angry lately, yelling at Justin when he does something you don't like and calling Zach names when he asks a question that you think is silly. What has your dad been talking to you about?"

Whitney's eyes grew big at the mention of her father. Valerie resisted the urge to sigh. Did her daughter honestly think that she didn't know that this behavior stemmed from Nick?

"Daddy has a new girlfriend," Whitney stated matter-of-factly.

Nick was seeing someone else? He hadn't said anything about that the last time he'd called to talk to Whitney. "Oh? What's her name?"

"Olivia."

As Valerie sat down on the bed, she couldn't resist asking, "What is she like?"

"She's really pretty. She's tall and has brown hair. She's skinny. And she wears pretty clothes." Valerie nodded, well aware of the fact that T-shirts and jeans had never been Nick's preference of clothing for himself or her.

But that was neither here nor there. Valerie's real concern was her daughter. "Is Olivia nice to you?"

Whitney seemed to hesitate before nodding. "She tells me I'm pretty. And smart."

"That's true, but sometimes people say nice things to convince others to like them. That's called flattery. Be careful, sweetheart. It's okay for you to like Olivia if she really wants to get to know you. All I ask is that you pay attention to other things about her too."

Whitney scrunched her nose. "Like what, Mommy?"

"You have to listen to what a person is saying with not only your ears but also your heart. Sometimes, a person leaves out important words when he or she is talking to others because they want them to believe something that isn't true. If you ever get a strange feeling about what the person is telling you, that's the Holy Ghost telling you to not believe it. When we know what people really mean when they speak to us, it helps us to know what is right. I learned this lesson the hard way when I married your daddy."

"You mean Daddy didn't tell you the truth?"

"Not all of it." Nick had wanted Valerie to think that he was such a nice, easygoing man. Charming. Smooth-talking. Charismatic. All of those qualities described him perfectly when, really, they'd been a cover for his selfishness and arrogance. Valerie jolted as she realized she'd compared Gage in much the same way when he'd first reappeared in her life. But now, through his thoughtful acts of kindness and genuine concern for her and her children, Valerie's opinion of him had changed dramatically.

Whitney's face contorted into a look of perplexity. *Oh, great,* she thought. *Have I confused the child beyond hope?*

"Hello, honey." Brande Levington's cheerful voice greeted Valerie. "I'm calling to tell you about a cute little duplex that a friend recommended to me for you to rent."

Valerie glanced at the clock. Gage would be here any minute to drop Zach off. Then it would be a race to get the kids out the door in time for swim lessons. "Thanks, Mom, but I've been looking around and have narrowed my search down to three apartment complexes."

"But apartments don't have yards for the kids to run around in. This duplex is owned by a member of our ward and has a terrific backyard where the kids could play. You'll need something like that if you want to continue to watch Gage's son."

As if on cue, the doorbell rang. Opening the door and motioning for them to enter, she whispered to Gage, "It's my mom." She then asked her mother, "Who did you say this ward member is?"

Brande hesitated. "The duplex belongs to Brother and Sister Merrill."

Valerie groaned. They were an older couple who had raised their children in a very strict manner. Valerie wasn't about to subject herself or her exuberant children to more criticism. When she'd moved out of her parents' home, she'd vowed that she would never live in their ward boundaries again.

"Thank the Merrills for me, but I would rather find an apartment on my own."

"Valerie, please consider it. Now that Justin is older, I'm sure he has improved a lot. The ward members will welcome you back with open arms."

"Hmm . . . maybe." In reality, she had no intention of finding out. "I'm looking around, Mom. I promise we'll be ready to move out by the time Grandma and Grandpa get home. No need to worry." She inflected a happy note into her voice to hide her discouragement. So few of the apartments in her price range suited her needs.

"Well, I'll keep my eyes open for more affordable housing for you and the kids. What did you say your price range is again?"

She wasn't about to divulge that information in front of Gage, who was once again studying the family pictures on the wall in a noble attempt to appear as if he wasn't listening to her end of the conversation. Valerie appreciated his discretion. "Um, I'll get back to you on that. Gage is here. I need to go. I'll talk to you later. Thanks, Mom."

"All right. I love you. Remember, your father and I just want you to be happy."

"I know. Love you too." Valerie soon ended the call, turning to Gage with a sigh. "Zach took off to find the others, I see," she said, grabbing his overnight bag.

Gage smiled. "I guess he's starting to think of this place as his second home."

"That's good."

An awkward pause followed. Gage cleared his throat. "So . . . I couldn't keep from overhearing. You're still looking for a place to live?"

"Yep. I've narrowed my choices to three."

Gage nodded thoughtfully as she gave him the rundown on each one. The rent was more affordable at one complex, but the surrounding neighborhood had gone downhill. Two other complexes were located in safer communities but required higher rent. The real drawback with them was that Whitney would have to attend a different elementary school and Valerie would have to drive further each morning to take Justin to his school. "So each choice has its pros and cons," Gage concluded.

"Mostly cons."

"Will you still be willing to watch Zach after you move?"

"I'm sure that won't be a problem. It's just that . . . well, as my mom pointed out, we won't have a backyard. But when the temperature outside skyrockets, the kids can't play outside anyway." Again, she inflected a falsely bright tone into her voice to mask her concerns.

"You could watch them at my house."

Valerie sucked in her breath. "I'm not sure that would be a very good idea. Especially after you gave the bishop a false impression of me."

"We cleared that up."

She shot him a dubious look. "When?"

"Right after you left to teach your Primary class. I spoke with him in his office."

"Oh." Nonplussed, she added, "I'm glad for you. But we still couldn't be at your house so late at night, then wake the kids to take them home."

Gage's brows furrowed. "Hmm. Yeah, that does present a problem. Especially for a good Mormon girl like you." He grinned to show that he was teasing.

"And don't you forget it," Valerie added in mock seriousness. "My reputation is on the line."

Gage grew somber. "Don't think I'm not aware of that, Valerie. There's not one day that goes by that I don't thank the good Lord for all you've sacrificed for me."

"I'm glad to help you, Gage." She gave him what she hoped was an encouraging smile.

Their gazes locked and time stood still. It was almost as if the spark in his eyes was meant solely for her. If only he would reclaim his faith.

He *was* changing a little at a time, she reminded herself. She'd felt his concern and protectiveness over her and Justin at the ball game. She'd heard his regret when he'd told her about his failed marriage. She'd seen his face light up at church.

Gage's gaze lowered to her lips and she knew he wanted to kiss her. Her heartbeat doubled in response. Would it be as wonderful as their first? If she took one step closer, she might find out. He reached behind her to pull her closer.

"Dad!" Zach came running down the hallway, followed closely by Justin and Whitney. "We found a cat in the backyard."

"Can we keep it, Mom?" Justin asked.

Startled, Valerie stepped back and pushed her hand through her hair. Was she mistaken or did Gage seem as disappointed as her? But his voice sounded perfectly normal when he answered, "It probably belongs to someone else. A neighbor, perhaps?" His raised eyebrows drew Valerie into the discussion.

Whitney was looking at them with a speculative gleam in her eyes. As if noticing it too, Gage dropped his arm from the small of Valerie's back. Poor Gage. It looked like the Whitney Patrol was back in full force. "I'm sure it does. Zach isn't allergic to animals, is he?"

The helpless look on Gage's face brought an amused smile to her lips. Gage was still learning the ins and outs of this parenting thing. For that, he deserved an A for effort.

G age called her five minutes after he left. "Forget something?" Valerie couldn't resist teasing him.

"Or missed out on something." That rich-as-chocolate voice was back, sending little shivers down Valerie's spine. "Listen, Valerie. I was going to ask you to come to my family's Fourth of July get-together when your housing dilemma distracted me. Or maybe it was that near-kiss. I'm not sure which."

"The near-kiss. Definitely." Valerie clamped a hand over her mouth. She wasn't a flirt and had never perfected the art because it wasn't her style. But bantering with Gage was coming more easily to her lately.

She could hear the amusement in his answer. "Yeah, that's it. We'll have to try it again some time. Speaking of which, I'm trying to ask you on a date. Er, rather, a get-together with the whole family tomorrow. But it's a start, right?"

Yes, and it was safer that way. Because while she was definitely attracted to Gage and growing closer to him on a personal level, Valerie still wanted him to be the kind of guy she'd promised her daughter that she would consider dating.

"My family usually goes to Tempe Town Lake," Gage said, "to see the fireworks. I don't get to participate in their festivities every year due to the team's schedule, but this year, I have the day off. And since Noelle's baby is due any day now and to avoid the extreme heat, we're having a barbecue at their house instead."

"That sounds like fun," she said cautiously. Low-key was always a good thing in her book. "Wouldn't that be making more work for Noelle, though? Especially when she should be taking it easy."

"Pierce and Noelle host get-togethers for their family and friends all the time. Besides, my mom will help her out."

"I will too."

"My mom mentioned that she'd like to see you again. And Whitney and Justin already know Pierce and Noelle. My brother, Craig, and his family will be there too. They have a daughter who is close to Whitney's age and a son who is the same age as Justin."

Hearing this brought back Valerie's insecurities. "Justin doesn't always get along with other children."

Gage's sigh conveyed his disagreement. But if he was serious about wanting to date her, then he'd need to understand and accept her cautious nature concerning Justin's limitations. "It's a common occurrence with kids. They'll be fine. And so will everyone else if something goes wrong. We're not made of glass, Valerie. We can bend and adjust to new situations."

"And we can leave early if things don't work out?"

Another sigh. "Are you going to spend the rest of your life running from everything, Valerie? If so, you're going to miss out. Instead of worrying about what might happen, have a little faith that things will work out."

The irony of his declaration wasn't lost on her. "When did we reverse roles?" she joked.

He laughed. "Maybe you're starting to rub off on me."

She hoped so. And maybe he was starting to rub off on her. Trust didn't come easily to her. His voice penetrated her thoughts. "If a situation arises where you feel the need to leave early, I promise that's what we'll do."

Instinctively, she knew that Gage would keep his word. She

appreciated the effort he was making for her, which convinced her to return the favor. "All right. That sounds like a plan."

Sarah Nielsen opened Pierce and Noelle's front door, waving Gage and Valerie and their children in. After greeting her son, Sarah exclaimed, "Valerie, it's so good to see you again!" She embraced Valerie tenderly, and Gage's heart lightened. Though he'd never admit it to Valerie, he was wondering if they could get through this celebration without a hitch.

Valerie returned the embrace until Sarah pulled back to examine her.

"You're lovely. Isn't she, Gage?" she asked, turning to him.

"Lovely indeed." Though the words weren't a part of his usual vocabulary, he loved the effect they created. A beautifully faint blush now graced Valerie's cheeks.

"Hi, Grandma." Zach ran in from behind Gage

"Hello, Zach." She hugged him and then turned to Valerie's children.

Gage made the introductions, knowing that if anyone could put Whitney and Justin at ease in this unfamiliar setting, Sarah could.

"I know your Grandma and Grandpa Levington. We used to be good friends while Gage and your mom were growing up." Sarah asked each of them their ages as well as a few other questions, appearing not to be bothered by Justin's minimal responses. She then led the children down the hallway where Gage's nieces and nephews were playing.

"Come this way." Gage led Valerie into the kitchen where his sisters-in-law were laughing and talking while preparing side dishes. "Hey, Noelle and Marissa."

They turned and smiled at Gage. "Hi, Gage!" Noelle greeted them enthusiastically. "Valerie, right? It's great to see you again. Marissa," she said, waving her over, "this is Gage's friend Valerie Hall. Valerie, meet Craig's wife, Marissa."

Marissa, who was a few inches shorter than Noelle, came up to Valerie to shake her hand across the countertop. "It's nice to meet you. I've heard a lot about you. It's great that you were able to help Gage and Zach. I understand the two of you practically grew up together?"

The corners of Valerie's mouth lifted briefly. Gage released the breath he hadn't realized he was holding. A dynamic duo, Noelle and Marissa were a force to be reckoned with. He hoped that Valerie could hold her own with these two. "You could say that," she stated quietly.

Just then, Noelle grabbed her abdomen during an obviously painful contraction. Valerie grabbed the colander to finish the pasta salad. "Here, I'll take that."

"Noelle," Marissa said in alarm, "are you okay? Here, sit." Bending over to pull a stool over, she gasped. "Noelle! Why didn't you tell me your feet were so swollen? You should have been sitting this entire time!"

When the contraction subsided, Noelle glanced down at her puffy feet. "Oh, that? That's nothing. You should have seen me when I was pregnant with Caleb. My ankles got so huge they swelled right up to my calves."

To Gage's surprise, Valerie joined in. "'Cankles,' you mean. I've had that happen too. It's so hot here, it's a casualty with most pregnancies."

"Cankles?" Gage gave a sardonic laugh. "Now I've heard everything. For a minute there, I almost believed you."

"It's true, Gage. It's very painful. Guess you'd have to experience it yourself to know," Noelle said tongue-in-cheek.

"Yeah, well, I'm glad you get to experience that particular joy instead of me."

Valerie's eyes narrowed dangerously. Gage gulped. Why did he get the feeling he'd said the wrong thing? Yep. Fire and ice. From where he was standing, it was hard to tell which one she was feeling.

"Oh, we know that you guys could never handle it. Right, girls?" Noelle's eyes glinted with amusement.

Now he'd really set the bloodhounds on him. Gage might not always know the right thing to say or do around a woman, but he was smart enough to know when he was outnumbered. He'd rather take a chance with the guys outside.

Noelle and Marissa burst into gales of laughter as soon as Gage beat a hasty retreat through the back door to find his brothers. "Can you believe that brother-in-law of ours?"

"Did you see his face?"

"Yeah, he walked right into that one."

"It serves him right. I don't think he always realizes what he blurts out."

Valerie bit her lip, feeling bad for having put Gage on the spot—although it had mostly been Noelle's doing. But then he'd made that ridiculous comment about the joys of pregnancy. Something he knew nothing about. But it wasn't his fault, she reminded herself. "I may have given you the wrong impression. Gage and I have had our ups and downs, but we're working it out. He's been jumping hurdles lately. Don't be too hard on him."

Compassion softened the women's faces. "We've all been worried about him," Marissa said.

"Life seems to be getting a little easier for him at this point," Valerie said.

"That's good. Because when he first brought Zach to our home, there was a huge rift in the family," Noelle confessed. "I'll admit, Pierce was too hard on him. But Gage impressed me when he didn't fight back. I hope they'll be able to work it out."

"I think Gage would like that too."

"So, Valerie," Marissa said as she began to load the dishwasher, "tell us about yourself."

Noelle clearly caught the mischievous look in her sister-in-law's face and grinned. "You said that you and Gage are working things out. Do I detect a love connection in the works? Give us the juicy details."

"We're just friends," she said succinctly, noting their dismay when they realized that they weren't going to get their "juicy details." Noelle and Marissa looked at each other, regret etched on their brows. Gage's sisters-in-law then toned down their questions, for which Valerie felt relieved. These two were an interesting mix of larger-than-life enthusiasm and gentle compassion for others. In some ways, they reminded Valerie of her own sisters.

When she told them how well Gage interacted with Justin, Marissa said pensively, "Hmm. Who knew that Gage could be so thoughtful? He is changing, isn't he?"

Valerie smiled. "He isn't the only one."

As far as Gage was concerned, the steaks sitting over the flames weren't the only things that were being grilled. His brothers were expert inquisitors, always had been.

"So, what's she like now that she's all grown up?" Craig asked.

"How serious are the two of you?" Pierce joined in.

"Does Zach get along with her kids?"

"What do *you* think of her kids?"

Honestly, Craig and Pierce were acting worse than Marissa and Noelle had. Maybe he would have been better off inside after all. Just then, Eric came around from behind Gage, slapping him on the back. "Guys, lay off him. Can't you see you're making him hyperventilate? He'll tell you what you want to know when he's good and ready."

"You mean he'll tell us only what *he* wants us to know." Craig lifted one superior eyebrow at Gage. While Gage had always felt that Craig was the perfect blend of both their parents, in that moment, he looked more like their father than ever before.

"What's that supposed to mean, Craig? You're not still mad about me keeping Zach a secret from you guys, are you?"

A tense pause followed with Craig and Pierce staring at him before Craig's face broke into a grin. "No. We're over that, bro. But we want to know about that blonde in there." He inclined his head in the direction of the house. "Are you dating her or what?"

"Or what," Gage retorted.

"You sure you don't want to tell us what's going on?" Pierce pressed. "Because we could find out from Kurt just as easily."

Gage released a long-suffering sigh. "Are we back in high school, guys? Valerie is Zach's babysitter, remember?"

"Then why did you bring her?"

Because I'm crazy about her and her kids. Because I'm trying to make a huge change in my life and I'm scared out of my wits about doing it. Because she's been my anchor in this storm.

"Because I love her."

The words slipped out before he could stop them. The shocked looks on Craig's and Pierce's faces would have been priceless if Gage hadn't been so worried about their reactions. He looked away only to see Eric grinning at him like a Cheshire cat.

"So when are you going to go back to church?" Pierce asked. "Because I'll have you know that the Levingtons take the gospel very seriously."

Gage sighed. Couldn't his brothers cut him any slack? Before he could answer them, however, Eric interrupted him. "He's already started going back."

Craig smiled. "Really, man? How long ago?"

"I just started," he mumbled, feeling uncomfortable with the conversation.

"And he's talking to Valerie's bishop." Again, Eric supplied this bit of information.

Craig and Pierce looked at each other in astonishment. "Is that true, Gage?"

"Valerie has helped me come to terms with my first marriage." With a self-conscious laugh, he added, "I guess you could say we've both 'been there, done that.' She's given me some great ideas for coping with Zach too."

Craig grinned. "That's awesome, Gage. Just make sure that what you're feeling for her goes beyond gratitude."

Gage sighed. *Brothers!* "I will, Counselor. As long as you make sure you really want to move back to this hot spot. You better hope your wife doesn't regret it later." Earlier, Craig had told his brothers that he had secured a new job in Arizona and would be moving down here in the next few weeks. Gage was excited for them.

"Nah. She'll get used to it."

They bantered with each other for a few more minutes before a loud shouting match hailed from inside the house. Gage took off running the instant he realized that it was Justin.

G age and his brothers found Valerie holding onto Justin to prevent his flailing arms from hitting Gage's nephew, Caleb. Justin shouted at the frightened boy being held against Noelle's rounded belly. Pierce pulled his crying son up in his arms while Gage rushed to Valerie's side. "What happened?"

His heart lurched at the stricken look on her face. "They had a disagreement over a game they were playing."

"That's more than just a disagreement," Pierce said loudly over Justin's screaming.

Valerie's face contorted at the candid remark. Gage gently placed his hands around each side of Justin's rib cage and pulled him gently while keeping his voice carefully modulated. "Let me take him for a little while, Valerie. Okay?"

She was starting to panic. He could see it her eyes.

"It will be all right. Just let me walk him around the neighborhood for a few minutes. We'll be right back."

She reluctantly withdrew her hands around Justin. "Okay."

Gage carried Justin out the front door. Dusk had fallen and the fireworks show, which he knew could be seen from the house at a distance, would begin soon. Justin was still writhing and screaming angrily. "Justin," he said in a steady voice. "Calm down. You're all right."

Not knowing what else to do, Gage kept repeating himself while rubbing his back. He managed to calm the boy down enough to set him on his feet and take his hand. "Let's go see if we can spot the fireworks from down the block, all right?"

Hiccupping, Justin nodded through his tears.

In the silence that followed, Valerie bit her lip while scanning the perplexed faces around the room. "Pierce, Noelle, I'm so sorry." She didn't know what else to say.

Apparently, no one else did, either. Noelle looked anxiously at her husband, whose tight expression mirrored her own. She ran her hand in soothing circles on Caleb's back and, after a few moments, turned back to Valerie with a sympathetic smile. "It's okay. Caleb's all right now." With obvious reluctance, Pierce set him down and sent Caleb off to play with the others.

Valerie should have followed Justin into the playroom to monitor his behavior. Justin wasn't very good at playing games. His skill level rarely matched that of the other players, yet he couldn't quite understand why he never won. Instead, he reverted to calling them names, accusing them of cheating or becoming openly hostile.

She'd known all of this, so why hadn't she listened to her conscience?

Because it'd been too long since she'd enjoyed living. Because a handsome man was paying attention to her again and because his family had invited her to participate in something that sounded so promising.

"Excuse me," Valerie whispered and made her way to the front door. Gage and Justin were nowhere to be seen. That was okay since she needed a minute to calm her nerves.

At length, the door opened softly behind her. Sarah Nielsen approached quietly and placed a reassuring hand on her shoulder.

"I'm sorry," Valerie said. Not sure how much Gage had told them, she added, "I wish it could be different. I wish that Justin was normal."

She knew she wasn't making much sense at this point, but Sarah let her blather on without comment. Then Sarah said softly, "It will get better over time."

"How do you know that?"

"Craig is a counselor at a high school. He's worked with several autistic adolescents. He was just telling me that he has seen vast improvements in many of them every year that he has worked there. But it takes time. And even though it will never be perfect or even what you'd prefer, the answers will come when you need them."

There was something to hang onto, Valerie supposed. "I don't understand why Heavenly Father gave Justin to me. I've seen so many other wonderful people whom I thought would be great parents for an autistic child. I feel so inadequate."

"He knew that you could do it." Sarah's quiet answer penetrated a place in her heart that she'd closed off to others' scrutiny. "He has every confidence in you, Valerie. And right now, you are the only parent Justin can rely on. He needs for you to be strong. Though, if I had my wish, Gage would become a supportive father figure to your children as well."

Valerie pulled back, startled. "You mean—you're not angry with us?"

Sarah smiled and pulled her back into a hug. "Goodness, no. Gage has explained Justin's disorder to us. Although we don't understand it fully, we know that you're doing all that you can to help him."

"I hope Pierce and Noelle aren't too upset with us."

Sarah shook her head. "They'll get over it. Noelle's not letting on, but I think she's experiencing fairly painful contractions. Naturally, she and Pierce are a little on edge. Also, Caleb is their only child. They'll soon learn the give and take of sibling rivalry and be able to deal with it in a more objective manner."

Valerie agreed. Yes, there were times when both children needed attention at the same time and she had to decide which child's needs took priority.

They sat on the porch and talked for another ten minutes. Valerie had always secretly admired Sarah Logan. She was beautiful and smart. She always had a smile and a kind word for everyone. Valerie had wanted to become like her. After becoming a mother to two rambunctious kids, however, she focused simply on surviving. But if Sarah could arise from the ashes of her own crumbled marriage stronger and with greater happiness to share, then Valerie knew she could too.

Gage and Justin emerged from the shadows of the night soon after. Much calmer now, Justin sat down beside his mother. Valerie put her arm around his shoulders and pulled him close. Gage knelt in front of them and told Valerie, "Justin has something to say to you."

Valerie waited. To her surprise, Justin mumbled the words, "I'm sorry," while looking down at the porch.

She gasped. "How did you—"

Gage's embarrassed shrug stopped her mid-sentence. He sent a silent signal toward Justin.

Valerie took a deep breath. Gage was right. Justin's apology was all that mattered at the moment. She leaned over and gave him a huge hug even though she knew that he loathed them. "Thank you so much, sweetheart. That means a lot to me. I want you to remember that the Logans are our friends. If we want to be invited back again, we need treat them kindly."

"Okay, Mom."

Gage lightly tapped Justin's knee. "Hey, buddy. I'm proud of you. But there's one more person I need for you to apologize to. Are you ready to go tell Caleb that you're sorry?" For a moment, Justin's face clouded. Valerie, along with Gage and Sarah, waited with baited breath for Justin to decide what he would do. "Okay."

Valerie let her breath out slowly. Gage had just performed a miracle with her son.

"That went well, didn't it?"

Valerie looked over at Gage as he drove them home, trying to decide if he was joking or being serious. His teasing grin gave him away. Okay, so they'd hit a rough patch at the family celebration, but all in all, everyone had had a good time, including Whitney, who had hit it off with Craig and Marissa's daughter, Sophie.

"I would still like to know how you convinced Justin to apologize," Valerie said. She glanced back, seeing her son leaning on Whitney with his eyes closed, his breathing even. It had been a long day for all of them.

"Remember when you told me that Justin responds well to being given choices? Well, the only choice I could think to offer him was to ask whom he wanted to apologize to first—you or Caleb." He shrugged. "I know that wasn't really much of a choice, but it worked in a pinch."

"It was perfect," she assured him.

In the silence that followed Valerie's declaration, Gage debated whether to test the waters as far as asking her on a real date. Now that the stressful moments were over, Valerie seemed a little less tense. Unfortunately for him, a nervous feeling twisted his insides, which also held some strange hold over his tongue.

"Hey, Valerie, I was wondering . . ."

Valerie turned to look at him. "Yes?"

If this was any other woman, Gage wouldn't hesitate. But this was Valerie, the girl of his dreams. Her standards for dating were undoubtedly high. And Gage was fairly certain he'd never been in the running for her affections. Until now.

"Gage?" she asked when he didn't respond. "What is it?"

"Well . . . I was hoping you might . . ." Again, his voice trailed off.

"Come out with it already, Gage. What's going on?"

Gage gulped. This was harder than he'd thought. Especially with sleepy kids in the backseat. He lowered his voice. "A date. I'm trying to ask you on a real date, Valerie. Friday night. Just you and me. Without the kids." Great. Now he sounded like a moonstruck teenager.

She lifted a skeptical brow. "Really?"

Why was that so hard to believe? "Yes."

Her expression eased and her mouth spread into that enticing smile of hers. "I would love to, Gage." And he loved it when her voice went all velvety like that.

He should have asked her sooner.

"You want me to go out on the lake with you in *that*?" Valerie looked at the pedal boat Gage had rented at Tempe Town Lake with a mixture of whimsy and uncertainty. "It looks like an oversized raft with wheels." Her voice was anything but velvety now.

Gage, however, was having a hard time keeping his excitement in check. "Think of it as a glorified bicycle."

"That floats on water." With an amused smile, Valerie shook her head. "Gage, only you could come up with something like this for a first date." She stepped into the contraption gingerly, holding on to the sides of the boat, and situated herself on the far seat. He then followed.

"It's a good thing it's getting dark," Valerie said, tugging her life jacket tighter.

"Hey! Are you saying that you don't want to be seen with the best-looking guy here?"

Gage's heart tripped over the delicate rise of her eyebrows. With the sun setting behind her, pinks and golds providing a nice backdrop, she was beautiful. A lump formed in his throat.

"Ha, ha! So how do we get this thing started?"

"Easy. We just start pedaling." Although it turned out to be harder than he first thought. Valerie controlled one side of the pedal while Gage controlled the other. They had to coordinate their efforts or be content where they were. Actually, he thought with a smile, he was a happy man out here on the sparkling water with the night sky deepening to shades of pink and indigo with gray-streaked cloud wisps. Even with the freeway so close, it seemed like it was just the two of them.

Gage stopped pedaling. "Let's sit here for a few minutes and enjoy the view."

Valerie smiled at Gage. "I bring my kids here to the splash pad often, but I've never been out on the water. It's peaceful in its own way."

"Did you know that the seats recline?"

"No, I didn't."

"Let's try it."

They found the levers on either side to pull the seat backs down. A comfortable silence settled between them as they drifted. When a blissful sigh escaped Valerie's lips, he teased, "Hey, no falling asleep. What would that say about being in my company?"

Valerie quipped, "It would say that you're a genius. You truly know what's important to this woman."

"Sleep?"

She chuckled. "Yeah. A mother of two kids doesn't get enough of that."

Point taken. Gage had needed time to adjust to Zach's schedule as well. However, he couldn't have his date falling asleep on him. If his brothers found out, they'd never let him live it down.

"It's too bad we're still in the city limits," Valerie said. "Then we'd be able to see the stars."

"The only time I've ever seen the stars were on those Scout campouts so long ago with your dad."

The sun had finally dipped below the horizon and the lake was bathed in soft lights outlining the bridge. "I take it you don't miss them."

Gage shook his head. "Not much." He'd always been a city kid.

But that didn't mean he wouldn't go for a star-gazing expedition with Valerie some time. Might be kind of nice. A realization hit him. "This isn't really your thing, is it?"

"What do you mean?"

"I mean, you're the kind of person who likes her solitude. Not so many people around as here."

As if just noticing her surroundings, Valerie raised her head to scan the shoreline. "This place is usually crowded but tonight's perfect."

That was because most people were inside enjoying the air conditioning. Even after the sun had dipped, the temperature had only marginally followed suit. It couldn't have suited Gage's purposes better. They'd eaten their fill at a bistro beforehand, talking all the while about inconsequential things. And now, with the romantic ambience of the soft lights and still water, Gage wanted to know more about Valerie. What she liked. What she hoped and dreamed.

"Tell me, Valerie. What is your dream for your future?"

She stayed silent for so long that Gage finally turned to look at her. Valerie was gazing out toward the water. "For the most part, I want my kids to be happy. Well-adjusted and able to cope in life."

It was a worthy goal. For Justin, Gage hoped it could happen. "What about yourself?"

"I hope to someday go back to school and study horticulture. I'd love to work in a nursery and maybe even become a manager someday. I've been taking classes that the Desert Botanical Garden offers from time to time. My garden has prospered from it and I would like to expand on that knowledge and perhaps help others do the same."

"You would do great." But what about her personal life? The tongue-tied sensation that nearly overcame Gage when he'd asked her out threatened to do the same again. Tempted to stay silent, he rallied for courage. "Do you ever think about remarrying someday?"

A heavy sigh was her response. Gage could only imagine the burden Valerie carried with such a loaded question. But he really wanted to know. "I would like to think there's someone out there for me who won't judge me too harshly for how I look or the way I raise my kids. But if it doesn't happen until they're grown, I guess I can live with that."

"What if you did find someone like that? Do you think you'd want to have more kids?"

"Nope!"

She said it with such force that Gage winced. "But why not? You're a terrific mother, Valerie. I can see you with a house full of kids."

She gave a humorless laugh. "I don't think so. Not after what I went through when Justin was born. I couldn't handle that again."

By her set jaw, Gage deduced that it must have been an agonizing experience for her. He knew there were no guarantees in life, but still, with April's deception and Gage's initial dismissal of fatherhood, he wouldn't mind being given a chance to try it again. He would do better the second time around. But if Valerie was dead set against the notion, should he continue to pursue her? How could he not?

Checking the time, Gage and Valerie decided to head back to shore. Then they stopped in a shop that was open late for a serving of gelato.

"Are you going to be at church on Sunday?" Valerie asked, startling Gage.

Setting the plastic spoon back into his dish, he said, "Yeah, I'll be there. The D-Backs will be back in town on Monday. Are you game for another date tomorrow?"

Valerie pretended to consider. "I might be. If I can convince my sister to watch the kids again. Where?"

"It's a surprise. But I hope you're still in the mood for stargazing."

She beamed. "Sure, if it doesn't rain." One could never tell during the middle of monsoon season.

"It won't. I promise."

She raised quizzical eyebrows to him. "You can promise a clear sky? Wow. You must be a magician."

"Not really. But I like my chances." He'd already checked the weather forecast for this week in anticipation of this outing.

Valerie nodded. "Okay. Then it's a date."

"So you never did tell me where we're going today, but from the looks of it, I'd say we're headed up to Canyon Lake." Valerie and Gage had just exited the Superstition Freeway and had turned north onto Highway 88.

Valerie grinned at Gage's double take. "How'd you guess?"

"My parents camped out there every summer."

"Your dad used to take the Scouts there too."

"I can imagine." With the exception of Whitney's stormy look, from the moment Gage picked her up for this date, conversation had flowed easily between the two of them. Poor Justin had asked if he could come too. Valerie's heart had melted as Gage had knelt at his level and ruffled his hair.

"Not this time, buddy. Tonight it's just me and your mom. But next week is All-Star Break. We'll do something together then, okay?"

Justin broke out into a grin. "Promise?"

"Promise."

"Okay."

Now, with the sky clear—just as Gage had predicted—and Gage's car smoothly eating up the miles, it seemed they'd never run out of things to talk about. Before she knew it, Gage was pulling into the Canyon Lake campground. After parking a distance away from the Ramada and the rest of the campers, Gage pulled an ice chest out from the back of his car. "How can I help?" Valerie asked.

"Want to grab that blanket and find a nice spot for it?"

"Sure."

It appeared that Gage had thought of everything. After spreading the blanket out, Gage set the cooler down. Valerie pulled containers of fried chicken, baked beans, coleslaw, and rolls out, along with disposable plates and cutlery. Plastic stemware and chilled sparkling cider rounded out the meal quite nicely. One thing was sure. This meal hadn't come out of a bucket or a box. The only item missing was dessert.

"Looking for this?" She turned to see Gage holding up a grocery sack with ingredients to make s'mores in one hand and roasting sticks in the other.

Valerie smiled self-consciously. "You read my mind."

When they were settled, Gage began awkwardly, "Um, I'll bless the food."

Though Valerie didn't say anything, she knew this was a big deal for him. And she was thankful to see this change.

They ate in silence until one by one, the stars lit up. "We're lucky to have such a clear night," Valerie said softly. "How many of the constellations do you know?"

Gage shook his head. "Not many. I can at least point out the Big Dipper."

"Which is actually part of a larger constellation, Ursa Major." Valerie traced what she could of the pattern overhead in the northeastern sky with her finger.

"Okay, now I see it. And there's the Little Dipper too."

"Part of Ursa Minor," Valerie added. "Of course, every good Scout should be able to locate the North Star."

"Who said anything about being a good Scout?" Gage joked.

Valerie chuckled. Trailing her hand down a bit, she pointed out Hercules, mostly from memory since not all of the stars that formed him were visible tonight. "Just below his leg, you can see the star, Vega. Aside from the North Star, it's one of the brightest and easiest stars to recognize."

She pointed out a few more constellations then quieted as they became lost in their musings. Valerie loved the cool crispness of the air and being out with Gage.

After some time, they got up to start a small fire in the grill. "Okay, so this isn't nearly as romantic as roasting them over an open flame, but we've got to observe fire restrictions and all that jazz."

"That's okay," Valerie said. "They'll taste just as good."

After a lengthy silence, Gage turned to her. "Whitney's still having a hard time with me, isn't she?"

Uh-oh. This was one subject she'd been trying to avoid. "I think it's because her dad has a new girlfriend and now that Justin has become so close to Zach, she doesn't quite know where she fits in anymore."

"What can we do about it?"

Valerie sighed. "The only thing I can think of that will help is time. Show her love. And patience. Lots of it."

With a smile of encouragement, Gage took her hand and pulled Valerie closer. The air had finally cooled to where it felt good to be wrapped in his arms. It would have felt nice anyway, but here in this moment, Valerie felt safe. Sheltered. And cared for.

"I hope Whitney knows that I'm not trying to replace her dad. I want to build a relationship with her, but she's not ready."

"No, she isn't," Valerie whispered.

"And I think that Justin could really benefit from having a guy in his life who can be a good role model for him. I haven't always been that guy, but I would like to be now, Valerie."

"Gage, what are you saying?"

"We balance each other out in a really good way. You're more serious while I can be impulsive at times."

"Just a little," she agreed with a chuckle.

"I think you like me just as much as I like you."

Feeling a little panicked, Valerie said, "Liking a person is different from loving a person."

Gage grunted. "Liking my friends was never like this. And what I'm feeling for you is way more intense than what I ever felt for April."

His lips came down on hers, softly at first and then with more pressure. Valerie responded by weaving her arms around his neck and pulling him closer. She couldn't deny the passion she felt or the disappointment that muddled her brain when it ended. But if Gage was hinting at a more permanent relationship—and she thought he was—she, like Whitney, wasn't quite ready. A *lasting* temple marriage was first and foremost her goal this time. Truth be told, she doubted Gage was ready for such a commitment as well.

"Gage, we can discuss this another time. Right now, I think it's best if we get back to our kids. Are you going to church tomorrow?"

"Yep. Zach and I will be there."

On the way back to Mesa, Gage's voice broke through the silence that had pervaded since departing the lake. "Valerie, I've got a fairly flexible schedule next weekend during the All-Star Break. I thought about doing something with the kids on Friday. Then maybe you and I could do something Saturday night?"

"What do have in mind?"

He shrugged. "For the kids, I'm not sure yet. Maybe a movie or bowling. I was thinking about taking you out for dinner and then a show afterward. Wear your most beautiful dress, although it could never compete with your beauty." He flashed her a brilliant smile. "Think you can convince Chloe to babysit for you one more time? Or is she getting a little tired of it?"

Hopeful that the darkness was covering her blush, Valerie said, "Not especially. But she's asking questions about us."

Gage gave a short laugh. "I'm fielding questions too. That's good. It means we're making progress."

Gage straightened his tie in the mirror, then ran his fingers through his hair. Once again, it was short, just the way he liked it. Gone were the days when Gage had hidden his face from others beneath the sleek curtain of his long mane. It felt good to face the world again with confidence.

On Thursday, Gage had bought a ring for Valerie according to her sister Chloe's specifications. Now, finally, it was almost time for their date. His palms were sweaty. He'd been on many dates with beautiful women through the years. But Valerie's beauty was very different. Refreshing. And although she didn't know it, this wasn't just any date.

Earlier this week, Gage had secured two tickets to a popular magic act in Scottsdale, for the renowned illusionist, Gordon Reno. In his excitement, an idea germinated, which prompted him to make another phone call.

"Hello?" His brother's voice came through on the second ring.

"Hey, Pierce. I need to ask you a favor."

"The last time I did a favor for you, bro, you dropped a bombshell in our laps."

Gage sighed. "Yeah. Sorry about that. This time, it's something better."

"Like what?"

"I want to ask Valerie to marry me. And I need your help." To his surprise and delight, after explaining his idea, Pierce agreed. Gage could hardly contain his excitement until today.

Now, Gage's phone buzzed just as he was heading out the door. Impatiently, he answered it. "Hello?"

"Gage?"

It was Travis from work. He and Gage had hung out in some questionable places a lot when Gage first became a member of the Diamondbacks organization. But Gage had been distancing himself from his friends more lately. "Hey, Travis. What's up?"

"The ladies and I were talking about checking out a new place that just opened up in Scottsdale this weekend." *What a coincidence*, Gage thought wryly. *So was I*. Although he suspected that the two of them were thinking of completely opposite venues. "You wanna come?"

Clubbing. That was about all his life had amounted to in recent years. While Gage missed the friends he no longer had time for due to tending Zach, he now realized how empty his life had been. The conversations they'd shared in those dim, hazy lights were nothing more than meaningless chatter. The more alcohol they consumed, the looser their tongues became, emitting vile and crude language that made Gage want to gag on his cola.

"I can't make it tonight. I've got plans."

"You sure you can't cancel them? Bridget will be there." The leggy brunette who didn't work with the rest of them but was a friend of Elise, their co-worker. Elise had introduced them in the hopes that she and Gage would hit it off. Gage had briefly thought about asking Bridget out, but the more she talked, the less he wanted to get to know her. She was just another knock-off of April.

"I'm going to pass this time. Good luck finding someone else to drive you."

Travis let an expletive fly. Gage cringed. Had he really fit in with that crowd not so long ago? Although he'd made relatively slow progress over the past five years, that kind of lifestyle seemed to be a thing of his distant past.

Ending the call, he breathed a sigh of relief.

It was time to face his future.

Gage rang Valerie's doorbell twenty minutes later. Brande Levington opened the door and waved him inside. "You're babysitting tonight?"

"Yes. Chloe had an obligation. I'll be staying with the kids here rather than taking them to our house."

Knowing the date would last well into the evening, Gage agreed it was a good plan. For that same reason—and because Zach had been missing Keith and Madeline—he'd set Zach up with a sleepover at his grandparents' house in Tucson. "I'll go see if Valerie's ready," Brande said and then left the room.

Whitney and Justin greeted him—Whitney, cautiously, and Justin, enthusiastically.

Whitney's brow puckered at the same time her little fist landed on one hip. "You're going on another date with my mom? Are you gonna marry her or what?"

He sure hoped so. But Gage wasn't about to reveal his plan to this sassy six-year-old who reminded him so much of her mom before he had a chance to ask the woman in question. Gage's fire and ice theory had just taken a turn for the worst. If he'd ever needed inspiration, now was the time.

Fortunately, it came. Whitney needed to know that her feelings mattered. "Would it be all right with you if I did?"

With her petulant expression, she made a good imitation of a worried mama. "But Mommy said that you don't have a testimony."

"I'm getting it back, Whitney. I've started going to church again. I want to be a part of your life too, not just your mom's."

Whitney looked at him dubiously, her mouth flattening into a straight line. Gage knelt down and peered into her eyes. The uncertainty he saw there twisted his gut. "Hey," he said softly. "It's hard when things change. You were probably hoping that your mom and dad would get back together, right?"

He waited for her reluctant nod before continuing.

"Sweetheart, I wish this could be easier for you. My own mom and dad split up and now they are both married to other people. It really hurt when that happened, but do you know what I learned from the experience?"

Entranced, Whitney slowly shook her head.

"Everything happens for a reason. A mom and dad have to work together to make their marriage succeed. When one or both of them are unwilling to do that, you have to accept it and move on."

Gage wasn't sure if he was making sense to Whitney. But she was no longer openly hostile toward him.

"My mom and dad are happier now because they both found someone else not only to love, but to work with and help each other. Moms and dads should stay together when they can, but that isn't always possible. I want you to know, Whitney, that I want your mom to be happy. And I want you and Justin to be happy because I care about you. No matter what happens, your mom and your dad will always love you. Remember that."

Oh, great. Now he'd made her cry. Gently, Gage pulled this precious but grown-up little girl into his arms. His heart ached for her.

"It will be all right, Whitney," he said softly. "Life will be different from the way you wanted it to be, but everything will work out as it should." He pulled back to look at her. "Heavenly Father knows how you feel. Pray to Him, okay? Don't get mad at Him like I did. It doesn't do any good. It only makes you feel worse."

She was nodding solemnly when Gage's senses suddenly went on alert. Looking up, he saw Valerie and her mom wiping their eyelids with the backs of their hands. He had been so engrossed in convincing Whitney to give him a chance that he hadn't heard them quietly enter the room. Terrific. He'd managed to make three generations of females weep with one blow.

Sniffling, Valerie stuttered, "Gage Logan, now look what you've done. My makeup was perfect. Now I need to go back and redo it."

"No, you don't." He hastily stepped forward to capture her hand. "You look gorgeous."

"You're being ridiculous." Valerie dabbed her face with a tissue.

"Not this time. You're stunning." Gage couldn't help staring at the vision that stood before him. Valerie wore a chiffon dress in dark amethyst with a sparkly beaded fitted bodice, which modestly showed off the feminine line of her hips. She had pulled her hair back in some kind of a stylish knot to reveal diamond teardrop earrings, which drew Gage's attention to her oval face. Gage's mouth went dry. While the dress and her makeup added glamour to her features, somehow, Gage knew they didn't attribute to her glow. His heart pounded at the thought that she might possibly return his feelings for her. He was tempted to kiss her right there and then to find out.

"Thank you," she said, her cheeks coloring delicately. "Not only for the compliment but for what you said to Whitney." Then she added lightly, "You look great, too, by the way."

"Thanks."

"Mommy, you look like a princess."

Valerie's mother agreed. "You sure do, honey. Have a wonderful time."

Dinner at the Mystical Cavern in Scottsdale was fabulous. Valerie had never eaten in such an elegant atmosphere. The restaurant had been built into the side of a hill with the dining room literally being underground. The same variety of vegetables Valerie grew in her own backyard were used in ways she had never dreamed of. Gage ordered the chipotle steak while she opted for the not-so-spicy-but-just-as-flavorful chicken Acapulco. Their entrées were cooked to perfection.

At first, Valerie's quivering nerves set her on edge. *Get a hold of yourself. This is Gage. Pretend you're back at Canyon Lake with him and you'll be fine.* Thankfully, Gage carried much of the conversation until she relaxed somewhat. She realized with a start that she was enjoying herself very much. Then Gage's phone lit up. Glancing at the text message, a hint of a smile teased his lips. Though she wondered about it, Valerie didn't want to pry.

Gage informed Valerie, "Noelle gave birth to a healthy baby girl on Tuesday. They named her Bethany Grace."

"Please congratulate her and Pierce for me."

After dinner, the conversation in Gage's car naturally turned to their children while he drove them to their next destination. For reasons unknown, Valerie had been so nervous about this date that she hadn't even thought to ask where they were going. Gage pulled up to the Scottsdale Center for the Performing Arts and led her into the glitzy building.

"The great and fantastical magic act of famous illusionist Gordon Reno?" She echoed the words in bold letters on her program.

Gage grinned, flashing incredibly white teeth. "Front row seats."

Her jaw dropped. "Are you serious?"

"Trust me. This is something you don't want to miss."

Valerie felt a thrill as the lights dimmed and the crowd grew quiet. Thunderous applause broke out when Gordon Reno appeared on the stage, wearing a white shirt and black pants with his long black cape flowing behind him. "Good eef-ning, ladies and gentlemen," he greeted in a thick eastern European accent. "Ve hope you vill enjoy ze show."

He introduced his scantily clad female assistant, Azalea, and warmed up the audience by turning a purple scarf into various shades of blue and green along with a few smaller tricks. His repertoire wasn't anything Valerie had never seen before on television, but seeing these tricks for the first time in person lent a whole new dimension to them. Her senses went on alert when Gordon Reno locked his assistant in a vertical box and he shoved first one, then another sharp-edged metal plate through staggered slits on each side. Almost without consciousness, Valerie gripped Gage's hand when the magician pushed the middle compartment off to the side, making a zig-zagging pattern with the three boxes. He raised his arms with a flourish and the audience erupted.

Valerie soon realized that Azalea was the real star of the show as Gordon Reno put her through one daring trick after another. Valerie's breath caught when he brought out a sword standing on end. As if casting a spell on her, he gently laid Azalea on the sword, chanting in a hypnotizing rhythm as her body fell lower and lower until the blade of the sword pierced completely through her flesh. An audible gasp escaped the crowd. Then, with precision, Gordon Reno repeated the same chants before raising Azalea up and helping her stand.

Azalea ended the performance with an acrobatic feat among the rafters that dazzled the audience, landing gracefully and giving a bow. "Let's hear it for my vunderful assistant, Azalea," Gordon Reno called, holding his arm out toward her. The audience roared. Ear-splitting whistles rent the building. "That is ze end of ze show. Thank you. Haf a goot eef-ning."

Valerie and Gage stood, along with the rest of the audience, for a lengthy ovation. When the crowd dispersed, Valerie bent to retrieve her handbag but Gage had already done so. Handing it to her, he lifted a brow. "I'm guessing you liked the show, judging from your beautiful smile?" The night air was still warm, but a gentle breeze was blowing as they left the building.

"I loved it." It had been a long time since she'd enjoyed an evening out with a handsome man. No checkbook to balance. No kids crying at her. No worries. "Thank you, Gage." She stood on her toes to plant a kiss on his cheek.

His eyes lit up and he wrapped his arm around her waist. "You're welcome." Gently, he pulled her toward him, his intention clear. People milled around them, the colors of their finery blurring in her vision as she focused on the man before her. His clean-shaven skin and dark, mysterious eyes drew her in like a homing device. A soft sigh escaped when his lips settled on hers. In that moment, she was exactly where she wanted to be.

Back in the Camaro, in the shadow of the streetlights, Gage looked over at Valerie. Soft music provided a nice ambience. He'd never seen her so relaxed or content. He was almost afraid to break the silence. "Valerie," he said, "there's one more place I'd like to take you, if you're up for it, before I take you home."

"Where?"

They'd crossed back into Mesa city limits some time ago and were now coming up on Main Street. "It's a surprise."

"The only place I can think of to visit around Main Street at this time of night is the temple." They both knew the Family History Center and Distribution Center, along with the other bookstores and shops around Main Street and First Avenue had long since closed.

"That's where we're heading." He couldn't resist grinning at her furrowed brows.

"Why?"

He shrugged nonchalantly. "Maybe I just want to visit the grounds."

If possible, her features creased even more. "But it's too dark to see the grounds. And the visitors' center is probably closed too. What are you up to, Gage Logan?"

Logan. Valerie Logan. He liked the sound. "You'll see." He parked the Camaro in the northwest parking lot by the visitors' center and came around to open her door. Holding his hand out to her, he asked softly, "Care to walk with me?"

Gage couldn't even begin to explain the enormous relief he'd felt from reading Pierce's one-word text message as they were finishing their dinner. *Done!* Knowing that his brother, who was busy with his own little family, had taken time from his wife and new daughter to perform this favor for Gage humbled him.

Gage wanted so much to hurry her along to the place where Pierce had hidden the surprise, but he knew that he needed to play it cool. The moonlight illuminated Valerie's questioning gaze. Not that he could blame her. The temple wasn't exactly a favorite hangout spot for Gage these days.

Finally, her face cleared and she tentatively took hold of his hand. Gage smiled in anticipation. He wasn't sure how much longer he could hold onto his patience. He led her past the reflective pool on the west side of the temple as they slowly walked the perimeter of the grounds, keeping the conversation light and their hands entwined. Gage's heartbeat sped up when they rounded the northeast corner of the temple. He led her to the stone bench located near the flower beds and water fountain, exactly where the photo sent from Pierce's phone indicated.

Gage leaned back slightly, feeling the tiny leaves of a potted fern brush up against the nape of his neck. As unobtrusively as possible, he reached behind him to feel around the base of the plant for the hidden object. His fingers brushed over something silky and smooth and he traced the curved edge just to be sure that it was really the object he was searching for. The fact that the object's color blended so well with the night was an added blessing. He brought his hand back into the pocket of his suit coat for just a moment.

Thankfully, Valerie didn't seem to notice his furtive movements. Extracting the small jeweler's box from his suit coat pocket, he slowly and carefully lowered it into the upturned hat. It was time to unveil his plan.

Valerie stared at Gage, absently wondering why he kept reaching behind him. Was it a nervous gesture or what?

His left hand found her right. With his other hand, he pulled a large, dark object out from behind his back and held it out to her. In the soft glow of the well-lit temple, Valerie could barely make out the shape of a—

Magician's hat?

Gage reached inside his suit coat and pulled out a magician's wand. He tapped the hat once. "Abracadabra, hocus pocus. I need you, my fair assistant, to pull the rabbit out of the hat for me."

What kind of silliness was this? A smile tugged at the corners of her lips. Cautiously, she lowered her hand into the cavity of the hat, aware that Gage watched her anxiously. She gasped when her fingers found a small square box inside. Shivers ran down her spine.

It wasn't!

Was it?

She lifted the lid. A diamond solitaire caught the reflection of the temple windows, radiating a prism of colors.

"Valerie Hall, I love you."

Valerie brought her hand to mouth. "You do?" she whispered.

He nodded. "Since you came back into my life, I've discovered a woman of strength and courage. A woman of compassion who has shared her testimony and given me hope for a better life."

Placing her hand over Gage's, she said, "I've only done what I would have wanted someone to do for me."

"You've done more than that. I feel like a new man because of you. I want to share my life with you and I hope that you feel the same. Would you do me the honor of becoming my wife?"

When she hesitated, he said in a rush, "I realize that you may not return my affection yet. But I think we could make a good match. We have a lot going for us. I am financially able to support a large family. I want to be a good husband to you and raise our children together."

Valerie's heart softened upon hearing the sincerity in his voice. It was admirable that he wanted to try, but could Gage, a long-time partyer, really change enough to stick a marriage with her and her children out? He'd been given a relatively easy child to raise. Could he handle Justin for the long term? He probably didn't realize the full extent of Justin's difficulties yet. "You've come a long way, Gage. But it's not as simple as you think."

Gage must have anticipated her objection because he said, "Justin would be welcome to live with us for as long as he needs to, though I feel that we should do everything we can to help him achieve the highest level of independence possible. But however his autism plays out over time, he'll always be an integral part of our family."

Tears clogged her throat from knowing that he genuinely wanted to make this work. "Wh-what about your inactivity in the Church, Gage?"

He smiled at her tenderly. "Valerie, honey, why is it that every time I lay my heart out, I make you cry? Is it really so hard for you to believe that I'm a nice guy?"

She swallowed hard. "No. But it has been a long time since someone has made me feel this way."

"Even though I can't come to church every week with you, I'll be there when I can. Please, Valerie. Give me some time to work this out. Hopefully, you can have your sealing to Nick cancelled by the time we marry."

His words brought hope. However, she wasn't sure if she could take such a risk. "Gage, that sounds wonderful. But are you sure you're ready for this step? I've known a few couples who were sealed in the temple only to get divorced a few years later. Marriage and parenthood aren't easy."

"And since I backed out of my mission call nine years ago and never returned to church, you're expecting me to do the same thing." The bluntness of his words cut through her heart. "I've made some bad choices in the past. But I'm in the process of repenting for those mistakes. Maybe someone like you, who has never lost your faith, might think those years were totally wasted. But they weren't. I've learned a lot about myself and I now know that what I want out of life can't be found in a nightclub."

"What does the Church mean to you, Gage?"

He paused to consider her question. "For the last nine years, the thought of going to Church was too painful, so I tried to block it out with other influences. But now I realize that without the Lord in my life, I can accomplish nothing."

"I feel the same way," she said softly.

Gage raised his hand to caress her face. "I honestly feel that He brought you back into my life at the point when I was finally ready to hear what He's been trying to tell me."

"Really?" she whispered, marveling at the Lord's timing.

He nodded. "I'm ready to take this step, Valerie. I want to marry you and have more children with you."

Just like that, Valerie's air supply dried up and she choked back a sob. *No, Gage,* she wanted to cry. She didn't want to talk about this right now.

Oblivious to her plight, Gage continued. "Valerie? I know you said you don't want to have more children. But I sincerely hope you'll consider the possibility. With me."

Oh, if only that *was* a possibility. But she knew better than to hope for a different outcome. "Gage, you know how I feel about that."

"I know what you told me. But I also heard what you didn't say. I'm not the only one with trust issues. Life didn't exactly turn out the way you planned. But you know what? I'm learning that the Lord usually has something better in store."

She pondered his words. "I'll have to pray about it."

He smiled. "I knew you were going to say that."

"Have you prayed about marrying me?"

He hesitated. "I haven't because it just feels right. But if you want me to, I will."

"I do want you to pray about it, Gage." Valerie paused and moved the diamond ring between her fingers. "I need some time to think and pray."

If he was disappointed about her cautious response, he didn't show it. "Take all the time you need."

Valerie was ecstatic when Gage made it to church for the third Sunday in a row. He cautioned her that his schedule would soon return to its normal craziness now that the All-Star Break was coming to a close. When Gage met with Bishop Gregory after church, the bishop encouraged Gage to call his dad. Apparently, during Gage's retelling of his father's rejection to his mission preparation and subsequent call, Bishop Gregory had sensed a lingering resentment toward Jared Logan for his callousness that Gage wasn't even aware he still harbored. He told the bishop that he would think about it.

He'd also mentioned to Bishop Gregory that he had proposed to Valerie and was giving her the time she needed. The bishop had counseled Gage to pray about it and if it was right, to be totally committed to the marriage not only in chastity but in his activity in the Church and devotion to his family.

Bishop Gregory had also kindly pointed out that Gage's job might be a hindrance to his progression in the gospel. Gage tried not to take offense at that. He loved his job. Though it was demanding, it was also very rewarding. Sure, he'd been juggling his time a lot more lately between taking care of Zach and spending time with Valerie. But all of that would subside once they got married, right? *If* they got married.

Very early the next morning, he drove to Tucson to pick up Zach. When Gage dropped him off at Valerie's before heading into work, Valerie seemed a bit tired and distracted and Whitney seemed out of sorts. Feeling certain that he'd made some good progress with Whitney on Saturday night, Gage sensed that her agitation stemmed from another source.

"What's eating at her?" Gage asked Valerie after Whitney stomped past them with a glare.

Valerie pinched the bridge of her nose in frustration. "She's angry with me."

"Why?"

"Because I don't prescribe to the same underhanded parenting methods as Nick. Apparently, Whitney has decided that going to church is pointless, especially since Nick took her out on his boat last Sunday with his girlfriend. I didn't even know he had a boat. We had a huge argument about it yesterday morning right before church. And then, to top it all off, she feels that I'm being too harsh by asking her to do her chores. As she put it, 'Daddy doesn't make me do anything!'"

"And you didn't know about the boating trip until yesterday?"

"No. I'm so upset, I could scream."

Gage pondered this before asking, "But what can you do about it? If he doesn't want to take her to church, then that's his choice, isn't it? Not that I agree with it," he said quickly when she looked like she was ready to argue. "I'm just trying to understand the legalities."

Valerie shook her head. "When we signed the divorce papers, it was agreed upon that whichever of us had Whitney for the weekend would take her to church. I guess I never considered the possibility that Nick might become inactive."

"Stand your ground." Hating the look of discouragement that came over her, Gage gently lifted her face toward his. "Be patient with Whitney while she figures things out. From what it sounds like, she's caught in the middle between two parents whose ideas and lifestyles are completely different."

"I know." She frowned. "I'm worried because Nick is making himself out to be the fun parent while I'm a fire-breathing dragon. She's too young to know the difference."

"Things will work out with her in time."

"But right now, she needs to know that skipping church and chores is not an option."

"I agree, at least during the time she's with you. And if you've got it in writing that Nick is supposed to take her to church too, then you've got a right to be that fire-breathing dragon."

"So what should I do?"

Gage thought about it for a moment. "Talk to Nick first. Then, if he's uncooperative, we'll call Noelle's father. He's an attorney who practices in family law. He'll be able to help you file a request for a modification of the custody agreement."

"All right."

He hugged Valerie, wishing that she would agree to become his wife. He wasn't foolish enough to believe that this would solve all their problems, but a marriage between them would give her some fighting powers that she didn't otherwise have. He was praying that she would soon come to the same conclusion.

The next morning, Valerie's phone rang as she was buckling the kids in the car for swim lessons. Glancing at the screen, Valerie grimaced when she saw that it was Nick. "Hello?"

"Val." His voice, which had once sounded pleasant to her ears when they were dating, was condescending now. "I need you to do me a favor. I want to take Whitney early this weekend."

"For what reason?"

"We're going to the White Mountains to stay with my girl-friend's family in their cabin."

"And is there a church nearby that you'll be attending?" she asked pointedly.

"There are several LDS church buildings in the outlying areas. But I'm not sure what Olivia's family is planning."

"You can plan on attending with her whether they are or not. And from now on, if you can't take her to church on your desig-nated weekend with Whitney, then I will be coming to get her," she declared, her voice rising with each word.

"Listen, Val." When he spoke like that, his voice oozing with false charm, Valerie wanted to grind her teeth. "I knew you would get all bent out of shape about the outing at the lake. We were bor-rowing a friend's boat. It was a one-time occurrence."

In the past, he had been able to sway her with his flattery, but now she recognized it for what it was. Manipulation. "You're right about that because I meant what I said. If you can't schedule these outings for more appropriate times, I will be contacting an attorney."

"Come on, Val. You can make an exception for Whitney. It isn't like she gets any attention at your house, anyway."

Valerie sucked in her breath. "Excuse me? What's that supposed to mean?"

"You've always ignored her and given more time to Justin than he deserved. That's how it was after he was born until the time you decided to leave. Whitney and I were never good enough for you."

"What are you talking about?" She'd had this same old argument time and again, yet she still couldn't unscramble his convoluted ideas.

"Come on, Val. Drop the act. You know that Whitney and I always took a backseat to that kid. You're still doing that now."

"Nick, get it through your head. Justin is a special needs child." She spoke very slowly and distinctly. "Special needs children naturally require more time and attention. And I didn't just walk out on our marriage. If you had been willing to give more of yourself to our son and help me out once in a while, we would still be married." She wondered why she was bothering to fight this same fight yet again, when a thought occurred to her. "Does Olivia even know that you have a son?"

"Of course she does," he replied. "But she agrees with me that kids like Justin have no practical sense or social skills. Frankly, he would just be in the way if we brought him along."

Which was just as well because Nick didn't even have the decency to keep the note of derision from his voice when speaking of his own flesh and blood. "You know, you can say it out loud, Nick. *Autistic.* It's neither a bad word nor a disease."

"This isn't the point of my call, Val. Are you going to let me take Whitney early this weekend or not?"

Valerie hesitated. While there was no solid reason to refuse

Nick, she hated giving in to him. "I guess. But I really need for you to take her to Eagar or Show Low for sacrament meeting, at least. I'll pack her a dress."

"All right then. I'll pick her up on Thursday morning."

"Can you pick her up Thursday afternoon instead? Her last swim lesson is in the morning."

"Fine," he growled. Valerie sighed. Nick Hall could be easy to work with as long as he called the plays, but the second a person crossed him, that person became his lifelong opponent. Lucky her.

An hour later, Valerie's disturbing conversation with her ex-husband was erased from her memory as she watched her little charges with pride. The kids had made enormous strides in improving their swimming skills. Whitney had learned the breaststroke and backstroke, and Justin and Zach were becoming more adept at swimming freestyle. The kids were chattering happily when she pulled into her grandparents' driveway. Parking the car, Valerie glanced up to say something to Whitney through the rearview mirror when she noticed that the front door was open. She peered at it closer, certain that it had been locked when they left. A feeling of unease crept up her spine. She told the kids to stay put.

Without stopping to think things through, she circled around to the back of the house, gasping when she saw shards of broken glass and dark red splotches dotting the concrete and grass. She stared at the back door, which also stood wide open, before her eyes darted to the cavernous hole in the window of the living room.

Peering through the window, Valerie gaped at the mess inside. More drops of blood soiled the carpet where the intruder, who'd apparently sliced a limb on the broken glass, had made his or her way into the living room and down the hallway toward the bedrooms.

Feeling sick, Valerie pulled her cell phone out of her pocket and dialed 911. In a shaky voice, she told them where she lived and gave the dispatcher the pertinent details. The dispatcher told her not to touch anything and to leave the property immediately as the intruder might still be there.

"Mommy, where are you?" Whitney's panicked voice sounded from far away.

Valerie turned to find the kids rounding the corner of the house. *Whitney must have helped the boys out of their seats belts.* Her heart dropped when they stopped to stare at the broken glass and blood. She was sure that the horror on their faces mirrored hers. "Watch where you step. Let's get back in the car."

Valerie's paralyzed brain could only think of one person to call. Her hands shook as she brought up his number.

She managed one word before the tears fell. "Gage?"

Gage stared at the disturbing scene in stunned silence. The trail of blood, which led directly into Valerie's bedroom where the intruder had upturned her mattress and rifled through her belongings, turned his stomach. Feminine clothing was strewn in every direction, making his blood boil.

The diamond teardrop earrings she'd worn on their date were now history as well as the rest of her jewelry. In a valiant effort to stave off the hysteria that he knew was settling in, Valerie jokingly claimed, "It's okay. Most of my jewelry came from Nick anyway." Gage enfolded her in his arms.

"Everything's okay now. You're safe." When Valerie had called him at work, Gage had had a premonition of sorts since she almost never called him there. He had arrived at the Skylars' house to find Valerie and the kids in the car with the engine running. In a jumble of "bad guy" and "broke into our house," Whitney, Justin, and Zach alternately told him the story he'd already pieced together on the phone. Gage let them talk their excitement out for a while. Then he quieted them down and said a prayer of gratitude for Heavenly Father's protection that day.

When the police arrived with their flashing lights and asked

Valerie to accompany them inside the house to take a closer look at the damage, Gage turned to the kids. "Who wants to go for ice cream?"

Whitney's lips trembled as she asked, "But what about Mommy?"

"She's with the policemen now so she's safe. We'll let her talk to them and come back in a little while."

Valerie was still inside the house when they returned. The wait seemed to take forever. "The police dusted for fingerprints and took a blood sample, although they cautioned me that it was probably too small to test for DNA," Valerie informed him as she met him outside. Her voice sounded a little calmer now. "Even then, if the burglar's blood isn't in the system . . ."

"They'll never catch the thief," Gage finished.

"At least nothing else is missing. The burglar left the flat screen television and my laptop alone."

Emerging from the house, Officer Jordan added, "In all likelihood, Mrs. Hall, the perp was watching your movements and knew you wouldn't be gone long."

"Watching me?" Valerie's eyes dilated to round saucers. Her face was white. "You think he knew where I was going?"

"He?" Gage echoed in alarm. Taking hold of her elbow, he led her to a nearby wicker chair and knelt next to her. "Who, Valerie?"

Gage had the feeling she wasn't really seeing him as she whispered, "Nick. He and I argued right before we left for swim lessons." Gage abruptly stood and flexed his fingers. He wanted to hit something.

The policemen soon left with a reminder to be safe and that they'd be in touch. Valerie took a shuddering breath. "I'll call Chloe and ask her to take the kids for the afternoon. There's so much stuff to clean up."

"I'll help you."

As soon as Chloe pulled up in her minivan, she got out and hugged Valerie. "I'm so glad you're safe. What's the damage?" While Valerie updated her, Gage patiently answered the kids' questions. Yes, the police would find the burglar. (He hoped.) No, nobody else's houses were broken into. Yes, they would be at Aunt Chloe's house for the duration of the afternoon. No, Whitney's dolls and Justin's car collection hadn't been touched. Neither had their bikes, including Justin's specially made model that Valerie's parents had given him for his birthday.

Gage peered at Valerie to see how she was holding up. The children's toys might not have been taken, but her sense of security had.

And that wasn't something that could easily be found again.

After Chloe loaded the children into her car and left, Valerie turned to Gage with such a defeated expression that he couldn't have stayed away if he tried. She threw herself into Gage's arms and wept. He stood there as solid as stone, holding her, hoping to give her comfort.

"Valerie? Gage?" They pulled away upon hearing Brande Levington's voice as she and John came through the back door. Brande's stricken face silently assessed the mess before she met her daughter's gaze. "Honey, I'm so sorry."

She came up to Valerie and hugged her. "Thanks," Valerie said.

Valerie and her mom swept up the broken glass and mopped the tile floor; then they packed some clothing for the children while Gage and John boarded up the shattered window and carefully picked up the shards of glass outside.

"Brande's parents are due to arrive two weeks from now," John Levington said as they worked together.

Gage raised his eyebrows. "That soon, huh?" Valerie hadn't told him that. And she still didn't have a place to live. He hadn't wanted to rush her with her decision, but he now felt a greater urgency.

John leveled a look toward Gage. He lowered his voice so that the women couldn't hear him. "Valerie is trying not to show it, but she's pretty shaken up over this."

How well Gage knew it. He remembered her shivering in his

arms a few hours ago. "She'll get through it. I'm amazed by all that she's accomplished on her own."

John nodded his agreement. "Always feels like she needs to prove something to us. That divorce sure did a number on her, as if we would think less of her for divorcing Nick."

As long as they were being frank with one another, Gage felt that he should level with John. "The thing is, she doesn't have to do this alone anymore. I've asked your daughter to marry me."

"I know. She told us."

"And?" Gage prodded when no further comment was made.

John brought his hammer down and looked at Gage steadily. "You're a good man, son. And I have no doubt that you'll be a good husband and father to Valerie and her children. But were you serious when you told her you'd marry her in the temple?"

"As soon as Valerie gets her sealing to Nick canceled, we'll be ready. That's a promise."

John must have heard the sincerity in his voice because he nodded his consent. "We'll get the ball rolling on that and welcome you into the family, provided that Valerie agrees to marry you."

Valerie opted to stay the night with her parents after she and Gage picked their children up from Chloe's house and Gage and Zach went home. All entrances to her grandparents' house were secured along with the window. But Valerie didn't feel very secure there.

Her mother helped her put Whitney and Justin to bed, at which point Valerie was able to take a much-needed hot, soothing soak in the tub. Donning a fluffy robe she'd borrowed from her mom over her nightgown, she went downstairs to fix a bowl of ice cream. Yes, she was splurging on calories, but after a day like this, she was trying to hold onto her last shred of sanity.

She blushed as she remembered Gage's departing kiss. He had no qualms about kissing her right in front of her parents. Knowing grins graced their lips as she and Gage parted. Maybe they knew something she didn't.

But you do know, her conscience whispered to her. *Gage is the man you love.* Valerie had known it in that moment when she'd called him at work. He was the one person she wanted there in her time of need.

As she ate her ice cream, Valerie's mind automatically replayed the day's events again and again. She was glad the intruder had ended up getting hurt rather than them, she thought darkly.

Forcing those morose thoughts from her mind, Valerie recalled the conversation she had with her father a few hours ago as he had put his hand out to stop her from leaving after finishing her dinner. "Valerie, may I talk to you for a few minutes?"

"Sure, Dad." She'd followed him to the back porch where they sat watching the sun set on a very long day. The pinks and oranges of the horizon refreshed her downtrodden spirit, reminding her of the evening she and Gage had spent at Tempe Town Lake.

"Valerie, I've had a chance to talk to Gage. I believe he's sincere when he says that he wants to marry you and be sealed in the temple. If this hold-up is a matter of you not loving him, then I can certainly understand that. But your mother and I both think that you do."

Valerie took her time answering. "I do love him, Dad. He's a great guy and has become a wonderful father to Zach."

"I believe he would be a good husband to you."

Valerie sighed. "I know. Like he said, we really do balance each other."

"So what's the problem? Are you nervous about taking on his son permanently?"

"No. Zach's a great kid. He and Justin get along really well."

"What are you afraid of then?"

"I've already gone through one divorce. I don't want to go through another." She decided not to tell him about Gage wanting more children. She figured if or when the time was right to do so, the Lord would let her know. For now, she could only cross one bridge at a time.

"You're afraid that Gage won't stick it out?" John asked gently.

"He's told me over and over that he's changed. But . . . how do I know for sure?"

"Have you prayed about it?"

Valerie nodded. "A few times. But I haven't received an answer yet."

"The answer will come when the time is right."

"Justin told me a few weeks ago that Gage would be his new dad. How could he know that when I don't even know it?"

"Hmm." He stroked his chin thoughtfully. "It seems to me that special needs children often see things we overlook. Could be that Justin is closer to the Spirit than you are at times. What else did he say?"

"That was it. He said it as a matter of fact. I was so thrown by it that I almost crashed my car."

"What happened after that?"

"Nothing."

"Are you sure?" John regarded her carefully. "Think back to that time. What did you tell Justin?"

"I started to explain that Gage couldn't be his dad, but I—I . . ." Valerie stopped midsentence when she remembered what had occurred next.

"What is it, sweetheart?"

Her heart beat rapidly. "When I began to dismiss his idea as a foolish notion, a warm feeling spread through me, like I was on fire. With all that's happened lately, I haven't thought about it since then."

"That could be the answer." They were both silent for a few minutes as they watched the sun slowly sink into the horizon. The crickets started their nightly chirping as the night air gradually cooled. "Pray about Gage's proposal again tonight, all right?"

Valerie was quiet as she lifted herself off the wicker chair. "All right, Dad. I will. Good night." She kissed his cheek.

When she reached the back door, her father called out softly, "Valerie."

"Yes, Dad?"

He smiled at her kindly. "I've learned through the years that when you want to know if taking a certain step in your life is the right thing to do, asking a yes or no question helps."

She returned his smile. "Thanks, Dad."

After a restless night and subsequent morning in which Gage had worried endlessly over Valerie, he brought Zach over to her parents' house earlier than usual to check on her and the kids. Valerie was already waiting at the door. Gage breathed a sigh of relief knowing that she was safe. Maybe it had been foolish to think that something might happen to her here, of all places, but the robbery had been nerve-racking for everyone involved.

Valerie greeted them and led Zach down the hallway to find Whitney and Justin. She then turned to Gage seriously. Backing up a few steps, she reached for the magician's hat that he hadn't noticed sitting on a decorative case. When had she snatched that from the house?

"I need to hand this back to you," she said solemnly.

His heart plummeted. "Okay." Gingerly taking it from her, he swallowed hard, not quite sure what to say.

"There's a rabbit in there."

Of all the things he'd expected her to say, that was probably the last. "What?"

A tiny smile peeked out from her serious expression. "You know . . . the rabbit that magicians pull from their hats? Look inside."

His sleep-deprived brain finally caught on to her meaning as he eagerly peered into the hat and thrust his hand into it to grab the white slip of paper, cut into the shape of rabbit's head, within. One word had been written in bold pink letters: *YES!*

"Are you sure?" And of all the things he wanted to say, that was possibly the most idiotic.

But Valerie didn't seem to mind. "Absolutely. I love you, Gage. I finally know what I want too. And I'm ready to take that journey with you."

Gage didn't waste any time. He poured all the love he felt for her into his kiss. When they finally came up for air, they were both breathing hard. "So what changed your mind about us, sweetheart?"

"The Lord answered my prayer last night. I felt the Spirit so strongly when I asked Heavenly Father if I should marry you. It feels right to me too."

"In that case . . ." He pulled the jewelry box out of his pocket and placed the ring on her finger.

Valerie's eyes bulged. "Wow. Were you really that confident that I would say yes right now?"

"No. But a funny thing happened when I was getting ready to leave. The thought came to my mind to grab the ring. I almost forgot about it as I finished helping Zach get ready. But then the thought came again just before we went out the door. So I stuffed it in my pocket, thinking I must be losing my mind to take it with me to work. I think this means we're on the same page now, doesn't it?"

She grinned happily. "It sure does."

Gage and Valerie waited apprehensively inside the Skylars' home with Whitney by the window for Nick to pick her up on Thursday after finishing swim lessons. The boys were in a back bedroom playing. In light of the events of Tuesday, Gage wasn't about to let Valerie face her ex-husband alone, especially considering Whitney's occasional outbursts expressing fear of "the bad man" coming again. Nick parked his convertible behind Gage's Camaro and Whitney lugged her overnight bag outside to meet him.

"That's odd," Valerie said, puckering her brows. "Nick's not getting out of his car to help Whitney, the way he usually does."

Gage squeezed her hand. "I'll help her."

As he approached the car, he noticed Nick rapidly drumming the fingers of his right hand on the steering wheel, as if the guy was anxious to be on his way. A little too anxious, perhaps? His left arm hung down by his side, hidden from Gage's view through the tinted window that was rolled a quarter of the way down. Gage would sure love to see if that hand sported a large bandage.

"Hi, there," Gage said lightly. "I see you didn't get out to help Whitney with her bag. Feeling a bit tired today?"

Nick's eyes narrowed. "Who's asking?"

Before Gage could answer, Valerie spoke. "My fiancé." Gage

wrapped his arm possessively around her shoulders as she stepped beside him.

Nick looked sharply from one to the other. "Your what?"

"You heard her," Gage said, struggling to keep his tone even. "We expect you to bring Whitney home on time. And in one piece. Her safety is important to us."

Instead of acknowledging Gage, Nick sneered at Valerie. "Is this guy for real, Val?"

Valerie stiffened. "Listen, Nick, we're all a little on edge because we had a break-in earlier this week. We're letting you know so that you'll be able to calm Whitney down if she becomes upset."

"A break-in?" With an inquisitive look, Nick glanced past Gage and Valerie to the house beyond. "Here? Wow, that's too bad."

"And we'd appreciate it if you'd give us a call in the event that she does. After all, our greatest concern should be for the welfare of our children, right?" Gage leveled his glare at the man who had made Valerie's life so difficult. If he tried any more tricks like he'd done in the past, Nick would answer to him. And Gage wanted to make sure the jerk knew it.

When at last Nick's gaze slid away from Gage's, followed by a thick swallow, Gage knew his message had been received.

After continual meetings with Bishop Ames (whom Bishop Gregory referred Gage to as the bishop of Gage's ward) and with his endorsement of Gage's renewed commitment to the gospel, the Logan and Levington families came together for Gage and Valerie's sealing in the Mesa Arizona Temple. For Justin's sake, they wanted to keep it low-key. When Valerie warned Gage that the stress of planning a large affair would likely push Justin to the limit, Gage agreed. "You won't hear me complaining," he said with a grin. "I can hardly wait."

Heat crept up her neck. "I feel the same way," she admitted softly. He was aware that it had taken Valerie this long since the burglary to feel safe enough to venture out alone on her shopping trips and other outings. In fact, her mom finally convinced her just a few days before the wedding to shop for a gown. Luckily, she found one near her size that Brande was able to hem.

Of course, all those practical reasons for marrying Valerie completely fled Gage's mind when he knelt before her at the altar. There, in the celestial room, surrounded by family, gazing at the woman he loved, this moment was forever etched in his soul. Looking into Valerie's eyes, he knew she felt the same way.

Later, when the wedding guests were gathered at Sarah and Eric's home, Gage's father and stepmother approached the happy couple. After Tamara squeezed Gage for all she was worth, he hugged his father awkwardly. "Hey, Dad," he asked, "would it be okay for Valerie and me to bring the kids for a visit later when base-ball season winds down?"

His dad's eyes lit up in anticipation. "That would be more than okay."

"We'd like to get to know your little bunch," Tamara added happily.

"I want them to get to know you too. We're also planning on taking the kids to Disneyland."

They both agreed that a short getaway would be better for their peace of mind and Justin's well-being than an extended honey-moon. Yet Gage wouldn't tell Valerie what he'd planned until he'd whisked her away from the crowd. Saying good-bye to Whitney, Justin, and Zach had been difficult, to say the least. "I wanna come with you," Justin whined.

"Shh, Justin," Whitney said. "Don't be such a bawl baby. Mom and Gage will be back in a few days. And we get to stay with Grandma and Grandpa."

Valerie looked at Gage, not sure what to say. Since that day almost three years ago when she and Nick returned home from Tahiti, Valerie had never been away from her son overnight. But the time had come to give him some growing room and enjoy time alone with her new husband.

"Justin, remember what we talked about." She bent down to his level. "You're a big boy and can handle this. When Gage and I get back, we'll do something fun together as a family."

"Hey, buddy." Gage stretched his arm to Justin for a fist bump. "I need you to be my helper. Zach is gonna be with you in a strange house with a new grandma and grandpa he doesn't know yet. He might feel lonely at times. Can you help him out?"

Justin's brow slashed downward as he pulled his head toward the floor. "Yeah, I guess."

"Justin," Gage said, waiting with his fist out. "Look at me."

Slowly, Justin raised his head. After another moment, he raised his fist to meet Gage's. "How many days are your mom and I going to be gone?"

He held up four fingers. "Four."

"All right, son. I knew you could do it. Remember—four days. Be my helper, okay? Make me proud."

Justin's face broke out into a huge grin. "I will."

"All right." After Valerie exchanged big hugs with both boys and Whitney, Gage gently pulled Valerie away.

Valerie and Gage enjoyed four of the most glorious days of their lives in Sedona. Valerie had never had much of an opportunity to explore the tourist town. They visited an art gallery and watched a pottery-making demonstration. Valerie laughed when the demonstrator invited her to give it a try. Hers turned out looking nothing like his. Early in the morning of their last full day in Sedona, Gage woke Valerie up with a long kiss. "Wake-up call, sleepyhead. We've got to get ready."

"For what?" she asked, her eyesight coming into focus. Gage was smiling down at her tenderly.

"It's a surprise." He bent down to kiss her again.

Several moments later, when they were both breathless, Gage broke away. "As tempting as it is to stay here this morning, I really think you're going to love what I've planned. Let's get up and get going. They'll be here soon to shuttle out us out to the landing spot."

"Landing spot?" she echoed in disbelief.

"Yeah. I hope you're not afraid of heights."

That made two of them. "Gage Logan, what did you sign us up for?"

"Oh," he said with a shrug, "nothing too spectacular. Just a hot air balloon ride with a catered picnic afterward." His boyish grin was contagious.

"Wow! Trying to impress your wife, are you?"

He quirked an eyebrow. "Is it working?"

With a flirtatious smile, she said, "Sure thing."

Gage's eyes turned to molten chocolate just before he kissed her again and in that moment, Valerie knew she'd never regret marrying this handsome, wonderful guy.

Gage's and Valerie's blissful honeymoon ended all too soon. Upon picking up the kids from her parents' house, they heard an earful from Whitney about Justin crying the entire first day they were gone. Grandma had come to the rescue, though, when she lassoed three helpers to bake chocolate chip cookies. All in all, Justin's reaction had been about what Valerie had expected.

Valerie's grandparents, who had returned home from their mission before the wedding, reported in their ward. As she sat with her children in sacrament meeting, looking at all the familiar faces, Valerie was saddened to realize this was her last Sunday with them. Valerie had grown to love these good people who had treated them with such kindness and respect.

Before their wedding, Gage had helped Valerie pack most of her belongings and move them to his house. Now that the task of unpacking lay before her, she was anxious to settle into her new home. Whitney and Justin immediately sorted through their toys to see if another burglary had occurred at their new home while they were gone. "It's going to take them some time to adjust," Gage observed.

Gage and Valerie and the kids began attending their new ward as a family. However, Whitney was now wavering in her desire to attend church, largely due to her father's penchant for taking off somewhere every weekend with his girlfriend. Nick's claim that it had been a one-time occurrence had been false. Valerie kept arguing with Nick about it, but it didn't seem to do any good.

"We're finished playing these games with him," Gage said to Valerie. "Let's call the attorney and get the ball rolling to end Nick's visitations, since he isn't holding up his end of the custody agreement."

Perhaps the most strenuous adjustment was the one that Gage was making in living with such a rambunctious crew. In spite of Valerie's warning, Gage acknowledged that Justin's disorder was more complicated than his public behavior indicated.

"Why does Justin do that?" Gage asked Valerie in a low tone one evening as the family sat down to watch a video. He gestured toward Justin, who was flapping his arms like wings and shuffling around the room making the sounds of a crow.

Valerie looked over to the television screen where an animated crow was emitting a sign of distress to the evil witch in the Disney movie. She replied, "Justin often becomes so engrossed in what he's watching that he literally forgets where he is."

Gage's eyes widened in awe. "He immerses himself in the action so completely that he loses his sense of reality?"

She nodded solemnly. "He has a difficult time distinguishing between fantasy and reality—much more so than the average child. Sometimes it's difficult to bring him back into the real world."

Once the school year began, Gage was in for another shock when he noticed Valerie following Justin around each morning as he got ready for school. She helped him pick out his clothes. Then she made sure he sat down to eat breakfast in a timely manner. She helped him tie his shoes. Then brush his teeth and comb his hair. And finally grab his backpack.

The third morning he saw her do this, he waylaid her in the hallway. "Sweetheart, surely Justin can do that stuff on his own by now."

She shook her head tersely. "Justin has difficulty monitoring himself because he usually gets too distracted. I have to keep him on task in order for him to be ready for school on time."

After thinking the problem through, Gage suggested that they install some shelving in Justin's bedroom to help him organize his stuff. With the help of Justin's speech teacher, they also implemented a picture chart to help him get ready for school each morning.

The time had come for the bedrooms to be painted. Dinosaurs for Zach and cars for Justin. Flowers with whimsical fairies dotted Whitney's room. The project soon took on a life of its own as more paint ended up on each other than on the walls. They were all laughing at how silly each other looked with blue-specked hair and green-streaked cheeks by the time they were finished. Gage shrugged sheepishly. "We may not be the Brady Bunch or the Von Trapp singers, but we are definitely making this blended family real."

"Yeah, real something," Valerie joked. "I'm not sure what, though."

"Real. As in genuine. This is the real deal. And I love it."

Coming home from work one evening, Gage discovered his extensive baseball card collection lying askew on the floor of Justin's bedroom. Several cards had been bent or torn. "Justin!" he thundered, growing angrier by the second as he waited for Justin to appear.

Valerie came running down the hallway instead. "What's the matter?" The self-explanatory evidence stopped her in her tracks. Her face turned white. "Please tell me Justin didn't do this."

"Who else would have done it?" he exclaimed. "Zach leaves my stuff alone. Whitney would have no interest in them. They're in his bedroom, for crying out loud!"

"Gage, I'm so sorry." She began sorting the cards into stacks that were still in good condition and those that were too far gone to keep. "I unpacked a few more boxes this afternoon. I didn't see him get into your things. I'll keep a closer eye on him from now on."

"You can't follow him around every minute of the day, Valerie. He's going to have to learn that certain things are off-limits." He knelt to help her. Picking a card up, he growled in frustration. "See this?" He thrust a card before her face. "That's a Billy Germaine rookie card. He was the star player of the 1989 World Series between the Oakland A's and the San Francisco Giants. He later admitted to using steroids along with Tim Davis." At least this one and a few others were in a protective cover. He rattled off more commentary about the players of the past as he picked up more cards.

Valerie was thoughtful as she handed her pile of cards to him. "Why don't you go through them and lock the valuable ones away and give some of the less valuable ones to Zach and Justin? Maybe you can help them start their own card collections. They would like that."

"Sure, but in the meantime, we need to talk to Justin about leaving my things alone."

"We'll do that," she said calmly, "and I'll try my best to keep an eye on him. But you do realize that we're not going to be able to keep him out of everything, don't you?"

Gage wanted to argue the point, but Valerie's penitent look pierced him. He sighed. "Yeah. I know."

"We'll keep our bedroom door locked and our most valuable possessions out of reach."

A sinking feeling settled in the pit of his stomach. His family was his most valued possession. "I'm sorry for getting so upset. I'll take the boys to pick out some cards of their own."

"I'm sure that Whitney would like to be included as well."

"Baseball cards for Whitney? I can't see it."

She answered with an enigmatic grin. "Maybe not yet, but you will."

Valerie woke with a start. The weather was turning cooler with the onset of October. On this particularly chilly night, with the wind howling outside, Valerie entered the kitchen in her nightgown and heated a mug of water in the microwave, yawning. She had fallen asleep but, in following the pattern of the past five nights, had woken upon hearing Gage's car pull into the garage. Though she'd tried to be supportive, there was no getting around it. Gage's crazy schedule was getting to her, interrupting her sleep patterns to the point where Valerie often felt so drowsy during the day that she crashed on the couch for thirty minutes each afternoon.

Valerie was steeping some chamomile tea when Gage entered the house through the kitchen, looking as tired as she.

Gage walked inside the house, wondering why the kitchen light was on, when he saw his wife sitting on the opposite side of the countertop. Her hair was slightly mussed and dark half-moons shown beneath her eyes. Still, the sight of Valerie in her nightgown kicked his pulse into an uneven rhythm. "Honey, what's the matter?"

She took a sip of what looked like herbal tea from a mug. Valerie yawned. "I'm having a hard time sleeping lately."

One look at her sunken eyes and he knew. "It's because of me, isn't it?"

She sighed. "I'm not trying to complain. I know you love your job, but I guess I haven't gotten used to your schedule yet. How do you do it for six months out of the year?"

Six months only covered the Diamondbacks' regular season. Wisely, he refrained from telling her that Spring Training was just as crazy. "It's a difficult schedule. But for me, it's never been a big deal because I was able to sleep late every morning. Now that I have a family—"

"—with rowdy kids who wake up insanely early," Valerie inserted.

A brief smile quirked his lips. "I'll admit I'm getting a little tired."

Valerie yawned again. "And without your caffeine fix, you're getting a little grumpy."

It was true. He'd given up coffee quite quickly, which had been a miracle. And energy drinks were not to his liking. So without a pick-me-up each morning, Gage was now struggling to function.

Gage ran his hand over his face, feeling the beginning of whiskers forming. "The season is almost over, Valerie. Hang in there for a few more weeks, okay? And that's only if the D-Backs make the playoffs." Right now they were going head-to-head in a wild pennant race.

"By the time I get used to your late schedule, it will change," she predicted. "Is there another position in the organization that would be less demanding of your time?"

"Yes, but most of the jobs I'm interested in doing entail being at the games. It's just like you said, Valerie. I love my job. I don't think I'll ever get tired of it."

Valerie lifted one shoulder. "I'm just saying that maybe there's a job with the Diamondbacks that would be more suitable to family life. And to church life too."

"Maybe but I'm not interested in those jobs." The D-Backs Foundation had, in fact, branched out in many outreach programs, and Gage was quickly moving up in the organization. His boss had been dropping hints concerning a possible promotion in the marketing department. He told her as much, adding, "Let's just wait and see what happens."

"And if you don't get the promotion, will you think about applying for another job or at least look into transferring into a different department?"

She was asking a lot of him. They both knew it. If there was a way to satisfy both of them, only the Lord knew. "Let's pray about it."

The Diamondbacks lost the seventh game to the Dodgers in a thrilling series. Gage, along with the entire team and crew, mourned the agonizing defeat. Gage completed his suite rental totals and end-of-the-season reports, looking forward to the vacation in San Diego his family had planned. Whitney and Justin were thrilled to be taken out of school for the occasion.

Gage sensed Valerie's nervousness increasing the farther they traveled. There hadn't been time for much conversing at the wedding and Valerie had only known Gage's dad as an aloof business tycoon while growing up. "Everything will be all right. My dad has completely changed from the time you knew him."

"Has he?" she asked as they pulled up in front of his father's five-thousand-square-foot mansion.

"You'll see."

Whitney and Zach exclaimed over the size of the house while Justin stared at it in wonder. Valerie shifted her weight from one hip to the other as they rang the doorbell. Gage threaded his fingers through hers to stop the trembling.

Jared and Tamara Logan promptly answered. After Tamara smothered Gage and Valerie in a gigantic hug, Valerie leaned over to whisper frantically in Gage's ear, "I just worry about Justin."

Gage whispered back, "Don't worry. He'll be fine."

Tamara hugged Whitney and Zach quite enthusiastically before her eyes landed on the five-year-old. "Hello, Justin. It's nice to see you again. How are you?" She carefully modulated her voice, which admittedly, was quite a feat for the older woman.

A lengthy pause followed. "Fine." Sure enough, his eyes were focused on the floor again.

Amazingly enough, Tamara seemed to sense that Justin was finished conversing for the time being and turned her attention back to the group as a whole. "Come on in, y'all. We're going to have us a good ol' time."

Valerie and the kids were struck speechless at the gorgeous layout of the rooms. Upstairs, an entertainment room boasted a supersized flat-screen television along with a video game console and a ping-pong table in the corner.

Zach was practically jumping up and down with excitement. "Cool. Look, Dad. Grandma and Grandpa Logan have all the fun games."

Gage smiled and said, "Yeah, Zach. I knew you'd like that."

Jared Logan chuckled. "Like father, like son."

Gage did a double take. "Really?"

"Definitely. High energy. Excited about life. Just like you were at that age."

Before everything changed. The unspoken words hung in the air between them.

"You must be tired, sugar," Tamara said to Valerie, breaking the awkward silence. "Let me show ya'll to your rooms."

She led Gage and Valerie to a bedroom complete with a reading nook, a king-sized bed, and a set of French doors that led out to a balcony. "Oh, my," Valerie breathed as she took in the spectacular view of the mountains in the distance along with the beautiful gardens below.

Gage glanced at the swimming pool, noting with relief that the cover was safely installed to keep excitable non-swimmers out of harm's way.

Though she was very different from their own mothers, Tamara brought her own special brand of magic to being a grandparent. Literally. Perhaps sensing that Whitney needed some extra loving, the two of them spent hours in Tamara's craft room with their supplies spread out everywhere. Nobody knew exactly what they were up to. Upon asking, they were promptly shooed away with the admonition that it was a surprise.

Later that evening, after dinner had been served and their craft supplies had been cleared away, Tamara and Whitney announced to the family that they would be presenting a magic show. Whitney, wearing a magician's hat made from construction paper and a cape that had been sewn with red and black felt, announced, "For my first trick, I will make a coin disappear." She directed the group's attention to a table with a sheet of paper and a clear plastic cup. From her pocket, Whitney pulled out a quarter and placed it on the paper. Carefully grasping the cup, she placed it on the coin and covered the cup with a small handkerchief. "Abracadabra!" When she lifted first the cloth, and then the cup, the quarter was gone.

Tamara cued the rest of the family in to applaud Whitney's first "trick."

Next, Whitney grabbed a paper bag that she'd set off to the side. "Now I will transform a toad into a prince. But first, I want to tell you a story." Whitney pulled a plastic toad out from the bag and showed it to her audience.

"There once was a fair maiden who was walking sadly down the road and spotted a toad. She said, 'Oh, Toad. I don't know what to do. You see, I was at this ball where a handsome prince was meeting all the eligible maidens in his kingdom. For you see, his father the king decreed that the prince needed to find a wife. Then this beautiful woman named Cinderella walked in and the prince took one look at her and forgot about everyone else but her. I've had my heart set on marrying a prince since I was a little girl. Can you help me?'

"Then the toad said, 'Why don't you kiss me and find out?'

"The lady said, 'Okay.' And she did." Whitney kissed the toad and placed it back in the bag while finishing her story. "As soon as she kissed the toad, POOF!" Whitney closed the bag and popped it like a balloon. She then pulled a plastic figurine of a handsome prince from the bottom of the bag. It was magic!

The family clapped their hands enthusiastically. While Whitney had her back toward the audience to prepare her final trick, Gage whispered in Valerie's ear, "Wow! Combining two fairy tales into one. And thinking about boys already. I can see what I'm up against in the years to come."

Valerie playfully smacked his arm and leaned over to whisper back. "You'll be fine. She's a great kid." They shared a knowing smile.

Whitney then turned back around and said, "Finally, for my last trick, I'm going to make this toothpick disappear into thin air." All of them could clearly see the toothpick she held up in her closed hand. Thrusting her hand toward her brother, she called, "Justin, catch!" Justin flinched, obviously expecting the toothpick to come flying his way.

"Wait! Where did it go?" Turning this way and that, he searched the floor around his seat.

"Whoa! It disappeared!" Zach gasped.

"It's magic," Tamara said in a stage whisper.

"Want me to make it reappear?" Whitney asked. They all clamored their consent.

Whitney then made a motion with her hand as if she were snatching the toothpick out of the air. Suddenly, it was in her closed hand again. "How did you do that?" Justin asked after Whitney bowed and they all applauded.

With a grin, she twisted her hand around to reveal the toothpick stuck to her thumb with a piece of tape. Impressive. The boys jumped out of their seats to ask Whitney how she had made the coin disappear and turned the toad into the prince. While Whitney was showing them the secrets behind her magic tricks, Valerie asked Gage, "How did Tamara know about our ongoing magic theme?"

"When she asked me what the kids would like to do while they were here, this idea came to mind. She looked for some magic tricks online and called me later to tell me about them. They were perfect, weren't they?"

"Absolutely." When Valerie smiled like that, Gage had a hard time remembering where he was. He loved seeing her—and their daughter—so happy.

Gage and Valerie took their bunch to Disneyland on the second day they were there, being mindful of Justin's limitations. When it seemed he'd had enough stimulation and was getting a little antsy, they left, promising to use their two-day passes again.

Jared and Tamara took them to the beach the next day for a picnic lunch and to let the kids play and explore. When the boys started wandering a little too far off for Valerie's comfort, she stood to follow them.

Gage squeezed her shoulder. "Sit down and relax. I'll follow along."

Valerie nodded and resumed her conversation with her in-laws while Gage tagged after the boys, giving them the distance they needed to feel a sense of independence while still keeping them in his sight. He soon became aware of someone walking behind him. Turning to see his father, he said, "Thanks for putting up with us, Dad. I know we're a noisy bunch."

Jared shook his head. "Not at all. You have a really great family, son, although I never imagined that you would someday marry John and Brande's daughter. I'm amazed and pleased by the fact that we'll be sharing grandchildren."

Gage mumbled, "Um, yeah." He wasn't about to tell his dad that he and Valerie would unlikely have any more, if Valerie had her way.

"Maybe some time you'll tell me just how you came back into the Church. I'd like to hear more."

Gage looked at him in surprise. In the past, that sentence

would probably have come out sounding more like a demand than a request. "It's because of Valerie," he responded lightly. "I know that the Lord worked a miracle in my life when He brought her back into it."

"Son, there's something I've been meaning to talk to you about, but it wasn't something that could be said over the phone or at your wedding."

"What's that?"

"Your mother brought something to my attention that happened a long time ago but that may still be causing some discord between us." At Gage's raised brow, he continued, "She mentioned that you felt slighted when you were preparing to serve your mission and my thoughtless behavior at the time dissuaded you from accepting the call."

Gage shook his head. "That was a long time ago, Dad. I don't want to rehash the past. My bishop has helped me to come to terms with the decisions I made."

"Forgiving yourself is one of the most important things you can do after seeking the Lord's forgiveness. However, Gage, I'm also asking your forgiveness. I was so wrapped up in my selfishness that I couldn't see how badly I hurt you."

Gage's heart ached. "It's okay, Dad. I just want to forget it and move on."

His dad smiled. Though slightly more wrinkled, Gage couldn't remember a time when his features had been so gentle. "I want that too. I think we've wasted enough time with regrets."

Gage and Valerie took the kids to Disneyland again on their last full day of vacation, wearing them out in the process. That night, after Gage had laid Zach down on his bed, he and Valerie stayed up to play a game of Monopoly with Jared and Tamara. The women found they were no match for the Logan men and soon gave up, heading into the kitchen to prepare some snacks. At eleven o'clock, an exhausted Valerie kissed Gage good night and left him to play it out with his father and Tamara, who said good night soon after.

Gage thought he was just coming out the victor when his dad surprised him with a sudden comeback. At half past midnight, they called a truce. As they were cleaning up the game, Jared said, "So tell me more about Valerie. How did the two of you meet again?"

Gage told his dad about the role Valerie had played in helping Gage to put the broken pieces of his and Zach's lives back together after April's death. Jared asked about Valerie's children. Although Gage had already given him a partial summary of his Valerie's struggles, tonight he shared them in greater detail. "I'm telling you this because we all need to be on the same page. Valerie has gone through so much with Justin, mainly because people don't under-stand. As her new family, we need to be patient and supportive. We already had one incident with Pierce and Noelle when Justin hit Caleb. It's bound to happen again at some point. I just hope that everyone can remain objective when it does."

"We'll certainly try. I'm proud of you and Valerie, Gage."

Their conversation drifted to other topics as they sat in the dimly lit room. For Gage, this was the most natural exchange he could ever recall having with his father.

"Tell me about your job with the Diamondbacks," Jared said. "You mentioned that you were a little worn out from the long season."

"Yeah. I hope that by next season, we'll be a little more settled into our lives and routines."

Jared looked at him pensively. "That's just it. How can you and Valerie establish a routine with your children when your schedule is so sporadic?"

Gage leaned forward to rest his elbows on his knees. "I don't know. Valerie and I have talked about this. But, Dad, I love my job and I'm good at it. I don't want to give it up."

"The Lord gave each of us strengths and weaknesses. Perhaps your love of the game is a little of both. You and I are a lot alike in that we have a tendency to become so engrossed in our careers that we forget about the people we love. It took me an absurd amount of time to recognize that. Surely there is a way for you to balance both your family life and career."

Valerie's suggestion of looking internally for another position came to mind. How quickly he had dismissed it as a foolish notion. But now all Gage wanted was for his family to be happy. "I'm going to miss being at the games."

"What is it about the games that you'll miss? The food?"

Gage grinned at his father's teasing. "No."

"The fans?"

He shrugged. "Yeah. Talking with them one-on-one, catching their excitement for the game . . . it's contagious."

"What about the players?"

"I enjoy interacting with them, for the most part."

"What about feeling like you're a part of something big?"

"Definitely. I love that feeling."

"Might I offer you a suggestion, son?"

"What's that?"

"Replace the big leagues with the Little Leagues. Get your kids involved in playing the game you love so much. Do your job and do it well, but allow some time to be a part of your children's lives. Before you know it, they'll grow up and be gone."

Gage nodded pensively as his father's words circled through his sleep-deprived brain. He knew he'd have a headache in the morning. But this talk with his dad had been well worth it.

The wheels on the minivan weren't the only ones turning. Valerie could practically see the gears grinding in Gage's head as they pulled onto the freeway to head home. However, she hadn't a hint as to what it was all about. She placed her hand on his shoulder. "Want to talk about it?"

He looked at her absently. "Talk about what?"

"Whatever it is you're thinking about."

"It's just something my dad said to me," he replied distractedly.

They'd only been married for a short time and were still learning to read each other's moods. She hoped that he would confide in her when his had improved.

"Hey, Dad, when will we get to see Grandma and Grandpa Logan again?" Zach asked from the backseat.

"Yeah, they were really fun," Whitney pitched in.

Gage grinned. "You had a good time visiting them, did you?"

"Yeah."

"What about you, Justin?"

Brownie points for Gage, Valerie thought. At least he had included Justin in their conversation.

"I had fun."

Gage turned toward Valerie with a determined expression, coming out of whatever fog he'd been in. "I've decided to look for a new job."

Her jaw dropped. "Are you serious?"

"Yes," he said quietly. "I've been wrestling with some things, and while I've made a lot of changes, part of me wanted to hold onto something familiar, kind of like a security blanket. But you were right. My current job is not allowing me to be a very good husband or father. I'm sorry that I've been so stubborn."

Valerie bit her lip, feeling guilty. "Gage, I don't want to take you away from something you love doing."

"No, working for the Diamondbacks has been an awesome experience. They're a really great organization to work for. But what I love doing most is connecting with people and turning their business assets into those of high demand. There are countless companies out there who need a marketing consultant or I could hire on with a marketing company with a large clientele base."

"Or you could start your own," Valerie added, catching onto his enthusiasm.

For a split second, his face brightened before it clouded. "Yeah, I've thought of that, but then we wouldn't have the benefits that we'd have from working for someone else. And let's face it, with Justin, we'll always need good health coverage, not to mention the possibility of needing maternity care." His warm gaze entreated hers before she averted her eyes.

Her face grew hot under his scrutiny. "It was just a thought. Let's keep praying about it. You'll find the right job when the time is right."

It was good to have Gage at church the next Sunday. Whitney was no longer fighting Valerie over going to church every week. Since she and Gage had filed a formal complaint about Nick's failure to uphold his end of their agreement, he'd started taking more care to do so. Menaces like him, Samuel Jensen had informed Gage and Valerie, knew how to stay just within the boundaries of the law. They would most likely never discover who had burglarized Valerie's home before their wedding.

Whitney escorted the boys to Primary while Valerie and Gage went to their gospel doctrine class. They sat by the Powells, who alternately held and chased down their fourteen-month-old daughter, Ruthie. Valerie's heart tugged at the sight of the adorable little girl, but she devoutly ignored the pang. *Forget about it,* she told herself sternly. *You weren't meant to have any more babies.* There were some things in this life that were irreversible and autism was one of them. She couldn't take that risk.

"Zach, do you want bologna or PB and J?" Valerie asked as she grabbed two slices of bread and a knife from the kitchen drawer for their late lunch after church.

"Peanut butter and jelly," he promptly answered. Valerie nodded as she began spreading peanut butter on one slice of bread.

Gage kept a close eye on her as he pulled a pitcher of juice from the refrigerator. Something seemed off.

Whitney entered the kitchen and began making herself a sandwich.

"Hey, Mom," Zach said after swallowing a huge bite of his sandwich. He'd recently begun calling Valerie by that name, probably because he wanted to feel like he belonged in this family of His and Hers.

"Yes, honey?"

"You have lots of brothers and sisters, right?"

"Yes, I have four brothers and three sisters."

"I'll bet it was fun growing up with all of them."

A whimsical smile escaped her lips. "Most of the time."

Gage listened closely as he poured a glass of juice for each of the children.

"And Dad has two brothers too. I'm glad Justin is my brother. But I wish I had another one. Then there would be three brothers in our family just like Dad's."

Gage stared at him in shock. Where had that come from? Ever since she had avoided his hint about wanting more children when they were driving home from California, he'd dropped the subject.

Just as he was about to say something, Whitney exclaimed, "No way!"

Gage set the glass of juice down on the countertop a little too forcefully, spilling a few drops while fully expecting to be called on to referee.

Whitney surprised him, however, by adding, "If Mom and Gage have a baby, they should have a girl. I want a sister."

He cleared his throat loudly, interrupting their argument. "Hey, guys."

When Zach and Whitney kept bickering back and forth, he whistled. Their mouths froze as all eyes turned to stare at him. Valerie's face had turned white. But he couldn't let his concern for her override the necessity to calm the children down.

"Your mom and I aren't having a baby." It was better to douse the flames of that fire right now before it blazed out of control. "At least not yet. So if or when that ever happens, we'll let you know. But it's not like you get to choose whether we'll have a boy or girl. Heavenly Father chooses for us. Isn't that right, honey?" he asked, glancing at Valerie.

What he saw tore his heart in half. Her chin quivered with the effort of holding her tears back.

"Valerie?" he said, coming closer to her.

Without a word, she left the room. Stunned, Gage watched her go. After making sure that the kids were okay and that their argument had been settled, he left them to find his wife.

Valerie heard the knob on the door turn before Gage entered their bedroom and came around the side of the bed. She'd fallen in love with the room the minute she'd laid eyes on it. The vases of flowers she placed around the room added a few feminine touches to the brown walls, stone fireplace, and walnut chest that sat at the foot of the bed. The French doors that were bursting with sunlight lent a warm and airy touch.

Now she sat on the red coverlet with her arms folded around her middle. She'd thought she'd recovered well enough from her emotional bout at church to convince herself that she was just fine. But when Zach introduced the topic of having more children, every ache, every longing for a normal life resurfaced.

Why hadn't Heavenly Father given her the large family that she'd always wanted? Why was that plan right for someone else but not for her? The questions plagued her.

"Why?" she whispered.

"Why what?"

"So many people seem to get exactly what they want out of life. Are they more righteous than me?"

"'Heavenly Father places each of us in the circumstances we need to learn and grow.'" When Valerie looked at him in surprise, he shrugged. "Bishop Ames said that to me the other day, just so you know."

She chuckled, though it came out sounding more like a coughing fit. *Well*, Valerie thought, *at least Gage had been listening.*

G age sat next to her on the bed. "What happened at church, Valerie?"

She flopped back, her hair splaying around her. Her lower legs dangled off the side. "It was nothing."

He placed his hand over her knee. "Tell me what upset you, sweetheart."

Gage listened patiently as she described her long-ago dream of having a large family and how, after putting that dream away, those feelings of longing had resurfaced as they sat next to the couple with the darling baby in church and as they watched little Ruthie nibble on her snack.

"I take it you were as shocked as I when Zach and Whitney expressed their hope for a new baby," Gage said.

"I almost fainted on the spot!"

He lay down beside her and stared at the ceiling. "What are we going to do about it?"

"Nothing," she said flatly.

Gage swallowed his disappointment, wondering if or when she'd ever be ready to face the obvious. After a few more minutes, he asked, "Are you sure this is what you want?"

"Absolutely."

Yet her strangled voice said otherwise. "You're afraid, sweetheart." Gage held his breath, waiting for a tongue-lashing.

She didn't disappoint him. "Gage, how can you even think of having another child when we're struggling with the three we've got?"

"When I think of how lucky I am to be married to you and raise the three wonderful children we've been given, how can I not?"

"What makes you think that everything will be all right?"

"How do you know it won't be?"

"Get real, Gage," she mocked angrily. "The odds are against us for having a normal child."

"I didn't know you were a fortune teller, Valerie."

"Even the best magician can't make things perfect."

"No, but I know who can," Gage answered quietly. "Once upon a time, you told me that you believe Justin will be made perfect in the next life. We don't have much control over what happens to us in this life. That's our test, isn't it? To learn to trust God?"

"You make it sound so simple."

"It is when you really think about it. Heavenly Father will give us the kind of child He thinks is best for us. Likewise, we'll be the kind of parents He thinks that child needs. Every kid has issues, Valerie. If it isn't autism, then it's something else. Whitney is dealing with being tossed back and forth like a tennis ball between two parents and Zach is dealing with having been rejected by his own mother before losing her altogether. The great thing about this is that we get to learn new parenting skills and techniques. And maybe even learn more about ourselves and our children in the process."

"And come closer to the Lord," she concluded, sounding somewhat in awe.

Gage hid a smile. She was catching on. "That too."

Whether it was from hearing their discussion the day

before or whether it came from his own conscience, Valerie would never know. But the next morning as the kids were getting ready for school and Gage was getting ready for work, Justin sat on the kitchen stool to eat his cereal after Valerie had called him in for the umpteenth time. "Mom, my brother and sister are waiting."

Thinking nothing of Justin's out-of-the-blue comment, Valerie poured milk into his bowl. "Well, of course they are, honey. Hurry and finish your breakfast so that we can take you to school."

Justin's face scrunched up impatiently. "No, Mom. Another brother and sister!"

Valerie paused. "What do you mean, Justin?" she asked gently.

"In heaven. They want to come."

She set the milk down with a thud. "Are you sure about that?" she whispered, mentally shaking her head. Her inner voice was screaming, *Not again! Please, no! Not again!* She closed her eyes to quiet her anguished thoughts.

"Valerie?" Gage's voice penetrated the train that was roaring through her head. Looking up, she saw him standing behind Justin, wearing a perplexed expression.

She cringed. "You heard?"

"Yeah." He glanced quizzically from her to Justin and back again. "So what gives?"

"Um," she hedged, knowing that she was going to sound like she had gone totally mental. "Justin has a knack for . . . well, let's just say he's very in tune with the Spirit. He actually told me that you would be his new dad before you asked me to marry you."

"He did?" Gage's eyes bulged.

I've rattled him, Valerie thought smugly as she watched him run his fingers through his hair. "I'm okay with the Lord using Justin as a conduit to His messages for us, but what I can't understand is why."

Gage teased, "Maybe it's because his mother is such a skeptic."

Great. Now he'd rattled her.

"Or maybe it's an opportunity for us to show our son that he's important, that we value what he tells us and that his ideas have merit, even when we don't always understand him."

Gage smiled. "I like your explanation a lot better."

Valerie sat in the Mesa Temple, waiting for the next session to begin. She'd asked Chloe to watch Zach for a few hours. With everything that had been happening lately, she felt unsettled. She'd awoken this morning with a burning desire to attend the temple in the hope that she'd receive some inspiration regarding Gage's job search and all this baby talk.

Now, as she prayed and listened to the prelude music, she was overcome by a feeling of peace. During a lull in the endowment session, Valerie's mind wandered to inconsequential matters. Gradually, she became aware of an intensely warm sensation spreading throughout her, eliciting the feeling of joy. Recalling the last thing she'd been thinking about, Valerie realized that she'd been praying concerning whether or not she and Gage should have a baby. She was given a very distinct impression that there were two more spirits eagerly awaiting their chance to experience life here on earth. Valerie could hardly wait for the session to end so she could tell Gage.

Six months later

"Nervous?" Valerie couldn't resist teasing Gage after watching his attempt to knot his tie for the third time.

"No. Incredibly excited." Grinning wryly, he turned away from the mirror and walked toward his wife, enveloping her in a warm hug.

Inhaling his wonderfully spicy scent, Valerie tightened her hold and looked up into his handsome face. "I'm so happy, Gage. For you and us."

Gage was now working as marketing director for the Arizona Office of Tourism. In addition to performing many of the same tasks he'd performed with the Diamondbacks, his job gave him the opportunity to help other government, public, and tribal entities to promote the terrific sights in Arizona.

Valerie pulled back slightly and placed his hand on her rounded belly. Once Valerie had told Gage about the prompting she'd received in the temple, they hadn't wasted any time. Now they were expecting twins. Gage, who had missed out on seeing Zach on the ultrasound machine, had been thrilled at seeing their babies for the first time.

Zach was thrilled with the prospect of getting his heart's wish for another brother and sister after being legally adopted by Valerie. He still visited his maternal grandparents and had even given them a Book of Mormon recently.

Today Zach would be sealed to Gage and Valerie. Gage's eyes lit up as he pulled her to him for a kiss. "I love you, Valerie Logan," he said with their foreheads touching. "More than you'll ever know."

"I love you too, Gage Logan. Everyday I'm grateful that you saw my worth when I didn't see it myself."

"I could say the same."

"The Lord saw it in both of us before we did. He knew what He was doing when He helped us find each other again."

The promise of brighter todays and better tomorrows was shining in his eyes. "He sure did!"

Author's Note

After I finished writing *Pierced by Love*, my mind started spinning with possibilities for Pierce's younger brother, Gage. As I began plotting, memories from my daughter's toddler years bombarded me, good and bad. My daughter is autistic, and even with the benefit of a very supportive husband, those years were exhausting! I initially dismissed these ideas. I didn't want to revisit the past. It was too hard to do so.

But then an interesting thing happened. Those memories became sweet to me and the moment I finally realized that the Lord wanted me to deliver a message of hope to the many parents of autistic children who struggle each day was the moment I experienced a true feeling of peace.

My prayer is that this story inspires you, whether you're a parent, grandparent, teacher, or friend of an autistic child, to look deeper into his or her heart, especially when that child may not be able to express his or her feelings clearly. We are children of God. He loves and cares about each of us.

Also, I want to express many thanks to those who helped me tell this story. The real-life experiences of my sister-in-law inspired the break-in scene. The second burglary occurred at Christmastime. When the family's presents were torn into and destroyed, her husband's coworkers stepped in to replace the stolen and damaged items. Goodness still exists in the hearts of many today!

I'm fortunate to have been tutored by some very talented authors from my writers' group, Typeractive. Janette Rallison, Randy Lindsay, Brock Booher, Adrienne Quintana, R. C. Hancock, Stephen J. Stirling, and Marilee Jackson have taught me to write more effectively. Through them I have grown as an author and been able to (almost) overcome my plaguing overuse of adverbs. If you would like to sample an offering of their work, you can download a free anthology of short stories for your reading pleasure at https://www.smashwords.com/books/view/583279.

I also belong to a local chapter of the American Night Writers Association (ANWA) and have benefited from my writing sisters' valuable insights on plotting and story structure. I thank authors Jennifer Stewart Griffith and Jennifer Bryce for their invaluable support. Jennifer Griffith has mentored me without complaint, helping me to navigate the confusing world of publishing, many times over.

I owe a huge debt of gratitude to Cedar Fort for allowing me a chance to share my stories with others. I appreciate their staff, especially my editor, Melissa J. Caldwell, for their hard work and upbeat attitudes. I've enjoyed working with them.

Most of all, I want to thank my family. My husband, Rob, and our six children are a source of inspiration in my life. I love you!

One more note of importance: Valerie's mother, Brande, was named after Brande Brock, who won a bid in a charity auction for her name to be used as a character in *The Matchup*. This auction was held in connection to author Brock Booher's launch party for his book, *The Charity Chip*, and benefited the House of Refuge, which is a faith-based non-profit organization located in Mesa, Arizona, that helps the homeless by providing transitional housing to families in need while at the same time helping them to become self-sufficient. You can find them at www.houseofrefuge.org. It was a pleasure to work with Brande. I hope that she will be pleased with my decision to cast her as a mother, which is one of my favorite roles in life!

Discussion Questions

1. How does Gage's childhood affect his decisions in adulthood? What is at the core of Gage's resistance to his family's overtures of love? Is he right when he states that Valerie would never go for a guy like him?

2. Have you ever experienced a prolonged period of discouragement such as Valerie experiences in struggling to raise her autistic son? Who or what lifted you up in your time of need?

3. Gage learns that Valerie isn't as unsympathetic to her children as she first appears. Name two or three examples that show Valerie's compassion for her children. Name two or three examples that show her inner strength.

4. Do you think true love can grow from a childhood love/hate relationship?

5. Did you enjoy reading Gage's transition into active parenting? What examples have you seen of parents giving in to their children too easily? What examples have you seen of parents being too strict? What do you feel is a proper balance between the two?

6. Have you known someone who came back into full activity in the Church after being away for several years? What was his or her biggest fear and how did he or she overcome it?

7. Gage married April for all the wrong reasons. How might hastily made decisions lead us into a trap?

8. While it's true that Gage was given an easy "out" in dealing with his ex-wife, real life rarely occurs that way. What are you willing to work hard for in your own life? How do you manage to work with difficult people?

About the Author

Photo by Katie Cluff

Laura Walker's first novel, *Pierced by Love*, was set in beautiful northern Arizona where she earned her bachelor's degree in elementary education. Being a native Arizonan, Laura Walker and her husband, Rob, think it's a great place to raise their six children. She and her family enjoy camping, swimming, reading, and learning history together.

SCAN TO VISIT

WWW.LAURALWALKER.COM